A big, work-roughened hand closed over hers.

Her eyes flew open and she stared at Riley's hand dwarfing hers. He placed their joined hands against the horse's firm, warm neck.

Her discomfort faded when she saw the mare standing calmly beneath Riley's touch. Susannah could feel his chest at her back, his warmth comforting. She tried keeping her mind on the horse. "She's soft."

"Yes."

"She's letting me touch her," she said, with both wonder and uncertainty.

"Just keep your touch easy. That's good." His breath washed against her temple.

Her hand molded to his as they stroked the mare's sleek firm flesh, and the slow, sinuous movement lulled her. Riley's strength wrapped around her.

She found her gaze fixed on him, not the mare. Raw desire shimmered in his blue eyes and Susannah felt her stomach clench in response. He looked as if he wanted to stroke *her*...!

Like many writers, **Debra Cowan** made up stories in her head as a child. Her BA in English was obtained with the intention of following family tradition and becoming a schoolteacher, but after she wrote her first novel there was no looking back. An avid history buff, Debra writes both historical and contemporary romances. Born in the foothills of the Kiamichi Mountains, Debra still lives in her native Oklahoma with her husband. Debra invites her readers to contact her at PO Box 30123, Coffee Creek Station, Edmond, OK 73003-0003, USA, or visit her website at: http://www.debracowan.net

A previous novel by this author:

WHIRLWIND BABY

WHIRLWIND BRIDE

Debra Cowan

MILLS &
BOON®

All the characters in this book have no existence outside the imagination of the author, and have no relation whatsoever to anyone bearing the same name or names. They are not even distantly inspired by any individual known or unknown to the author, and all the incidents are pure invention.

First published in Great Britain 2011
by Mills & Boon, an imprint of Harlequin (UK) Limited,
Eton House, 18-24 Paradise Road, Richmond, Surrey TW9 1SR

© Debra S. Cowan 2004

ISBN: 978 0 263 88791 4

Harlequin (UK) policy is to use papers that are natural, renewable and recyclable products and made from wood grown in sustainable forests. The logging and manufacturing process conform to the legal environmental regulations of the country of origin.

Printed and bound in Spain
by Blackprint CPI, Barcelona

Chapter One

~~~~~~~~~~~~~~~~~~~~~~

West Texas, 1883

"Hello, Mr. Holt. No, Riley. I should call him Riley." Two hours after arriving by stage in Whirlwind, Texas, Susannah Phelps stood on the wide, dust-covered veranda of Riley Holt's large frame house. During the ride out here, she'd tried to think of the best way to start this conversation. Blurting out "I'm here to marry you" would not do.

Susannah felt like a mail-order bride who hadn't been ordered, and it didn't sit well. The October air was cool, but the sun, glaring down from a clear sky, kept the temperature from being sharp. She stayed warm with her blue wool cape and gloves. Red Texas dust hazed the air, coating everything with a rusty film and settling in the creases of her navy serge traveling skirt.

This was a lonely, isolated pocket of the plains.

Sprawled in the middle of browning pastureland, the white house with black shutters looked conspicuous and stark amid the red bluffs and short, endless grass. She'd never imagined

Riley would have such a grand home; her expectations had been of a crude log cabin or a sod house.

For the third time since arriving, Susannah tugged at her bodice and smoothed her skirt, then paced the few steps to his front door. Sweat dampened her palms. She'd worn her gloves all day, but now they were too hot. She peeled them off.

A man named Matthew Baldwin had been kind enough to drive her from Whirlwind to Riley's ranch, the Rocking H, but his buckboard had added to the bruises on her derriere. Four days of travel from St. Louis by train and stage, combined with her pregnancy, had left her more than exhausted. Her legs and feet were swollen to the size of German sausages, and she really wanted to sit down. But, having made up her mind to accept Riley Holt's marriage proposal, she was ready to settle things.

Miss Elmira Wentworth of Miss Wentworth's Finishing Academy in St. Louis would fall to the floor in a dead faint if she knew what Susannah was about to do. This was the most unladylike thing she'd ever done.

Susannah glanced down at her belly. Well, not the *most*.

As always, the reminder of her disgrace brought searing memories of the horror and anger on her parents' faces. Her mother and father had actually let her leave St. Louis without saying a word! She'd eagerly agreed to Adam's plan to come to his friend in Texas. Not because she shared the man's desire to marry. No. She, like her brother, had thought their parents would relent before she left, would put aside their anger. They hadn't.

So here she was in Whirlwind, a dusty Texas town that might as well be on the other side of the world. She was the one who had been hurt in this whole mess, the one person whom everyone had turned on. Paul LaFortune, especially, had betrayed her. She'd loved him with all of her young, innocent heart. His talk of "their future" had seduced her, had had her believing his sweet, empty promises that he'd loved her as much as she'd loved him.

She'd given him not only her virtue, but also her heart. She wouldn't be so foolish again. Wherever Paul was, things were probably perfect for him. She was the one who'd been banished, the one who was slinking away to an unfamiliar town to marry a stranger.

True, Riley Holt was one of her brother's best friends, and Adam trusted him implicitly, but Susannah had never met Riley.

She rested a hand on the barely visible swell of her stomach. She was just beginning her fifth month, and so far her condition had been concealed by full skirts and looser clothing. At first, the baby had been only an extension of the scandal that had disgraced her and forced her to leave St. Louis. But now the reality of this tiny life, and the enormous responsibility it brought, had sent her to Riley Holt's door. This trip was not just about her. She was all this baby had.

It was up to her to provide for her child's every need—food, a home, love and security. Even if it meant marrying a man she didn't know.

Miss Wentworth and her parents aside, Susannah had to go through with it. Squaring her shoulders, she knocked.

When there was no answer, she knocked again. Uncertainty tightened her already dry throat. Surely Riley was here. He *had* to be here.

Skirting the mound of baggage Matthew Baldwin had stacked before she'd insisted he leave her alone at the ranch, she walked to the east end of the veranda. The long stretch of porch that ran the length of the house was empty. Only a whitewashed windmill broke up the expansive acres of prairie grass. She certainly hadn't expected a windmill, usually rare in these parts. Down a soft slope, red long-horned cattle roamed.

Susannah walked back across the front and to the opposite end of the porch, her gaze skipping over a spring house next to the main house. A weathered but sturdy barn stood several yards away. A clang sounded from inside. She straightened.

Nerves prickled at the back of her neck and she balled her gloves in one hand. She returned to the steps, her lace-up travel boots clicking hollowly on the wood. After a slight hesitation, she started toward the barn. The clanging sounded again, sharp and metallic. She sucked in a deep breath and struggled to calm her nerves.

The pungent odors of animals and manure drifted to her. She wrinkled her nose and kept moving, despite feeling disconnected and a little lost.

Wide double doors were slid back, revealing the barn's hazy interior and another opening of the same size at the opposite end. Metal smacked metal twice, then was followed by a curse.

The husky baritone caused an odd flutter in her stomach, a flutter that had nothing to do with the baby. She stepped forward, out of the cool sunshine and into the dim barn.

After a moment, she was able to define the row of stalls on either wall, the slatted doors, bridles hanging neatly on each wooden beam that separated the cubicles. Saddles were draped over the stable walls, from behind which big, dark eyes stared at her.

Horses. She inched back against the door, curled her fingers around its edge. The sharp clang of metal sounded to her left and she turned.

A man bent over a pump, his back to her. Despite the shadows, she could see the span of broad shoulders beneath the white shirt. Even thinking himself unobserved, he seemed to command attention, filling the space with some undefinable aura of power.

Suddenly, as if he felt her presence, he straightened and turned, freezing when he saw her. He moved out of the shadows, holding a greasy wrench. His hard, even features were blatantly male, compellingly confident. Had Adam told her Riley was so big?

So…intimidating?

Spurred by nerves and uncertainty, she blurted, "I'm here."

One dark brown eyebrow arched. "Uh, yes, you are."

Oh, bother. She hadn't once practiced saying *that*. Frustrated and uncertain, she rubbed her forehead. "I mean, hello."

Riley stepped into the light then, and she saw that his eyes were a piercing blue. "May I help you, ma'am?"

"I'm Susannah. Phelps?"

He grinned. "Are you asking me?"

"No! I am. Susannah Phelps, I mean." She gave a wobbly smile.

"Adam's sister?"

"Yes." Relief washed through her and she smiled more widely, dismayed to realize she'd crushed her gloves into a ball. "You received Adam's telegraph?"

"Yes." Still looking surprised, he tossed the wrench aside, then pulled a rag from the back pocket of his denim trousers and began wiping his hands. "What are you doing out here? How did you get here?"

"I thought…didn't Adam tell you I was coming?"

"Yes. Well, to Whirlwind."

"Oh, good." A beam of sunlight showed up the gold in Riley's sun-streaked brown hair and angled over his bronzed features. His blue eyes set her pulse to pounding.

Nothing about this man was pretty or soft or gentle. Strength and power carved every line of his body. His worn white shirt molded a wide shelf of shoulders, a deep chest. He was commanding and rugged and authoritative.

That intent gaze suggested a leashed restlessness, as if he were surrounded on all sides by walls or worse, a firing squad. A raw tension vibrated from him, belying the polite smile that never really reached his eyes, the low calm voice. Everything about him spoke of hard work and labor and sweat, a far cry from the men who'd squired Susannah about, men who spent their days in their father's law office or shipping business. Riley was a man of the land who owned his world.

His gaze skimmed over her, from her loose chignon to her dusty shoes. A wariness slid into his eyes, and something sharp, hungry.

Though he'd become fast friends with Adam at university nine years before, Riley had never returned Adam's visits or come to St. Louis. But Susannah had seen a photograph of him with her brother. The grainy image looked nothing like this man. The poor reflection certainly couldn't capture the blue of his eyes or the power in that body.

His gaze dropped to her lips and her pulse tripped. Taking a step back, she pressed closer to the door. He made her as nervous as those horses did. There was a restive energy about him that reminded her of the animals, as if he were too wild to be confined.

He looked away, shifted from one foot to the other. "I didn't realize you were coming to the ranch."

"Oh. Yes." She tucked a strand of loose hair behind her ear, glad she'd taken the time at the stage depot to brush out her skirt and wash her face. Still, she would've liked a bath. She felt awkard and unwelcome. "I've interrupted you."

"Just working on the pump."

He seemed to be waiting for her to say something else. When she didn't, he frowned, tucked the dirty rag back in his pocket. "How was your trip? Did you take the stage?"

"Yes."

"Where are you staying?"

Maybe that jarring stage ride had addled her brain, but she suddenly felt as if she were in the wrong place. Susannah frowned.

Riley studied her. "Adam sounds happy in his new marriage."

"Oh, he is." Pressure tightening her chest, Susannah rushed to take advantage of the opening Riley had given her. "Pardon me for being forward, but don't you think we should discuss the marriage?"

He stared blankly at her.

"I'm in agreement. Are…you?"

Tilting his head, he studied her, shadows softening the hard angles of his face. "Sure. I think Adam will be happy."

Oh, dear. Her hands fluttered to her throat. "I didn't mean—I wasn't talking about *Adam's* marriage."

"No?"

She swallowed. Why was he making this so difficult? Was he teasing her the way he had a moment ago? She could see no humor in those dark blue eyes, only a mild curiosity. "I know you never spoke to me directly, but Adam said you were in agreement."

"*I* was in agreement?" Riley's eyes narrowed dangerously. He took a step toward her; his hard body seemed to close off what little air she had. "About what?"

Feeling as if she were being cornered by a wild stallion, Susannah noted how her heart was thudding painfully against her ribs. Adam had said Riley wanted her and she'd believed him. However, at the moment, Riley didn't seem like a man who wanted her. At all.

Unsettled, she rushed on. "I realize my coming to you was forward, but I had to. Since you'd already spoken for me, I didn't think it would be too much a breach in etiquette."

"*Your* coming to *me?*"

"Yes."

"Spoken for you? Are you saying…" He cleared his throat, his gaze locking on hers. "You think we're going to get married?"

"Yes." She nearly shouted in relief. "Everything's in order. I'm in complete agreement. There's just one thing—"

"I'm sure as hell not in agreement," Riley exclaimed.

"What?" Susannah squeaked.

For just a moment, his eyes hardened and he paled as though she'd stuck a gun to his head. Then he grinned and stepped around her to move outside. "Where is he? Adam!" he called. "Come on out! The joke is over."

"This is most certainly not a joke," Susannah huffed, turning in a swirl of skirts. Panic flared. What was going on? The only reason she had come to this godforsaken dust pit was because Adam had said Riley wanted to marry her, and she needed security for her baby.

"Phelps, you snake!" Laughing, Riley started for the house, his strong legs eating up the distance over the hard ground.

Susannah followed, her senses spinning. Honestly! "He isn't here. I'm alone." And destined to remain that way, it seemed.

Riley pivoted, causing her to stop abruptly or run into his massive chest. He braced his hands on his hips. "What's all this talk about marriage then?"

Temper flaring, she mimicked his pose. "Didn't you say you wanted to get married?"

"Me? No." He chuckled.

"You *didn't* tell my brother you wanted to marry me?" she demanded with a jerky wave of her hand.

"No. Absolutely not."

It took a second for the full import of his words to sink in. "No?" she said weakly, her hand falling to her side.

He must've seen the color drain out of her face because his smile faded. His voice softened. "No."

She thought she might be sick all over his dusty boots.

Chapter Two

He'd never even met the woman and she thought he wanted to marry her. Amazing.

Riley watched Susannah's face grow pale. The disbelief in her eyes shifted to shock. She swayed and he stepped toward her.

"Are you okay? You look like you might be sick."

"I'm fine." She marched around him toward the house. "I won't bother you any longer."

For a moment, Riley stood there. Adam had sent her to him, and for some ridiculous reason, Susannah believed Riley might actually want to marry her. Not so ridiculous, he reminded himself as he followed her. People agreed to arranged marriages all the time. Mail-order, too. But not him.

He caught up to her. "I'm sorry I reacted badly. You took me by surprise."

She looked away. "I noticed."

"I have no idea why Adam would say I wanted to marry."

"Marry me?"

"No, anyone. I don't know what he was thinking. He knows I have no intention of doing that again."

She glanced over, skirts swishing against the ground, stirring up little puffs of dust. "Would it be so awful?"

How was he supposed to answer *that?* "Well…"

"Don't worry. The misunderstanding is cleared up."

His gaze traced her slender curves. Silver-blond curls gleamed in the sun, revealing a long elegant neck. Her light vanilla scent drifted to him and his heart gave a hard kick. He squared his shoulders against the reaction.

After his wife's death four years ago, he'd focused all his attention on building the Rocking H with his father. A short three years after their marriage, Maddie had been suddenly wrenched from him, her life snuffed out when she'd lost her way in a dust storm and broken her neck. Riley hadn't been interested in another woman since, nor had the inclination to find one who did interest him.

He slowed as he neared the porch, while Susannah steamed ahead, sweeping past him and up the steps, her skirts brushing his boots.

She bent to pick up two small valises, stuffing one under her arm and gripping the other in her hand. "Just what did my brother's telegram say?"

"That you were coming to Whirlwind."

"That's all?"

"Yes." He wondered what Adam had told Susannah. Before the sun set, he intended to find out. Whatever it was had convinced her to travel hundreds of miles to marry a man she didn't know.

Marriage?! Riley had thought he might swallow his teeth when she'd made that little announcement. He wasn't marrying her. Not because she was the sister of one of his good friends, but because she didn't belong here. Look at her! She was too soft, too delicate for life in the Texas plains. His past made him an expert on beautiful outsiders, especially those who believed they were strong enough to survive in this sometimes-merciless land. Hooking up with Susannah Phelps would be like carrying china on a cattle drive. Not smart. Not practical. He hadn't built the reputation of the Rocking H by being stupid or impractical.

"Humph." She yanked at the strap on the largest trunk and stumbled backward.

Riley cleared the steps in two strides and reached out to steady her. She regained her footing, straightened away from him.

He eyed her mound of luggage incredulously. "Are all these yours?"

She shot him a glacial look and shifted the valise under her arm, then grabbed the strap of the smallest trunk. The valise crashed to the ground.

"What are you doing?"

"Leaving, of course." As she bent toward her bag, he scooped it up.

He glanced around. There was no horse or buggy. "Just exactly how did you get out here?"

"Matthew Baldwin."

Matthew? Riley lifted a brow. Matt Baldwin hadn't been called by his full name since they were fifteen.

Puffing out a breath that lifted a stray curl over her forehead, Susannah reached for the valise he held, then wrapped the strap of the smallest trunk around her other hand. "There."

Dragging the piece behind her, she clomped down the steps, then stopped. She stared down the long, dusty road, past the crude log archway where he'd carved his rocking *H*. Did she think she was going to carry all that luggage? The three pieces she held now looked heavy enough to break her. She was so fragile and small-boned, Riley didn't think she could carry even one of those valises all the way to town. He wanted to ask if she'd brought everything she owned, but he kept his mouth shut.

Hefting the bag under her arm, she looked over her shoulder. "How far *is* Whirlwind?"

"Three miles."

"Three..." After a long moment, she turned, lifting her chin. "I'd like to leave my luggage here, if you don't mind. I'll send someone for it."

"How are you planning to get back to town?" He couldn't stand it anymore; he moved down the steps and reached out to pry the small trunk from her grasp, then slid it onto his shoulder. "Walk? I don't see a horse."

"Oh, I don't ride horses."

He grinned. "What do you do with them?"

"I..." She blinked, then recovered. "Nothing."

"You certainly can't walk all that way. I'd be more than happy to give you a ride." He glanced at the two large trunks still on his porch. "And your luggage."

"I'm sure you have better things to do. Fix your pump, for one."

"I've got time. I feel badly about what happened back there." Not as badly as Adam was going to, though.

"Let's just forget that, shall we?" she asked primly.

"Sure." Remembering the hurt that had flared in her eyes when he'd laughed at her assumption of marriage, Riley felt his conscience twinge. "If you need anything while you're in Whirlwind, anything at all, you let me know."

He reached out and took the valise from under her arm. The back of his hand brushed the underside of her breast, and she stiffened, her gaze flying to his.

Damn.

For an instant, they stared at each other.

Susannah stepped away, nervously fingering the fastening of her cape. Her movement jerked him back to attention.

His hand burned as if he were still touching her. She might be slight, but there was nothing wanting about those breasts, which were fuller than they appeared under her wrap. He turned for the barn. "Let me hitch Pru to the wagon. I'll get you back to town."

Susannah Phelps wasn't his responsibility, but she was the sister of his good friend. He would get her back to Whirlwind, even back to St. Louis. And he would get some answers in the process.

After hitching the bay mare to the buckboard, he drove around to the front of the house and loaded Susannah's trunks into the back. Lines of fatigue pulled at the magnolia-smooth skin around her clear blue eyes, tightened lips that were temptingly kissable. He wished he weren't so aware of the exhaustion etched on her face, the slight droop to her shoulders, the careful stiffness of her movements as he handed her into the wagon. If she'd ridden the stage all day, and then Baldwin's buckboard out to the Rocking H, she had to be sore. He hated riding in both contraptions.

"You all right?"

"Yes," she answered a touch impatiently.

Reaching under the seat, he pulled out a blanket. He shook out the dust, then refolded it and handed it to her.

"Thank you." Looking surprised, she gave him a grateful smile.

She was a dandy, sleekly curved just like a Thoroughbred. Her creamy skin begged a man to touch it, see if it was as soft as it looked. Her eyes reflected every emotion like a pool of clear water.

Hell. He pulled himself into the wagon and picked up the reins. Adam knew Riley would never marry again, certainly not a lady who probably couldn't even lift a full bucket of water on her own. It took a special breed of woman to live here. Even those who could didn't always survive. Riley's own mother had been strong, had birthed two big sons, but she had died in her sleep two years ago. Her heart had just given out.

His father, Ben, had passed last year, still grieving for Lorelai Holt. He'd built her this ridiculously fine house in the middle of the plains, and she'd lived in it less than three years.

Already Susannah's magnolia skin had reddened under the October sun and she looked about to wilt. Riley would take her town, wire Adam to let him know his plan hadn't worked. Whatever that plan was.

Riley clucked to the horse and slid a sideways glance at Susannah. She sat straight and stiff as a rod next to him, her skirts pressed as tight to her as she could get them. Her other hand, white-knuckled, gripped the seat.

"Adam's been known to play a practical joke, but never anything like this."

She murmured something incoherent.

"Why do you think he did it?"

She glanced over, a sudden wariness sliding into her blue eyes. "I guess he had his reasons."

And she knew what they were, the little baggage! Riley knew by the set of her jaw as she turned away that she wasn't going to tell him. He resented the flicker of admiration he felt at the sight of a little backbone. Little sister could keep Adam's secrets. Riley would get his answers soon enough.

The silence between them swelled. She looked uncomfortable and color rode high on her finely honed cheekbones.

"Peppermint?" He offered her a short stick of the candy, fresh from his shirt pocket.

Her gaze dipped to his hand, lingered on the sweet. "No, thank you."

He nodded and popped the candy into his mouth. He understood her embarrassment. Adam had put them both in an awkward position.

They rode with only the noise of creaking wagon wheels and cawing crows until he topped a hill and saw Whirlwind sprawled out in front of him in its neat T-shaped layout. To the northeast, about eight miles from town, sat Fort Greer.

"Where should I take you? Do you have a place to stay? I can get you a stage ticket to Abilene, so you can catch the train back to St. Louis."

"I'll be fine."

He slid her a look. "I'll take you to the Whirlwind Hotel. It's not fancy, but it's clean."

And Riley would pay for her room. He told himself that should've eased his conscience. He was doing what he could, what he *should*. She certainly couldn't stay with him at the Rocking H, not without a chaperon.

A hammer rang against metal as they approached a barn-like building at the edge of town, and Riley lifted a hand in greeting as he drove past Ef Gerard's blacksmith shop. The burly man, with muscles bulging in his glistening, thick black arms, returned the wave. Blatant curiosity burned in his coffee-colored eyes as he caught sight of Susannah.

Being a Friday afternoon, the town was still relatively quiet. There was no activity outside the livery or the saloon right across the street. Cowboys from nearby ranches or passing cattle drives would change that in a few short hours. They would come to town to spend their pay on whiskey and women, but Susannah would be safe inside the hotel.

Businesses lined both sides of the double-wagon-width main street, with the church-cum-schoolhouse crowning the center point of the T, a north-south street aptly named North. Homes were scattered on either side of the steepled frame building. As his wagon ambled up Whirlwind's main thoroughfare, Riley caught sight of his brother, Davis Lee Holt, in the sheriff's office. Good. Riley wanted to talk to him.

The mare plodded past Pearl Anderson's restaurant, the Pearl, then the telegraph office, which also served as the post office. Across the street, Haskell's General Store was doing a brisk business. On the same side as the saloon, the store was flanked by the newly opened *Prairie Caller* newspaper on one side and Cal Doyle's law office on the other. A neat, tidy frame building on the corner was home to the other Doyle brother, Jed, a gunsmith.

Easing the wagon to a stop in front of the hotel, Riley set the brake and looped the reins around the handle.

Susannah reached into her reticule and offered him a silver dollar. "Thank you for the ride. I appreciate it."

Immediately indignant, he growled, "Put that away."

"But—"

"I won't take your money," he said evenly, not liking the way she made him feel like a hired hand.

Irritation zipping through him, he hopped down and started around to help her down.

"Miz Phelps!"

Riley rounded the back of the wagon, halting when he saw J. T. and Matt Baldwin standing next to the wagon, both offering a hand up to Susannah.

She smiled, erasing all fatigue from her face. "Hello, Mr. Baldwin, Matthew. How nice to see you again."

The warmth in her greeting to father and son stirred something deep inside Riley, and he felt an unfamiliar heat charge through his chest.

The elder Baldwin elbowed his son aside. "Let me help you down, Miz Phelps. You boys get her luggage."

Russ Baldwin appeared suddenly beside his brother. While their father handed her down, the Baldwin brothers moved toward Riley and reached for the trunks in the back of the wagon.

All three Baldwins easily had three to four inches on Riley's six-foot height. Their broad shoulders and massive thighs made them the biggest men around; one or another of them won the arm-wrestling match every year during the Fourth of July picnic. But they were known to be gentlemen in every sense of the word. Riley had always liked them.

The Baldwin men were more than capable, but shouldn't he be the one responsible for making sure Susannah was settled?

J.T. deposited her beneath the hotel's green awning as carefully as if she were blown glass.

"You've already had your visit with Riley?" Matt stepped onto the boardwalk, balancing a trunk on his massive shoulder.

She didn't so much as glance Riley's way. "Oh, yes. I'm sorry I asked you to lug all my baggage out to his ranch, but I wasn't sure where I'd be staying." She gave the three men a blinding smile.

They nodded, each grinning as if they'd tipped back a bottle of Pete Carter's best whiskey. All kept their gazes locked on her with rapt attention. Riley frowned, but told himself to be glad that she hadn't shared with them the real reason she'd come out to his ranch.

"I'll be staying here."

"Good," both brothers said in unison.

Riley's jaw clenched as he turned to retrieve the remaining luggage.

Russ, who had already unloaded the largest trunk, plucked the two valises from the wagon before Riley could. "How are things going at the ranch, Riley?"

"Very well, thanks." He smiled at Russ, trying to figure out why he was annoyed. He'd done the right thing by bringing her to town. She wasn't his responsibility. Hell, he hadn't even known she was coming to see *him*.

The three men asked after Susannah's health at least twice each, and she didn't seem to mind at all. Clearing his throat, Riley said, "I'll get you a room, Susannah."

She turned, gave him a cool smile that made her look regal and damn infuriating. "That won't be necessary."

His lips tightened and he stepped up on the boardwalk. "I'll be right back."

He returned a few minutes later and folded a room key into her hand. "Here you go."

Her eyes darkened. "Thank you."

Matt Baldwin swept off his hat. "Let me escort you inside."

Susannah smiled and took his arm.

Russ shifted her valises to one hand and opened the hotel door.

Gritting his teeth, Riley stepped down into the street, then climbed into the wagon. "I'll check on you later."

"There's no need. You've done enough."

If she didn't wipe that haughty look off her face, he was going to come up there and do plenty more.

He nodded and clucked to the mare, glancing over his shoulder when he heard Susannah's light laughter mix with the deeper sounds of the Baldwins'. She didn't even glance Riley's way as he turned the wagon and headed back up the street. As if he were invisible, as if they hadn't discussed marriage.

She needed him about as much as a boar needed a teat. She was fine. He was relieved.

Relief was the last thing he felt, Riley admitted as he braked the wagon in front of the post office a few moments later.

Irritation, sympathy, even a grudging fascination flickered inside him, but not relief.

He went inside to send a wire to Adam. With his blood doing a slow simmer, Riley found thoughts of Susannah harder to shake than a burr in his sock. When she'd realized he had no intention of marrying her, hurt had darkened her clear blue eyes. At the sight, a fierce protectiveness had flared in his chest. He seemed unable to squelch that, even after seeing her surrounded by the hulking Baldwins. *Especially* after that.

At least she wasn't planning to stay in Whirlwind. St. Louis was definitely the place for her. The brutal Texas climate, the unforgiving land, the isolation of ranch life whittled away at women like Susannah. This land had killed his Maddie, hadn't it?

After he'd turned eighteen, at his parents' request, he'd spent a year in Boston at university. He hated that closed-up life, the air and sky squeezed out by buildings and countless homes. Except for the friends he'd made—Adam Phelps being one of the best—Riley hadn't liked anything about the big Eastern city.

As Tony Santos read back his message, Riley thought about apologizing again to Susannah. But another apology, no matter how compelled to make one he felt, wasn't going to erase the embarrassment between them, the awkwardness. Fishing another peppermint stick out of his shirt pocket, he broke off a section and slid it into his mouth.

Cutting off further thoughts of the curvy blonde, he told the rotund telegraph operator he'd pay extra to have Adam's reply delivered to the Rocking H as soon as it arrived.

After he left, he walked past the Pearl Restaurant and to the jail for a quick talk with his brother. Davis Lee, older by almost three years, sat on the edge of his scarred, but polished desk, whittling. Wood shavings littered the otherwise spotless pine floor. A single door behind Davis Lee's desk opened to the four cells of Whirlwind's jail.

Riley stepped inside the building and closed the front door, noting the quick peel and flash of Davis Lee's knife. Davis Lee liked to whittle; he was good at it. But he only did it when something bothered him.

"More trouble?"

The eldest Holt, lanky and two inches taller than Riley, looked up with somber blue eyes. "Just came from Cora Wilkes's house. The McDougal gang held up the stage today and killed Ollie."

"Damn. Anyone else?"

"No. He'd just brought in three passengers and was headed to Abilene to pick up some supplies for the fort."

"They killed him on the way out of town?"

"Yes."

That explained why Susannah hadn't mentioned any trouble. Sharp relief stabbed at Riley's chest.

He removed his hat, hit by sadness at the stage driver's death. "I'm sorry to hear about Ollie."

"Damn those McDougals. J. T. Baldwin happened upon the scene, sent Russ to town to let me know, but none of us could catch them." Davis Lee stood, his wiry frame as taut as strung barbed wire. He and Riley had done their share of wrestling and fighting growing up. Despite the two inches in height he had on Riley, it was always a draw. "You should've seen Cora."

"Is there anything I can do?"

"Check in with her off and on. With winter coming, she'll need wood and someone to help with the chickens."

Riley nodded, made a mental note to stop by and offer his condolences on the way out of town. And he'd help out often, too, even though he hated chickens.

Ollie and Cora Wilkes had lived in Whirlwind as far back

as Riley could remember. Cora supplied all the fresh eggs in town. Ollie used to let him and Davis Lee ride the boot on short stagecoach runs.

"I've had all the trouble I want out of those outlaws." Davis Lee slid his knife into the top drawer of his desk. Both brothers had blue eyes like their father, but Davis Lee's dark brown hair testified to their mother's brunette coloring, whereas Riley had their father's sandy hair. "I spoke to a Ranger a week or so ago. He thinks they're closing in on them. 'Course, they've been chasing those Irish bastards as long as the rest of us have."

"They need to be stopped," Riley agreed. "I'll join up if you want to put together a posse and track them."

"We're better served to patrol Whirlwind. I plan to do that twenty-four hours a day, especially after what happened today. The McDougals killed Ollie a scant two miles from here. It's not like them to strike so close. I don't want to leave the town unprotected."

"I guess the Rangers are tracking them, anyway."

"And every bounty hunter who hears about them." Shaking his head in disgust, Davis Lee ran a practiced hand over the row of rifles in the open gun cabinet behind him. "I can help them out best from here. I've already deputized all three of the Baldwins, plus Jake Ross and one of your ranch hands, Cody Tillman."

"Five deputies? Where do you think you are, Dallas?"

His brother gave a small smile. "I need enough men so that someone can stand watch in town while others patrol. And I need someone here at the jail round the clock. I've got a murderer in the back, waiting on the circuit judge for his trial."

Riley cleared his throat, his nerves still jumping at how close Susannah had come to harm. "Adam Phelps's sister, Susannah, came in on the stage this morning."

Surprise spread across the other man's features. "What's she doing *here?*"

Riley saw no reason to humiliate her or himself by telling his brother the truth. "Visiting, I guess."

"Staying long?"

"No." He walked to the window, wondering if she was settled into her hotel room or if she was off with one of the Baldwins. Whatever she was doing was none of his business, he reminded himself.

"Where's she staying? The hotel?"

"Yeah." A glint of blond hair drew Riley's eye, but it wasn't her.

"I'll go say hello." Davis Lee walked up next to him, looking toward the hotel.

"There's no need," Riley said quickly. Too quickly.

His brother sent him a sideways look.

"She probably won't be here long, is all." He wondered if she had any idea what trouble she courted by traveling alone, especially through the outer edges of Texas. "Well, I'll leave you to it."

"See you Sunday for lunch?"

"Yeah." Riley and Davis Lee never missed Sunday lunch together, especially since their father had passed on last year. Davis Lee still had a room at the ranch, but he'd taken to staying in town after returning from Rock River to Whirlwind and being elected sheriff two years ago.

Riley left the jail and headed up the street toward his wagon, which he'd left in front of the post office. Other rigs lumbered up and down the street. A group of boys, whooping and hollering, darted out of the schoolhouse.

As he started to climb onto his buckboard, he glanced up and saw Susannah headed his way. He considered letting her pass, but the reminder of how close she'd come to Ollie's fate changed his mind. Removing his hat, he stepped up onto the planked walk in front of her.

Her step faltered. Sunlight gilded her perfect magnolia skin, lit her eyes like endless pools of blue.

"Susannah," he said quietly, suddenly uneasy. He had to force himself not to crush his hat.

She stopped and gave him a curt nod. "Mr. Holt."

"Are you getting settled? Do you need anything?"

"I'm fine." Her gaze was guarded.

"Good." He ran a hand over his jaw, wishing they hadn't gotten off to such an awkward start.

She smiled brightly and he thought she was easily the nicest sight he'd witnessed all day. It was a shame she wasn't cut out for life here.

"Will you be leaving soon?"

"Leaving?"

"For St. Louis."

"Oh, I'm not leaving. I'm staying in Whirlwind."

His eyebrows shot up and he couldn't stop the sudden quirk of his lips. "Really."

"Yes, really. That amuses you?"

"Hardly. You don't belong here."

"Pardon me?" Her shoulders stiffened and her gaze turned downright frigid. "I wasn't aware I was in *Riley,* Texas. Are you the mayor? The sheriff? Is this *your* town?"

"Life here is hard." He flexed his hands on his hat to keep from shaking her. "This land is unforgiving, sometimes brutal."

"Evidently some people are, too."

That made him feel lower than a whipped dog, but the possibility that he might someday find her pale and lifeless pushed him on. "I just mean it's not easy here like it is in St. Louis."

"You might be surprised to learn life isn't that easy in St.

Louis, either,'' she said quietly, making him wonder at the shadows in her eyes.

He had no intention of telling her about Maddie, but he had to make her understand. "We have Indians—"

"We have outlaws."

"We have snakes."

"We have floods." Her gaze stayed stubbornly locked on his.

"Things happen here that you'd have no idea how to handle. Things that could get you killed."

"You think I'm stupid, is that it? Lacking in some way?"

"No, stop twisting my words around. I'm just trying to warn you."

"And you have." She smiled, a patently dismissive smile, and started forward. "Nice to see you again, Mr. Holt."

Frowning at Susannah's formality, he moved to the edge of the walk so she could pass. He knew it wouldn't matter a damn if he pointed out that at least in St. Louis she had her father and her brother for protection. "If you need anything at all—"

"Don't give it another thought." She tossed the words over her shoulder. "Truly. I'll be fine."

She continued down the walk, heading toward the post office. No doubt she planned to wire her brother, just as he had.

Riley's gaze locked on Susannah. The petite blond beauty's hair caught the sun and glittered like a star. Dragging his gaze from the enticing sway of her skirts, he climbed into the wagon and picked up the reins, snapping them against Pru's rump. Damn Adam, anyway.

Chapter Three

If you need anything at all, let me know.

How many times had Riley said that? She *needed* a husband, but she didn't see him offering to help with that, Susannah thought indignantly as she walked away from him toward the telegraph office. She could feel him staring.

His gaze burned between her shoulder blades, causing her skin to prickle. She fought the urge to smooth her hair or turn around.

Her voice had come out more stiffly than she'd liked when talking to him, but seeing him reignited the embarrassment she'd felt in his barn. Adam had a lot to answer for.

Couldn't Riley have married her just because she was told he wanted to…even if he didn't make the promise himself? Evidently not. She wondered why he'd been so mean. Maybe he was merely concerned. His dire warnings sounded like something her brother might say. But Susannah was staying. She was glad she hadn't told him about the baby, but what was she going to do now? She *wasn't* going back to St. Louis.

Her entire family would be in even more disgrace. First

the baby, then this. Paul hadn't wanted her. It wouldn't do to advertise that Riley didn't, either.

Susannah tugged on her gloves and opened the door to the post office, which also served as the telegraph office. She needed a place to live, which she could secure using the money she'd received from the sale of some jewelry before she'd left home.

She sent a curt telegram to her brother, ordering him to respond immediately and tell her exactly what he'd said to Riley. She also asked that he not tell Riley about her "situation," hoping her choice of words would keep eager-to-please Tony Santos from figuring out that she was expecting. She'd endured all the embarrassment she could for a while. A final plea for her brother to wire some money ended her telegram. It was the least he could do after sending her to Whirlwind under false pretenses.

After leaving the post office, she started back to the hotel, stopping at the Pearl for a dinner of stew and fresh bread. The rich, meaty meal wasn't the roasted pork with pearlized onions Minnie the cook served every Friday night at the Phelps's house, but the meal was good and very filling.

Susannah traced a square on the red-checked tablecloth, hit with a pang of homesickness as the aroma of fresh pie and bread drifted around her.

A shadow fell across her plate and Susannah looked up. A tall, lanky man with dark brown hair stood there. "Evenin', ma'am."

"Good evening." Her gaze skipped over a handsome face, then dropped to his tin star. "Sheriff."

The blue eyes beneath the dark slash of brows reminded her of another pair of blue eyes.

"You'd be Miz Susannah Phelps?"

For one heartbeat, she thought perhaps her parents had sent someone after her. "How did you know?"

"I'm Davis Lee Holt." A broad smile split his face. "Riley's my younger brother."

"Riley's brother." Relieved that Davis Lee wasn't here on behalf of her parents, she kept her smile in place, but her thoughts whirled. Had Riley sent his brother, the *sheriff,* to kick her out of town? "It's a pleasure to meet you."

"Same here. My brother thinks a lot of yours. And you, too."

She wasn't so sure about that, but nodded, anyway. What had Riley told his brother about her? Whatever it was, the eldest Holt seemed too polite to say. Though he didn't look much older than Riley, his features were sharper and just as compelling. But Davis Lee didn't make her nervous the way Riley did.

"Riley says you're here visiting."

"Uh, yes." She dabbed at her mouth, then returned her napkin to her lap. She hoped that was all Riley had said.

Davis Lee's gaze searched her face and she recognized the probe beneath the question. Intelligence glittered in his eyes. She sensed the sheriff knew there was more to her story. If Riley had enlisted his brother to send her packing, he was going to hear from her.

Instead of the leashed wildness she detected in Riley, she recognized a calm in his brother. But he had the same restrained power in his broad shoulders.

After a short exchange about the food and her accommodations, the man bade her good-night. "Hope you have a nice visit in Whirlwind. Please let me know if there's anything you need. Drop by my office anytime."

"Thank you, Sheriff."

"Davis Lee, please."

"All right, Davis Lee." Susannah smiled up at him, relieved that he was leaving. She wondered how Davis Lee would've responded if she'd shown up on *his* doorstep instead of his brother's.

She paid her bill and went up to her room, looking forward to sleeping on a mattress, despite its lumps.

It was a relief to take off her dusty traveling clothes. She'd let out the seams in a few dresses. The roomier garments, along with her cape, had hidden her expanding curves, but she could no longer lace her corset. In days, her condition would be obvious to the whole world. Soon she'd need a couple of new dresses. Clothes were easy to find, but what about a husband? She couldn't advertise. It simply wasn't done.

Pulling the pins from her hair, she tilted her head back and let the heavy mass tumble down her back. She dug her brush from her smallest valise and walked to the window, staring out at the sky, which was turning a vibrant orange and pink. She dragged her brush through her hair, enjoying the comfort of the familiar routine.

Who would want to marry a woman carrying another man's child, anyway? The stigma of Susannah's illegitimate child was one reason she'd left St. Louis. Despite its distance from big cities, Whirlwind wasn't removed from convention.

The land stretched forever, vast and unending, golden plains melting into the flame-colored horizon. Susannah felt small and out of place. Just then, the baby kicked.

Placing a protective hand over her belly, Susannah determined her baby *would* have a place here, somehow. She'd figure out a way.

And suddenly she had an idea.

For the third time, Riley unwadded the crumpled telegram and stared at it, his shocked numbness edging into a quick flare of temper.

She was in the family way, dammit. A baby!

All last night he'd wondered why she would marry a man she didn't know, and he'd never once considered *that*.

Miz Susannah Phelps had some explaining to do. Riley told himself it should be enough that he'd escaped her marriage trap. It wasn't. Aware now of the real reason she'd come to Whirlwind—to him!—he had to know what would've happened if he'd agreed to marry her. Would she have told him she was expecting?

Trying to calm the angry disbelief perking inside him, he saddled Whip. He made it to town in record time, going straight to the Whirlwind Hotel. She wasn't there. He asked the desk clerk, Penn Wavers, if he knew where Susannah had gone, but the nearly deaf old man just smiled and told Riley to sign the register.

Jaw clenched, he walked out and looked up and down the dusty street. Just like yesterday, cool sunshine glittered off the plate glass of Whirlwind's businesses. There were only so many places she could be; if he had to go in every one of them to find her, so be it.

Turning, he moved quickly down the planked walk, going into the bank, the Pearl Restaurant, peering into Davis Lee's office, but there was no glint of silvery-blond hair. Just as he turned away from the sheriff's window, he saw Susannah coming out of Haskell's General Store across the street.

"Miz Phelps!"

She turned and he saw apprehension flicker across her pretty features.

As he neared, she backed up against one of the rough wood columns that supported the awning. Shoulders taut, she looked poised to bolt. He figured if the lady thought she had a prayer of outrunning him, she would've chanced it.

She held a soft, lumpy package wrapped in brown paper and tied with string. She clutched it closer as he stopped inches away from her.

Her delicate scent teased him. She wore a white, soft wool dress with thin red stripes, too pretty and frothy to be practical for this part of the country. Thick, gleaming hair was piled atop her head like silky sunshine. Just the sight of her made Riley's mouth watcr, and it wasn't because she reminded him of his favorite candy.

She looked cool and sweet; he just bet she would taste that way, too. Damn.

Sky-blue eyes regarded him warily. Her chest rose and fell rapidly. The fabric of her dress pulled taut across her breasts with each breath. She was one fine-looking woman. He might not want to marry her, but that didn't mean he was blind. He forced his gaze to her eyes.

"Mr. Holt."

He doubted she'd be so formal once he told her what he knew. "I need to talk to you."

"I'm on my way to—"

"Now." He gripped her elbow, not hard enough to bruise that creamy flesh, but firmly enough that she knew he meant business.

He tugged her over so that they stood away from the street and against the wall of the store. The wall *without* a window.

She pulled away from him, paper crackling as she hugged the package to her. "What do you want? I don't like to be manhandled."

"There are a few things I don't like, either, such as being lied to."

She went as still as a spooked rabbit. "What are you talking about?"

"I'm talking about your little secret."

She started to turn away. "I don't have time for—"

"Your baby."

The words were enough to stop her. She faced him, eyes wide with horror. "Adam told you?"

"Damn straight."

Tension vibrated in her body, and he knew if he touched her, she'd be as rigid as a wagon axle.

"I asked him not to say anything," she whispered harshly, her gaze darting around.

"He didn't say it plain. Still protective as all get-out." She was so pale that Riley thought she might faint. That wouldn't surprise him a bit. "He reminded me of a situation with a girl we knew at university. The same thing happened to her."

"So he didn't—"

"No. Your secret's safe, though you can't keep it quiet forever."

She let out a slow breath, a hint of color returning to her face. "I don't know why you're concerned. It's not your problem."

"I have to wonder if you would've told me the truth, had I agreed to marry you."

"Of course!"

"Now, how do I know that?" His gaze skimmed over her full breasts, her still-defined waist.

Before he could ask when the baby was due, Tony Santos rushed up. Doffing his hat, he gave Riley a quick hello before turning to Susannah. "Miz Phelps, did you get the telegram all right?"

"Yes, thank you, Mr. Santos."

"I sent my nephew as soon as it came in, just like you asked."

"I appreciate that." She smiled, not showing any signs of the impatience clawing through Riley.

He cleared his throat, giving the older man an expectant look.

Tony shifted from one foot to the other, then smiled at Susannah. "I hope you're having a nice day, ma'am."

"Thank you."

Riley stared hard at him until the older man stammered a goodbye.

As Tony walked away, she glared at Riley. "There's no need to be rude."

"How far along are you, anyway?"

"Just at five months," she said tightly, flushing a dark rose. "I hardly think this conversation is appropriate."

"Honey, you tried to hitch up with me. It doesn't get more appropriate than that."

"Must you keep bringing that up? We were both there. It's not as if I don't know what an idiot I made of myself."

"I wouldn't say you were an—what is that?"

"What?" Still sounding vexed, she looked over her shoulder.

"On your hand." He'd caught a glint of something shiny, something gold. On her third finger. Lifting her left hand, he felt his jaw drop. "What is this?"

"A ring."

"A wedding ring," he clarified, his gaze shooting to hers. Her hand was stiff and hot. And tiny. Surely she hadn't already married? He'd dropped her off at the hotel less than twenty-four hours ago!

"Yes, a wedding ring." She snatched her hand away.

"You move fast."

"It's none of your concern."

"I may not be marrying you, but I am still a friend of your family. I can't just let you—"

"You have no say, Mr. Holt. None." Color blazed in her high cheekbones, turning her eyes the color of heated sapphires.

In spite of the irritation spiking inside him, Riley's body

hardened. She scrambled his thoughts quicker than a kick to the head.

He gestured to the ring. "What about this poor clod? Did you tell him? Who is it? One of the Baldwins?" For some reason, the possibility made him sick.

"I'm not married. I'm…a widow."

For a full two seconds, he stared at her. "You're what?"

"A widow. A woman without a husband."

"I know what a widow is!"

"Keep your voice down," she whispered, looking around nervously.

"You've never been married." What did he really know about her? "Have you?"

"No." She stepped closer and he felt anger and desperation pouring off her. "But I refuse to let people know my baby as a bast—as illegitimate. The child is the innocent party here."

Riley agreed. Susannah's delicate scent tugged at something inside him. How long had it been since he'd smelled anything besides himself and horse sweat? He cleared his throat. "Your condition will be obvious soon—"

"And by then people will have seen the ring." She touched the band on her finger. "Hopefully, they'll draw the conclusion that I'm a widow."

"Who's gonna believe that? You didn't have the ring on yesterday."

"I wore gloves," she said defiantly. "Except at your ranch. Don't you think this has gone on long enough? We're starting to draw attention. Surely you can't like *that*."

He glanced around and noticed several people walking past with curious looks on their faces. Others stopped in the street, watching openly.

Riley lowered his voice. "What about your last name? It's the same as your brother's."

She looked stricken for a moment then brightened. "I'll say I married a distant cousin."

"That would work."

Jake Ross, a widower whose ranch adjoined the Rocking H, ambled up. Tipping his hat to Susannah, he said, "Mighty nice day, Miz Susannah."

"Yes, it is." Her eyes lit with hope, as if she thought Jake might rescue her.

Riley exchanged greetings with the typically shy man, waited until he'd moved on before turning back to Susannah. "I want you to tell me why you cooked up this scheme."

"I don't owe you any explanations."

"Lady, you came here because of me."

"Only because Adam assured me you wanted to marry me."

"And you would've gone through with it, too. For that reason alone, I deserve an explanation."

The color drained from her face. "All you need to know is that I'm posing as a widow so that I won't bring disgrace to my child. I know how cruel people can be."

Pain flared in her eyes, then was gone. Riley wondered what experience she'd had with cruelty. If Adam had sent her all the way to Texas, there must've been some. No doubt from wealthy families who called the tune in Susannah's circles.

She was so delicate looking. His voice softened. "What happened to the father?"

"That's none of your business." Her face closed up. "I have it in my power to protect my child and that's what I'm doing. You know what it's like for an unmarried woman in my condition. Adam sent me here because of the scandal in St. Louis. This is my chance to start fresh, a place to give my baby a life where he or she isn't shunned because of being illegitimate. I'm asking you to keep this between us. Please."

Riley had already shot to hell the one plan her brother had

for keeping her respectable. Now Adam's presumptuous plan didn't seem so presumptuous; instead it seemed protective and desperate. He'd sent her far away, where no one knew her, yet where he had a friend he could trust. Someone she could lean on if necessary.

J. T. Baldwin's big voice boomed behind Riley. "Miz Phelps, how are you feeling today?"

"Fine, thank you, J.T."

"You're the loveliest thing this old town has seen in quite a while."

Fighting a sharp surge of impatience, Riley chewed on the inside of his cheek.

"You're quite the flatterer, J.T."

"Only when called for. Say, my boys and I are heading over to Abilene for a horse race this weekend. Would you care to join us?"

Riley saw her face pale at the mention of horses, but she smiled. "Thank you, J.T., but I have some matters I must attend to."

"Well, maybe next time."

The big, ruddy-faced man bid them good day, but before Riley and Susannah could continue their conversation, Davis Lee stopped to inquire after Susannah's health. "Hello, Miz Phelps."

"Davis Lee." A soft smile curved her lips.

"You two have met?" Riley leveled a look at his brother.

Davis Lee grinned. "Last night in the restaurant."

"I suppose you were just out for a walk?"

"Yep."

Riley knew he shouldn't have discouraged his brother from meeting Susannah. That had been like waving scent in front of a bloodhound.

"Have a nice day, ma'am." He clapped Riley on the shoulder as he stepped around him. "And *you* behave."

Had she already met every man in town? Riley was starting to think he should've dragged her behind a building so they would have some privacy.

Once they were alone again, he picked up where they'd left off. "What happened between you and the father?"

Her lips tightened and the ice in her gaze could've frozen a Texas summer day.

"Were you betrothed?" he pressed.

"It didn't work out."

"I'm sure Adam knows." Riley couldn't imagine any man—or woman—walking away from a child.

Her lips twisted. With a look of determination, her gaze locked onto his and she said in a fierce, low voice, "His name was Paul LaFortune. I fell in love with him. I thought we were to be married. He said he wanted that. But when I told him about the baby, he disappeared. I thought it was from shock or surprise. After two weeks, Adam hired a private investigator. They found him and he wasn't interested in the baby."

"Or you," Riley said softly, reading volumes beneath her careful words, the too-smooth, emotionless speech.

She lifted her chin, eyes bright with anger. "Have you heard enough?"

"He seduced you."

She blinked in surprise, then said stoically, "I was also party to the deed. He didn't take advantage."

"I imagine it depends on who you ask." Riley found himself strangely compelled to touch her, reassure her in some way. He stuffed a hand in his pocket.

"My *idea* of love seduced me. I realized then I didn't know what love was, but that's all right. What my baby needs is security."

"Miz Susannah?" It was Russ Baldwin who interrupted them this time. "You ready to drive out to Widow Monfrey's old place?"

Susannah gave him a blinding smile. "I'll be right with you, Russ." She turned back to Riley, her voice urgent and pleading. "You won't say anything, will you?"

"Why are you going out to the Monfrey place? It's been empty for about three months."

"Promise you won't tell anyone about my ruse or the baby. Please?"

"Are you looking to live out there?"

"It's none of your concern."

"That place is run-down." Riley turned and waved off Baldwin. "Miz Phelps isn't going today, Russ."

The big man looked at her. "Ma'am?"

"I'll be with you in one minute, Russ," Susannah said with a forced smile.

"Go on, Russ," Riley said. "I'll take Miz Phelps wherever she needs to go. She did come to visit *me,* after all."

"All right, Miz Susannah. If you change your mind, let me know." He touched a finger to the brim of his hat and strolled off.

Her eyes sparked with anger and her lips tightened in a way that made Riley want to kiss her until they went soft beneath his. "How dare you!"

"You can't stay with me," he blurted, then cursed silently.

She stiffened. "I never asked—"

"I mean, it would be improper for you to stay with me," he said in a more gentle tone, "but I can find you a place. I already know of one."

"There's no need," she said hotly.

"*I* feel a need."

"No," she said.

"Let me make up for the way I acted yesterday. It was poorly done."

She looked at him a long minute, then her features

softened. "We were both under false assumptions. And you can rest assured Adam has already heard from me for his part in that."

Wanting to coax a smile from her, Riley grinned. "I would've paid good money to see that telegram."

A smile curved her lips, and it kicked through him like a steel-shod hoof.

"What did you have in mind?"

He stood there, a bit stunned, before he realized she'd asked him a question. "Oh. You can stay with Cora Wilkes. She's newly widowed. Just yesterday, in fact."

"She doesn't need someone invading her grief."

"She needs someone to help her," Riley said firmly. "And so do you. It's a good arrangement. I'll take care of everything."

A tiny frown puckered the smooth skin between Susannah's eyebrows.

"I'll come by the hotel in a few days and take you to meet her."

"I don't know."

He took off his hat, stepped close enough that he could feel the warmth from her skin. "Let me do this."

The struggle to refuse was plain on her face, but finally she nodded. "Thank you," she whispered.

Her eyes, endlessly blue and liquid, did something to his insides. And when she smiled, his muscles clenched as if she'd run those small oval nails across his bare belly. Had any man *ever* turned her down? Probably not.

"Let me walk you back to the hotel."

She nodded, but didn't take his arm. As they walked, she kept a wary distance between them. They reached the hotel in silence, and after agreeing to meet on Friday, Susannah disappeared inside, skirts swishing.

Hell. Irritation shot through him and he pulled his hat

lower on his head. Reaching into his pocket for the last piece of peppermint, he popped it into his mouth despite how it now reminded him of Susannah. She'd been here twenty-four hours and it seemed that every male in town—except him and Lester Hedges, who was just this side of dead—was already panting after her.

Yes, he would keep her secret, along with a healthy distance. Something about Susannah Phelps made him wonder about things he'd never given a second thought. Such as what it would be like to have a woman like her again. And then he remembered the agony of losing one woman to the ravages of this land, and felt himself take a mental step back.

He'd gotten his answers, found out why she'd really showed up in his barn yesterday. She was expecting, but she was just fine. That was all he cared about.

Only then did he wonder what she'd meant about providing security for her baby. Even though Adam's plan had failed, did she still plan to marry? Judging from what Riley had just witnessed, Susannah wouldn't lack for suitors.

For some reason, that thought had him clenching his jaw tight enough to snap.

Chapter Four

In the last three days, Susannah had barely spared Riley a thought. When she was asleep.

She stifled a groan of frustration and smoothed a hand down the skirt of her rose plaid day dress. After wrapping her chignon with a matching ribbon, she put on her short gloves.

As she waited at the Whirlwind Hotel for Riley to collect her and take her to meet Cora Wilkes, Susannah determined that the flutters in her stomach were due to wanting to make a good impression on the widow. They had nothing to do with the way Riley's blue gaze seemed to see right through her. Or the fact that she hadn't seen him since that day on the boardwalk in front of Haskell's General Store. Had he been to town at all?

Drat the man, anyway. He vexed her, but she found herself easily vexed these days. Her emotions had played havoc with her in the last few months. Riley was helping her find a place to live, so she couldn't be angry at him, but she didn't want to think about him. Nor did she want to be beholden to him.

The small watch pinned to her bodice showed it was a little

before three as she made her way downstairs and out to the front of the hotel. She smiled as she passed Mr. Wavers behind the desk. As she stepped out into the cool October day, she saw Riley in the street several yards away. One broad hand caressed his black-and-white paint's nose as he looped the horse's reins over the hitching post.

The short collar of Riley's white shirt skimmed the back of a strong, tanned neck. He was broad and powerful from his chest to his legs. Intimidating even. Though not as intimidating as that horse, which made Susannah stay right where she was under the hotel's awning. Riley Holt wasn't the most handsome man she'd ever seen, but she couldn't seem to take her eyes off him.

He wore a broken-in, gray felt Stetson today, reminding her that the small flat-brim on her head would serve only as decoration in the strong Texas sun.

He stepped up onto the walk before catching sight of her. "Hello."

The pleasant surprise in his voice caused a new set of flutters in her stomach.

"Hello." She twisted the satin strings of her reticule around her fingers. "I'm ready."

"You look real nice." His gaze skimmed over her before coming back to her face. Wide shoulders blocked the sun, threw a long shadow across the planks. "We'll walk if that's all right. Cora lives just at the end of town."

"Yes, I'd like that." In truth, Susannah had walked a bit already today and her ankles were starting to swell, but she preferred walking to riding in something that might force her to sit too close to Riley.

Heading west, the direction Riley lived, they made their way down the wooden walk past the post office and the Pearl Restaurant.

"What have you been doing with yourself?"

"Did you think I might have left?" she asked coolly.

"I figured you stayed. Just to show me." He grinned, taking any sting out of his words.

Released from school moments ago, children darted past them, skipped into the street to dodge horses and a lumbering wagon driven by an old man.

Riley waved as they passed his brother's office, and Susannah glanced at the window to see Davis Lee lift a hand. She waved, too. Her skirts swished softly against the planked wood.

"Thought you might've missed me the past few mornings." Riley gave her a teasing smile. "You doing all right today?"

"Yes, thank you." She didn't like him asking after her all the time. It made her think he cared, made her wish…

"Do you need anything?"

"No, thank you." She'd had no luck finding a job and was growing concerned, but she wouldn't tell Riley that. As they stepped off the walk and into the street, she slid a look at him. "What have you told Cora about me?"

"That you need a place to live."

"Nothing about…my condition?"

"No. That's for you to tell her."

Grateful, she studied him for a moment. "Are you sure it's all right to call on her? Her husband has only been gone three days. At home, mourners don't receive visitors for at least a month."

"Well, things are different here."

"Yes, so you've said." His reminders were starting to fray her nerves. "I assume you still observe some niceties."

"Some."

He sounded amused, which caused her jaw to set. "I thought you said Cora lived at the end of town?" The clang of metal on metal sounded sharply as they reached the blacksmith's barn.

"She does. Well, outside of town a bit." He guided Susannah to the left and they walked past Ef Gerard's smithy. Riley pointed. "See the stage stand?"

Susannah followed his gaze down a gentle slope to a small house behind the shed-size building that served as the stagecoach stop. She hadn't noticed the house when she'd arrived in Whirlwind, but then she'd been more than preoccupied with the thought of marrying Riley. "Oh, I see."

A few minutes' walk brought them close enough for Susannah to see the house was made of rough, unfinished wood. The well-kept home had a certain charm for all its sturdy practicality.

Riley pointed to the side of the house where a wall protruded. "Ollie built on an extra room there. I thought it would be nice for you. It's not large, but it's private."

Touched at his thoughtfulness, Susannah reminded herself that he was looking after her out of a sense of obligation to Adam. And that was fine. Soon she'd be able to take care of herself.

She lifted her skirts to climb the two rough-hewn porch steps. Riley swiped his hat from his head and knocked. She barely had time to smooth her hair before the door was opened by a slender woman.

At least six inches taller than Susannah's five foot three, the woman smiled, though it didn't reach her hazel eyes.

"Good afternoon, Cora."

"Hello, Riley." Patting her neat brown hair, Cora turned to Susannah. "You must be Mrs. Phelps."

"Yes." Susannah shook Cora's hand, marveling at the strength in her long fingers.

She stood straight and tall, putting Susannah in mind of her posture lessons from Miss Wentworth. The sun picked up an occasional gray thread in Cora's sleek bun. Her slightly lined face bespoke someone who usually met life's challenges with a smile.

Susannah's heart tightened at the woman's recent loss. "I appreciate your seeing me."

"I welcome the company. Gettin' a little sick of my own."

"I'm sorry to hear about your husband. If this isn't a good time, we can come back later."

"No, no, come on in. Now is fine."

Riley put a hand to the small of Susannah's back, sending a burst of warmth through her as he guided her into the house. She stepped away once they were inside.

"Let me show you the place." Cora closed the door behind them. "It's not much."

A colorful rag rug warmed the rough pine floor in front of a dormant fireplace where a kettle hung. Savory scents of meat and bread lingered in the air. "This is the kitchen and back there is our bedroom. We have a room built onto the side. Ollie did it so we'd have an extra if we ever needed one." Her voice drifted off.

Susannah caught a flash of pain in the other woman's eyes.

"Sometimes stage passengers rent the room," Riley explained.

Sunlight streamed through plate glass windows on either side of the front door and two windows along the wall to her left, giving the small space ample light. Oil cloth tacked above each window could be let down for privacy.

A deep sink, complete with pump handle, stood against the far wall next to the center fireplace. From what Susannah could tell, this front room served as a gathering place for visitors and meals. She speculated that the door behind Cora led to a bedroom. On the wall to her right was a doorway covered with a long, blue calico curtain.

Cora walked over and pushed aside the fabric. "Ollie was always thinking ahead."

"It's a nice room," Riley stated.

"It's private." The older woman patted the door frame. "If you'd like, Susannah, I can probably talk Riley into putting on a real door."

"I'm sure this will be fine." She moved over to stand next to Cora and look into the room that would be hers. "I don't want to be any trouble."

Across from her, a narrow bed stretched against the long wall. Within arm's reach to her right, a wide washstand with two drawers held a pitcher and basin on top. A window near the foot of the bed drew Susannah. She walked over to stare out at the prairie grass. The throaty cluck of chickens sounded from behind the house. She turned, spying a wooden-framed mirror over the washstand. The three hooks on the wall beside the mirror weren't nearly enough to hold her clothes, but she would make do.

"It's very nice. I'm definitely interested."

The bed was half the size of hers at home, but it looked sturdy and comfortable and clean.

"Wonderful," Cora said. "We can work out the terms in the other room."

"I think you should know that there will be two of us." In an effort to still the sudden trembling in her hands, Susannah placed them on the slight swell of her stomach.

"A baby?"

She nodded, carefully keeping her gaze from Riley, who leaned one shoulder against the jamb and watched with that unsettling intensity.

"Wonderful!" the other woman exclaimed. "When do you expect the little one?"

"Sometime in February. You don't mind about another person?"

"Goodness, no."

"I'll pay extra, of course." She'd figure out a way.

"We'll talk about that if we need to."

"Yes." Susannah slid a look at Riley to see if he might say anything about the baby. He stood silent, a message in his eyes that told her this was her decision.

Cora laid a comforting hand on Susannah's arm. "Riley told me you're recently widowed yourself. I'm sorry to hear it."

"Thank you."

She looked down, her conscience twinging. She didn't like deceiving people, but she wouldn't allow her child to be treated badly because of her foolish belief in a man who didn't love her. "How long has it been, dear?"

Susannah froze. She hadn't given a single thought to when she'd lost her fictitious husband. Or how. "Uh, n-not too long," she stammered, a flush working under her skin.

"I'm sorry. The memories are probably too fresh for you to want to discuss it."

"Yes, I'm afraid so." At least Cora's kindness would gain her some time.

"Susannah was supposed to meet her husband in Abilene, and arrived there to find him ill," Riley said. "Unfortunately, he didn't make it, but she came on to Whirlwind, where they'd originally planned to settle."

Susannah struggled to keep the surprise from her face. She certainly hadn't expected him to help her with her deception. His explanation was simple and easy to remember, thank goodness.

"Bless your heart," Cora said. "You don't have to talk about it. That will come in its own good time."

"Thank you."

Tears glimmered in the other woman's eyes and she glanced

down quickly. Susannah threw a grateful look over her head to Riley.

He gave a small nod.

Cora ran a hand along the edge of the washstand. A simple scroll pattern bordered both sides and was burned into the top. "Ollie made this washstand. And that bed."

"Is there anything you need done around here, Cora?" Riley asked. He was obviously trying to change the subject.

Susannah glanced at him before saying, "Seems like Ollie could do just about anything."

"He could." Tears swam in the woman's eyes and Susannah's heart went out to her.

Behind Cora, Riley shook his head at Susannah, clearly not wanting her to pursue the topic. Her lips tightened. She hadn't lost a husband, but she had lost her home and family. "How long were you married?"

"Thirty-five years."

Riley's frown deepened and he gave a more violent shake of his head. His features twisted as if he'd been seized by a cramp. Susannah shot him an irritated look. Why did he keep interrupting the widow every time she talked about her husband?

"We met in Dallas and came out here as newlyweds."

"My goodness. Did he always drive the stage?"

"Yes." Cora turned to Riley, her voice cracking. "Remember how you boys used to beg to drive it?"

"Yes, ma'am." He shifted from foot to foot as if the floor had suddenly gone hot. "I think I'd better check on the chickens."

His boots thudded heavily across the wooden floor as he walked out.

Cora wiped at her eyes and a smile touched her mouth. "He doesn't want me to be upset."

"Would you prefer not to talk about it?"

"I'd like to, since you asked. It's nice having a woman around. These kinds of things make those boys uncomfortable. His brother, Davis Lee, is the same way."

"I know what you mean. My brother can't take his leave fast enough when subjects like this come up."

The other woman smiled. "Let me get you some tea. You look like you could sit a spell."

"That would be wonderful."

Several minutes and one cup of tea later, Susannah had reached an arrangement with Cora about the room. She'd also learned that Ollie Wilkes had been killed the same day she'd arrived. A band of outlaws called the McDougal gang had been responsible not just for widowing Cora, but also for robbing other stages and a train in Abilene, and killing people throughout Texas.

Cora was obviously hurting, but going on with her life. Susannah hoped she herself could be as strong in her present circumstances.

She paid for the first week's room and board. "I'd like to help around here. I'm afraid I don't know how to cook, but maybe I could help with the chickens?"

Cora tucked the money into an old tin. "No offense, dear, but do you know anything about chickens?"

"No." Susannah smiled brightly, swallowing her uncertainty. "But I can learn. Don't you think?"

"Of course. Let's go out and have Riley show you."

She followed Cora out a side door hidden in the corner next to the sink. A fence squared off a large area. A barn stood several yards directly behind the house; next to it was a fenced-in round pen.

"Chickens are in there." Cora pointed at the rectangular building to their left.

A curse sounded from inside the long shed and she

chuckled. "My hens don't like Riley any better than he likes them."

Here, the grass was cropped close to the ground; near the barn, it grew high enough to brush Susannah's hem.

As she and Cora approached the barn, red dust puffing around their feet, a big, black horse appeared in the barn door.

Susannah froze, her heart hammering painfully against her ribs.

"Hello, Prissy," Cora crooned, changing direction to stop and stroke the huge animal. A white star between its eyes was the only color on the coal-black beast. Dark eyes stared unblinking at Susannah.

Aware of the size and power of the horse, she stayed where she was, falling into step when Cora rejoined her. Even though she knew the horse was a safe distance away, she couldn't help looking over her shoulder.

A clatter, then the angry flutter of wings sounded as Cora opened the door to the henhouse.

"Give me that egg, you witch."

"She's my best hen, Riley. She doesn't like to be upset," Cora said.

He turned, sunlight sliding through the planked roof to light one side of his face. He looked more than vexed. Susannah would've grinned, but she was debating the wisdom of offering to care for the chickens.

Dusting off his hands, he stepped forward into full sunlight. He gestured toward a small pile of eggs just inside the door. "You're the only one who can handle that old grouch, Cora."

"Nonsense."

"What happened to you?" Susannah glimpsed a raw place on Riley's hand and tried to squash the alarm that shot through her. "You're bleeding!"

He glanced down, then shrugged. "The old witch pecked me."

She fumbled in her reticule for her handkerchief. "We'd better clean it up."

"I'm sure it's fine."

She took his hand, dabbing gently at the blood across his knuckles until she'd cleaned the deep scratch. As she worked slowly around the wound, she realized the air had suddenly become thick and hot. Charged.

She looked up into his eyes, saw a flash of raw hunger that tripled her heart rate. His thumb came up and covered hers. Oh, mercy!

He jerked away the same time she did, and turned to Cora. "What are y'all doing out here?"

"Susannah is going to help me with the chickens," the older woman said.

Susannah crumpled her handkerchief and pasted a smile on her face, hoping Riley couldn't see how his touch had affected her.

He arched a dark brow. "Do you know anything about chickens?"

"Not yet." She lifted her chin, not liking the skeptical tone in his voice. "Maybe you'd better show me, Cora. I don't want to end up like Riley."

Cora chuckled. "Use a gentle touch. Just talk to them and nudge your hand under their bellies like so...." She demonstrated on a sedate looking bird. "You don't have to try and wrangle them like a steer," she said with a meaningful look at Riley.

He gave the widow a crooked grin, and Susannah bit back a smile.

"You try it, Susannah. This hen usually lays this time of day, though I've never figured out why. The others typically lay at night or early morning."

Susannah stepped up, apprehensive but trying to copy Cora's movements exactly. She slid her hand beneath the hen's plump, soft belly and touched a warm, smooth surface. She drew out an egg while the bird blinked sleepily.

"Look!" She held up the object, thrilled that she had managed to retrieve it without incident.

"Good." Cora tucked the egg into her skirt pocket. "We'll come out again in the morning."

As the three of them walked back to the house, the older woman invited Susannah to bring her things from the hotel and move in that evening.

Susannah smiled. "Thank you, I will. In the next few days, I'll be able to pay you for the whole month. My brother will send me some money, and I'm looking for a job."

"A job?" Riley halted in midstep. "Just what kind of position do you think you're going to find in Whirlwind?"

"I don't know." She stiffened. "Please don't sound so shocked. I didn't say I was going to become the sheriff. I have excellent penmanship and I'm fair with figures. I'm sure I can find something," she said with a lot more confidence than she felt.

"I'm sure you can, too." Cora patted her arm and gave Riley a look Susannah couldn't decipher.

She and Riley bade the other woman goodbye and started back toward the hotel.

"Thank you for introducing us. I think things will work out wonderfully."

"You think the room will suffice?"

"Oh, yes. I don't need much."

If he disagreed, he kept it to himself. "I'll help you move your things."

"Thank you." She slid a look at him, thinking about the way her nerves had hummed when he'd touched her hand out behind Cora's house. "I appreciate you helping me with the story about my husband. I haven't thought out everything yet."

"You're welcome." He stopped in front of the Pearl. "Are you serious about finding a job?"

"I have to. I'm responsible for another person now."

"Look, I could get you a ticket back home. Or I'm sure Adam would come for you himself, if you asked."

Reminding herself of Riley's help today, she tried to squelch the burn of irritation his offer caused. "I'm not going back to St. Louis. I appreciate your help in finding me a place to live and I can tell I'm going to love Cora, but I think I can handle things from here."

"Are you telling me to mind my own business?"

Heat flushed her cheeks, but she held his gaze. "I wouldn't put it so bluntly, but…"

"All right, but if you need anything, let me know."

"I appreciate the offer, but I'll be fine."

"Life out here can be pretty unpredictable."

"You've made it plain you don't think I'll last, but you're wrong."

He stared into her eyes for a long moment, then touched the brim of his hat. "Let's get your things and get you out to Cora's."

"I'm sure I can manage."

"I'll help you."

"It will take me awhile to pack—"

He was already walking into the hotel.

Puffing out an exasperated breath, she followed, staring a hole in his back. It wasn't hard to see why he got along so well with Adam. Men!

Chapter Five

All the next morning and into the afternoon, Riley tried to shake thoughts of Susannah, but they clung like a cobweb. Until yesterday, he'd managed to stay away from her for three days. He'd agreed to mind his own business. Maybe being left alone was the only way she'd realize she didn't belong here. Maddie had been determined, too. And she'd paid a steep price for it. Riley would hate to see that happen to Susannah.

He glanced down at the still-red scratch across the knuckles of his right hand. The memory of her touch on his skin, her scent drifting around him, had his body going tight. She was a fine piece of woman and he didn't have any business thinking about her.

He stepped up on the stall slat he'd just replaced. Even though it held his weight, he cussed. His concentration was shot clean to hell and supper was still two hours away. Joe and Cody Tillman, the father and son who worked as Riley's ranch hands, were stringing fence in the south pasture, and would probably stay out there again tonight. He might as well go to town and check on that pump part he'd ordered.

An hour later, Mr. Haskell looked at him as if he'd asked

to try on a bonnet. "That pump part won't be here for at least a month, Riley. It's coming from back East. Didn't I tell you that the other day when you ordered it?"

"Did you?" He thumbed back his hat, trying to recall.

"Is there anything else I can do for you? Need any supplies?"

"No, I'm all set." He glanced over his shoulder and out the large plate glass window, turning slightly when he caught sight of Cora rushing past the store. "Maybe some peppermint. A quarter pound. Thanks."

Mr. Haskell measured out the sweets, wrapping them in brown paper. "Here ya go. That'll be a nickel."

Riley handed him the coin and took his candy as he moved away from the counter.

Cora was alone and covering ground fast. Holding her hat onto her head, she rushed as if she were being chased, into the sheriff's office.

Something had happened. The McDougal gang? Susannah?

Riley strode over to the jail, stepping inside in time to hear Cora say "...should've been back by now."

"I agree," Davis Lee said, rising from his chair behind the desk. "Abilene is a trip that can easily be made in one day."

"What's happened?" Riley shut the door, noting the frantic look on Cora's slightly lined features.

"That's what I'm trying to find out," his brother said.

"Susannah headed out to Abilene this morning and she hasn't returned."

"Why did she go to Abilene?" Riley and Davis Lee asked in unison.

Riley's brother shot him a look, but he ignored it and kept his gaze on Cora.

"She said she had business there."

"Maybe she boarded the train," he said. "And headed back to St. Louis." *Where she belonged.*

"No," Cora said. "That girl intends to stay. Besides, she took only her reticule. All her things are still at my house."

He leaned against the door. "What kind of business would she have there?"

"That's what *I'm* trying to find out." Davis Lee came around his desk and took a seat on the corner in front of Cora. "Do you know?"

The older woman frowned. "She didn't say."

Riley recalled her declaration to find a job. Surely she wasn't looking in Abilene. "Why would she do a fool thing like take off alone for Abilene? She knows about the McDougal gang."

"Oh, she wasn't alone," Cora said.

Of course she wasn't. One or more of the Baldwins had probably swooped in and carted her over.

"Miguel Santos went with her."

"Miguel?" Riley straightened. "He's just a boy."

"He knows how to drive a rig," Davis Lee reminded him.

Cora added, "They took his uncle Tony's old mare."

"Oh, well." Davis Lee shrugged. "She's as easy to handle as a pup."

"But if something happened…" Cora's concerned gaze swung from Riley to his brother.

Davis Lee patted her shoulder consolingly. "The boy has been to Abilene plenty and he has experience."

"With outlaws?" Riley fought the urge to hightail it out of town and start searching for the pair.

Davis Lee heaved a sigh. "Brother, you're not really helping."

Unease pinched between Riley's shoulder blades. "What time did she leave?"

"She showed up here at the jail a little before eight," Davis Lee said.

"Why would she come to see you?" Riley swallowed a bark of impatience. *And since you saw her, why did you let her go?*

Davis Lee leaned over his desk and opened a top drawer, taking out his revolver. "She asked me about the McDougals, wanted to know if I thought they were still in the area."

"I'm sure you told her they were nearby."

"They're not. I got a wire last evening telling me the McDougals robbed a train yesterday between Dodge City and Wichita."

"Thank goodness, they're gone!" Cora put a hand to her chest.

Riley crossed his arms and said in a low voice, "Maybe they're not *all* up in Kansas. They could've split up."

"They never have before," Davis Lee said evenly. "All four of them were spotted at the holdup."

"Someone could've made a mistake." Urgency coiled through Riley. Just because Davis Lee was so all-fired certain the McDougals were gone didn't mean they were. "People do it all the time."

Davis Lee buckled on his gunbelt. "I'll ride that way and see if I can find Susannah and Miguel."

"Oh, thank you, son." Cora pulled her shawl tighter around her shoulders.

He moved to the wooden gun cabinet behind his desk, unlocked it and pulled out a rifle. Glancing over his shoulder, he held it toward Riley. "Do you want one?"

"I'm sure you can find her."

Davis Lee laughed. "You might as well come along. You're about to crawl out of your skin just standing there."

"She's a grown woman—" Riley began.

"I'll feel better if you go, too." Cora squeezed his arm.

Why couldn't he just mind his own business where Susannah Phelps was concerned? Like yesterday, when he'd piped up with that story about her fake husband dying in Abilene. Even so, this was different, possibly dangerous. Riley couldn't face Adam if something happened to his sister.

"Let's go." Davis Lee tossed him the weapon.

Riley caught the Winchester, grabbed a handful of shells from his brother's desk drawer.

"I'm sure she's fine, Cora." Davis Lee gave the woman a quick hug.

Riley kept his mouth shut, but gave the older woman an encouraging smile. He truly hoped Susannah *was* all right.

He and his brother mounted, riding east out of town past the church. After covering more than a mile, Riley saw a buckboard moving slowly through the prairie grass.

As they neared, sunlight glinted off silvery hair, and relief swelled sharply in his chest.

"It's Susannah," he called, loudly enough to be heard over the horses' galloping hooves.

Davis Lee nodded to show he'd heard.

A few short moments brought her and the young, dark-haired boy into clear sight.

Miguel walked in front of the buckboard, leading the mare by her harness. Susannah rode in the weathered wagon, her hands clamped onto the edge of the seat as if welded there. Her face was pale as chalk, and Riley didn't miss the brilliant flash of relief in her blue eyes.

She met his gaze briefly, then looked away.

"Are you two okay?" Davis Lee reined his horse on Susannah's side of the wagon, while Riley did the same on the other.

She nodded. "Yes, we're fine."

"Cora's pretty worried."

"It's my fault, Sheriff." Miguel uncomfortably met Davis

Lee's gaze. The boy's hair stuck straight up in back, as if he'd just rolled out of bed. "The mare was spooked."

"It's not your fault she saw a snake." Susannah shuddered.

"She bolted off the road," the boy explained.

"But not very far. Miguel got her under control quickly."

Despite Susannah's defense of the boy, Riley noted that she trembled. Was she all right? What about the baby? He wanted to ask, but he didn't think Davis Lee and Miguel were aware of Susannah's condition. Concern hollowed out a hole in his gut.

"This mare's well-trained." Davis Lee looked her over with a critical eye.

Riley dismounted to check the horse for injuries, running a hand down both her back legs to her fetlocks before moving to the front. She was fine. While he stood stroking a calming hand down the bridge of the mare's velvety nose, he studied Susannah. Her hair drooped from its usual neat chignon. A streak of dirt ran across one cheek. Her hat dangled precariously off the back of her head. Wisps of silvery-blond hair blew around her face and straggled down her neck.

She slid a glance at him, then turned her attention back to Davis Lee.

If Riley weren't so aware of the sheer terror swimming in her blue eyes, he might think she'd just tangled the sheets with someone.

That thought heated him up as much as the possibility that something could've happened to her and the baby.

"Looks like everyone is okay," his brother said.

Riley clapped a hand on Miguel's shoulder. "You did a fine job, boy. The mare isn't injured and you and the lady are fine."

Miguel smiled.

Susannah's lips curved, but she didn't relax her hold on the wagon seat.

Davis Lee pushed back his hat and stared toward town consideringly. "I'll drive Susannah back in the wagon. Miguel, you can ride my horse or in the back of the wagon, whatever you want."

"I can really ride your horse?" he asked excitedly.

"Yep." Davis Lee walked around to the other side of the buckboard and stepped in front of Riley to climb up beside Susannah.

He inched back, swallowing the insistence that he drive her. Davis Lee was more than capable, and it was better for him to drive her. If Riley got any closer, he might try to shake some sense into her.

As the four of them rode back to town, he let the soft wash of their voices play over him. He was glad both Susannah and Miguel were all right, so why did this restlessness churn inside him?

Whip yanked on the reins and Riley realized his hold was too tight. He loosened his grip and struggled to level out the tide of relief choking him. Susannah was still pale, but appeared composed. A spooked horse could be as dangerous as anything out here. He wondered if this incident would send her packing. She sure didn't like horses much.

Sliding a sideways look at her, he watched as she shakily unpinned her crooked hat and resettled it properly on her head. That damn fake wedding ring glittered. It didn't go down easy to realize that he wanted to put his hands on her. To shake or comfort, he wasn't sure which. Questions boiled inside him, but he bit them back. He wouldn't even be here if Davis Lee hadn't insisted he come along.

The sun dipped below the horizon in a blanket of amber fire. Just outside of town, Creed Carter, Pete's boy, ran toward the wagon waving his twig-thin arms. "Sheriff! Sheriff!"

Davis Lee slowed the wagon to a stop within sight of the church. "What is it, Creed?"

Riley and Miguel reined up.

"Luther and Odell are at it again." The spindly young man bent at the waist, panting. "They're threatening to duel."

Riley grinned, shooting a look at his brother.

Davis Lee sighed. "Does either of them have a gun?"

"Luther does."

"Is it loaded this time?"

"I don't know, but he's waving it around like he means business."

Davis Lee turned to Susannah. "Excuse me. I need to handle this."

"Go on. I'll be fine. I can walk from here." She smiled, and though it flattered her lovely face, Riley could still see fear in her eyes.

Davis Lee pulled the brake and left the reins draped loosely over the buckboard's front. "Riley will see you to Cora's."

"I'm sure I can see myself home," she said primly.

"Riley?" His brother's gaze swung to him, burning across the space between them.

"I'll see that she gets there."

"Thanks." Davis Lee climbed out of the wagon and smiled up at Susannah. "I'm glad you're all right. Cora will be glad, too."

"Thank you, Sheriff. I'm sorry if I caused any trouble."

"No trouble." He gazed at her as if he didn't have anything better to do than chase around after silly women all day.

Riley doubted she would apologize to him.

His brother touched the brim of his dark hat and followed Creed, who zigzagged ahead as if dodging hot coals.

Riley dismounted and walked over to Miguel. "Why don't you leave the sheriff's horse at the jail? I'll bring the buckboard and your uncle's mare once I deliver Miz Susannah to Miz Cora's.''

The boy's dark eyes went to Susannah. "Is that all right, ma'am?''

"It's fine,'' she said with a gentle smile.

He looked down at the ground for a moment. "I'm sorry about what happened today.''

"Nonsense, Miguel. You handled it beautifully. If it weren't for you, that horse would still be running.''

Despite her kind words, Riley noted that she still gripped the seat hard enough to leave nail marks. He tied his horse to the back of the wagon and moved up to the front in time to see Susannah press a coin into Miguel's hand.

"But, ma'am, you've already paid me.''

"That's extra for the way you handled yourself. Just think how frightened I would've been if I'd been alone.''

A broad grin split his face. "Thank you, Mrs. Phelps. Thank you!''

Riley helped him mount Davis Lee's buckskin gelding, and waited until the horse ambled toward town before climbing up into the buckboard. His gaze flicked over Susannah's dusty navy traveling suit and white shirt. "Is the baby all right?''

"Yes.'' She laid a visibly shaking hand on her stomach.

"You're sure?''

"Yes, thank you.'' After a pause, she insisted, "I can see myself to Cora's.''

The relief he'd felt about the baby evaporated. Riley set his jaw and settled into the seat beside her. "I'll have you there before you know it.''

He slapped the reins across the mare's rump and the wagon lurched into motion.

"Who are Luther and Odell?'' she asked.

"Two of the saloon's most loyal patrons.''

"Oh.''

Her soft vanilla scent blew gently across his face. The sight of wispy hair blowing around her face and trailing down her neck pulled Riley's gut tight. She looked sweet and vulnerable. Dangerously so. Enough to make it an effort to keep from asking the questions boiling through him. He lasted until they reached Cora's.

He helped her down from the wagon, his lungs filling with her warmth, his nerves pinging. His hands flexed on her waist as he thought about the way she'd tended to him yesterday. As he set her on her feet, he forced himself to remember another woman who'd once tended him, to recall what had happened to her. "What in the heck were you thinking? You shouldn't be gallivanting around out here."

"I wasn't gallivanting." Her head came up sharply and she stepped away. "I had business."

"What was so important that it couldn't wait?"

"Adam wired me some money. I needed it."

"You should've waited until someone other than a boy could go with you."

"Oh, I suppose you mean you?" She looked down her nose, twisting the strings of her reticule. "The arrangements I made worked out fine. Your brother said the outlaws weren't nearby, so I didn't see the harm."

"Yeah, your wagon was nearly wrecked because of a snake."

"That could've happened no matter who went with me. I admit I was terrified when that horse ran away, but Miguel quickly got her under control."

"You shouldn't have gone without an escort. An *older* escort."

"I imagine I'll be going a lot of places without an escort, Mr. Holt."

He hated when she called him that. "Well, Miz Phelps,

down here you can't just wander willy-nilly around these parts."

"I was not wandering willy-nilly." She gritted her teeth, her fist closing over the bag. "I had business to attend to, and I did that. If you don't approve, then maybe you shouldn't ask so many questions."

Seething, and not sure why, Riley stared into her blue eyes. They were troubled yet determined. Unyielding. Just like another woman he'd known. Another woman who hadn't belonged here.

He valued his friendship with Adam too much to turn his back on Susannah, but Riley couldn't let his life get tangled up with hers, either. "You're right. You're a grown woman, and not accountable to me."

She gave a sharp nod of agreement, but he caught a flash of confusion and surprise in her eyes.

He climbed up in the wagon and tipped his hat. "I'm glad you're unhurt. And the baby, too."

"Thank you," she said grudgingly. "For coming to look for us. And for driving me back."

"You're welcome." He clucked to the mare. As he rode away, Riley told himself the hollow ache in his stomach was because he was hungry, not because of what might have happened to her. Frustration had him jamming his hat farther down on his head. He'd managed to stay out of her affairs for all of one day.

The protective feelings that dogged Riley all the next week weren't any more welcome by him than they would be by Susannah. An obligation to keep Adam's sister safe was what he felt. Was *all* he would feel. Putting up hay for the winter, replacing rotten planks in his shed and barn, and working his three-year-old filly, Storm, had kept Riley busy. His body at least. His mind was plumb tuckered out trying to sidestep insistent thoughts of Susannah. Curiosity over whether the incident with the spooked horse might have sent her packing was wearing a hole through him. If the horse hadn't scared her away, maybe her inability to find a job would.

As he rode toward Whirlwind the next Saturday for one of the fall horse races, he hoped Susannah had left town, but he had no way of knowing. With her delicate build and ignorance about life on a ranch, she reminded him of Maddie. Neither woman was suited to life in a hard land.

A land that had killed his wife.

A vicious dust storm had disoriented Maddie and caused the fall that had broken her neck. Riley would always feel some responsibility over that. The whirling, blinding clouds of dust had come up suddenly, while he'd been in Abilene at a horse sale. There had been no way he could warn her, nothing he could do. Hours after arriving home, he and his father had finally found her at the bottom of a shallow gully not far from the house.

Riley had blamed himself for a while, and then he'd felt nothing. Since Maddie, he hadn't found another woman who had been able to stir even a passing interest. The fact that Susannah Phelps stirred much more than that needled him. A woman like her was just flat-out wrong for him. He knew what kind of woman fitted him and his life. It wasn't Susannah.

He repeated that to himself when he saw her standing under the awning in front of Haskell's Store. Sandwiched between the giant Baldwin brothers, with her silky hair piled atop her head, she looked like a specially wrapped package. Bright and shiny and too pretty for either one of those hairy sidewinders.

The dainty blue parasol Matt held for Susannah looked like a twig in his large hands. Russ leaned close to point out one of the horses in the street, where the race would take place. She listened attentively, turned her head when Matt indicated Jake Ross on his bay. She stayed against the storefront, not even within spitting distance of the animals. She must be really terrified of horses.

Riley dismounted in front of Haskell's and stepped up on the boardwalk. People wove around him, moving down to the street for a place near the action. Children's laughter punctuated the buzz of adult conversation. Hurrying feet and restlessly stomping horse hooves stirred up the smell of dirt and animals. It looked as if the whole town had turned out. Riley squinted against the glare of the sun. Occasionally a stiff breeze shot through the crowd, bringing a crispness to the sunny fall day.

Susannah looked warm enough in a navy coat, which made her eyes even more blue than he remembered. A soft, becoming blush highlighted her cheeks, and a wisp of blond hair blew across her face. She was so pretty his whole body hummed. She looked fresh and…in the family way.

Her condition had become evident in the week since he'd last seen her.

"Good day, Susannah." He touched the tip of his hat. "Russ, Matt."

"Hey, Riley," Matt said.

"Riley." Russ grinned.

Susannah nodded primly, her gaze on a point past his shoulder.

"I didn't expect to see you here today," he said.

Rather than look at him, she smiled at both Baldwins. "I couldn't say no to two such charming invitations."

Matt switched the parasol to his other hand. "Even though I asked first."

"Did not," Russ said pleasantly, arms crossed over his chest.

"Ever been to a horse race before?" Riley asked her.

"No."

"I thought you didn't like horses—"

"She'll like the race," Matt interrupted with a grin. "I promised she would."

Susannah's lips curved as she glanced at the big man, who was standing a little too close to her for Riley's liking. So far she hadn't looked at *him* once.

"They'll start down by the church, race through town and around twice," Matt explained. "The winner takes home a money prize, the total of the entry fees."

Riley was starting to feel like a spare wagon part. He glanced around. "Where's Cora?"

"She isn't feeling well." Susannah finally looked at him, her blue eyes concerned. "I think she's missing Ollie."

Riley nodded, his gaze meeting hers in sympathetic understanding. "What about J.T.? Surely he's around. He doesn't miss a race."

"He's on watch at the other end of town." Russ hooked a thumb toward the smithy. "Your brother needed another deputy."

On his way into town, Riley had seen Davis Lee at the smithy, and had stopped. Since the McDougals had hit so close to town, Davis Lee wasn't taking any chances. He'd posted a guard at either end of town for the race today.

"Are you racing today, Riley?" Matt asked.

"Yes."

"On Whip?"

Riley nodded.

"I'll put some money on that." The younger Baldwin turned to Susannah. "Excuse me, Miz Susannah. I'll be right back."

As he moved behind her and into the store, she glanced at Riley, then Russ. "Is he betting?"

"Yes, ma'am."

"On Riley?"

"Yep." Russ chuckled. "Riley always gives Banker Dobies a run for his money."

"Banker Dobies? From Abilene?" she asked.

"That's the one." Riley set his teeth at the memory of her ill-advised trip to Abilene. He needed to get inside and pay his entry fee. "He's a good rider. We've traded off winning this race the last four years."

Susannah's gaze scanned the people hurrying across the street, the groups already in place on the other side. "There he is."

She nodded toward the east end of town, where Francis Dobies sat astride a gray-white gelding lined up with several other horses and their riders.

Riley flicked a look at her dewy skin, the sweet curve of her neck. That damn gold band gleamed on her finger. No doubt the Baldwins now knew her as a widow. For her baby's sake, he hoped her masquerade worked. Of course, the best thing for both of them would be for Susannah to realize she didn't belong here. Not his affair, he reminded himself. Slamming the door on the thought, he tipped his hat to her and walked inside the store to pay his fee.

Several minutes later, he took his place in the line that stretched across Whirlwind's main street in front of the church. Susannah's hair, gleaming like cornsilk, made her easy to pick out. The Baldwin brothers dwarfed her small frame.

Pete Carter limped to a spot in front of his saloon and raised a pistol. "Take your marks!"

The riders lined up.

"Get set." After a few seconds, Pete fired the pistol.

At the gun's crack, Whip leaped off the start. Riley automatically leaned into the gelding, blanking his mind of Susannah and keeping his gaze fixed ahead. The ground blurred beneath his paint's hooves. He and Dobies were neck and neck down Main, around the first turn at the smithy and behind the stretch of buildings. Just as they turned to circle through town again, a black horse streaked past on Riley's right.

He cut his gaze to the side, then back. He didn't recognize the animal. He leaned forward and let Whip have his head.

Riley and the banker tied for second. The rider on the black horse, whose face was covered by a brown slouch hat and a dark bandanna, came in first with a modest lead. Amid the cheering, Riley slowed his mount, catching a glimpse of the banker's face.

Hard and set, Francis Dobies's eyes followed the unfamiliar figure on the black horse as the pair disappeared around the blacksmith's barn.

Riley stuck out his hand to the banker. "Good race, man. Maybe we'll both have better luck next time."

"Who is that?" Francis ignored Riley's outstretched hand and swung down from his saddle.

"I don't know." He lowered his hand, dismounted. "Never seen that horse before."

"Neither have I." A flush rimmed the banker's jaw and he strode over to Haskell's.

Francis must've been set on winning that money, Riley guessed. He left Whip at the hitching post and started for Haskell's to congratulate the winner and introduce himself.

People on either side of the street poured into the middle, talking and cheering. More than once Riley caught the same question that Dobies had asked about the stranger. Whoever the man was, he'd collect some nice winnings today. At least twenty people had paid the dollar entry fee. Anyone who'd bet on the stranger would have made a nice haul, too.

As he neared the store, Riley caught sight of the Baldwins talking to Jake Ross and Tony Santos. All four men were shaking their heads.

"...couldn't see his face."

"Didn't know that horse at all."

Where was Susannah? Ah, there, against the plate glass talking to Miguel.

Riley stepped up under the awning. Color flagged her cheeks as she smiled at something the boy said.

Dobies stalked out of the store. "Haskell said the winner already picked up his money and left out the back. Not very sociable, is he?"

Riley shrugged, slightly annoyed by Dobies's attitude. "He did beat you fair and square, Francis."

The banker gave him a flat stare and stepped into the street, elbowing his way through a crowd of people still standing there. All around, voices chattered like squirrels. Riley caught smatterings of conversation, all about the identity of the mystery rider.

"Hey, Riley," Russ called out. "Who *was* the winner?"

He shrugged. "Don't know."

"That horse didn't have a single marking," Matt observed. "Like pure midnight."

The other men murmured agreement.

"Yeah," Riley said.

"That just beats all," Jake Ross said quietly.

"It's the fastest horse I've seen in a while," Tony Santos added.

From the corner of his eye, Riley saw something flutter. He turned his head and spotted a piece of paper tacked to a post in front of the store. He stepped closer to read the neat print and his eyes widened.

Susannah Phelps will offer an eight-week charm school on manners, dancing, courtship and other matters of etiquette. A distinguished graduate of Miss Elmira Wentworth's Finishing Academy For Young Ladies in St. Louis, Missouri. For more information, see Mrs. Susannah Phelps, now residing in the home of Mrs. Cora Wilkes.

A *charm* school? And who the hell was Elmira Wentworth?

Riley looked up in time to see Susannah squeezing her way through a throng of people in front of Haskell's door. He yanked the paper down and stepped over to her.

"You're offering a school?"

"Yes." She looked startled, then caught sight of the paper he held. A tinge of pink warmed her skin.

He bit the inside of his cheek. "You created your own job?"

"I can't take all the credit. Cora and I came up with the idea together."

"Cora."

"Yes. She suggested I consider my strengths, and when I did, a charm school seemed like a good idea."

Very resourceful, he admitted. And persistent, though he didn't hold out much hope for her success. "Good luck. I hope some people will show up."

"I think they will."

"Where you planning on having this school?"

"Cora's house. She's also offered the barn if I need more space."

Riley didn't figure she would. "How many women do you expect?"

"Oh, I expect both men and women," she said pleasantly.

"Men?" He couldn't see many of these men showing up to learn how to eat with fancy utensils and flutter napkins around.

"Yes."

"Will there be any women there?"

"At least Cora and I. What about you? Don't you need lessons in at least one of my subjects?"

He raised a brow. "I don't have any trouble getting food in

my mouth. I already know how to dance, and I'm not courting anyone, so I guess not."

Matt and Russ drifted away from the other men and closed around Susannah like guards.

"You thinking about going to Miz Susannah's school?" Russ pointed to the flyer in Riley's hand.

"We are," Matt added.

Of course they were. "I'm sure she'll be plenty busy trying to teach the two of you a little polish."

"Too bad you won't be getting any of it, Holt." Russ grinned. "You're a little rough yourself."

"It's hard to polish a diamond, boys."

Matt and Russ chuckled, each offering an arm to Susannah.

She tucked one hand into the crook of Matt's arm and one into Russ's. As they walked away, she said to Riley over her shoulder, "If you change your mind—"

"I won't."

"Classes start Monday evening."

The possibility that more than one or two men might show up was slim. Riley hoped she wouldn't be too disappointed.

Chapter Six

Riley Holt made her as nervous as any horse ever had, with all that muscle and power and intimidating presence. His blue gaze tickled something deep inside her. Something she'd tried to bury since Paul's rejection.

Just before dark on Sunday, Susannah slid the basket handle over her arm, took a deep breath and let herself into the henhouse. Ugh! The sharp, dirty smell threatened to overwhelm her. Morning sickness had ended a month before she'd arrived in Whirlwind, but when she gathered eggs for Cora, her stomach rebelled, both in the morning and in the evening.

Forcing her thoughts in another direction would help the time pass faster and perhaps dull the pungent odor of the hens and their litter, but it wasn't Riley she wanted lingering in her mind. After seeing him at the horse race yesterday, he'd been in her thoughts enough that she'd slept poorly last night. Even now, images of him taunted her. She hadn't been able to take her eyes off him during

that race. The talk about the winner, whose identity was still a mystery, had flowed around her, but all her senses were attuned to the man whose name had brought her to Whirlwind.

She might be afraid of horses, but she could admire someone who wasn't. And Riley definitely wasn't. The man probably wasn't afraid of anything, she thought with wistful envy. He moved easily among the animals as if they were no danger, and Susannah knew from experience they were.

He and his horse seemed as one, a blend of masterful teamwork that illustrated a power and fluid grace she'd never seen. A power she wanted to get closer to.

She put her apron over her mouth to help cut the sharp stench of ammonia as she breathed deeply, then resumed gathering eggs. Why couldn't this odor burn thoughts of Riley out of her mind? Just the way he looked at her made her pulse skitter. Neither of the Baldwin brothers did that. Only Paul had ever affected her that way. Which was why she was glad Riley had refused to marry her. She would never again let her heart overrule her head, and Riley Holt could make her forget all about common sense.

The slanting light inside the henhouse changed as the sun dropped lower in the sky. Fighting the onset of nausea, she choked in a deep breath and hurried to check the nests at the other end, even though the birds had laid this morning. Coming out of the henhouse, she latched the door, then rested her forehead against the rough wood, dragging in deep gulps of fresher air. Her queasiness slowly subsided.

She didn't want to be involved with Riley, but she did want his good opinion. The amusement in his eyes when he'd learned of her school had told her he didn't believe she would succeed. But she would.

Just then something hard hit her elbow and hot breath blew against her sleeve. She screamed, flinching. The basket flew out of her hands and crashed to the ground, eggs cracking audibly. Moving on adrenaline and instinct, she darted to the corner of the henhouse, horrified to see Cora's mare toss her head and run the other way.

The horse galloped to the fence, and Susannah cringed against the weathered wood of the henhouse. Her heart kicking painfully against her ribs, she curved a hand over her belly. Why had Prissy come up to her? What had the mare wanted?

The horse slowed to a lope, her long legs carrying her up and down the fence line. She kept her dark eyes fixed warily on Susannah.

"Are you okay?"

She jerked at the sound of Riley's voice. Her body shook, just like her voice, as she answered, "I think so. Yes."

"Stay there for a minute." He walked slowly toward the mare. "Shh, girl. It's all right."

Prissy wasn't the one who'd had the life scared out of her, Susannah wanted to snap. But she kept her mouth shut.

The horse stopped pacing and watched Riley approach. He continued to talk softly to her. When he reached her, he put one hand on the white star in the middle of her nose and the other on her neck.

Susannah trembled, her emotions swinging from fear to relief to disgust. What about Cora's eggs? She glanced over and saw a mess of yolk and shells. Oh, no!

Tears burned her eyes. Hugging the small building, she edged toward the basket, picking it up gingerly, then eyeing the mess of broken shells at her feet. Selling eggs was how Cora made a living.

"No, no," Susannah whispered. Clutching the basket, she knelt and tried to salvage at least one egg.

"Are you sure you're all right?"

"Cora's eggs. They're completely ruined."

"It's fine—"

"No! It's a day's wages."

"Susannah." Riley reached down and took her arm, gently pulling her to her feet. "Cora will understand. It wasn't your fault." His gaze skipped over her before he studied her face. "You're sure you're fine? And the baby?"

She nodded, then frowned at him. "What are you doing here?"

He dropped his hand from her arm, the absence of his warm touch making her aware of the slight chill in the air. "Davis Lee and I thought we should check on Cora. We didn't see her at church this morning, and yesterday you said she felt poorly. Pearl wanted us to take her some pie, too."

"I'm sure Cora appreciates it." Susannah's gaze swept the bits of egg at her feet. "I don't know how I'll pay her for these. I can't believe I dropped them."

"It was a natural reaction."

"You saw?"

"Yes, from the side window. Prissy was just being friendly."

"She scared me to death." Susannah placed a hand on her chest, urging her heart to slow down. "I feel like a ninny."

"There's no need."

"I wish I could be as calm as you."

"You just need to get comfortable around horses."

The memory of nearly being run down when she was nine flashed through her mind, and she shook her head. "I don't think that will ever happen."

"Look." He walked over to Prissy and smoothed a broad hand down her neck. The mare stood motionless beneath his touch. "Why don't you come over, just touch her?"

"I don't think so."

"I'll be right here holding her. She won't hurt you."

Susannah's shoulders knotted up. She didn't want to, but she and the mare both lived here. What if she were alone with Prissy sometime and got startled again? Or what if something happened to the baby or Cora and Susannah needed to go for help?

"I promise I won't let anything happen." Riley smiled, setting off a flurry of sensations in her belly.

The mare stood placidly. Even Susannah felt herself responding to Riley's soothing presence. "What should I do?"

"Just stroke her. Start slow. Here, come closer."

She took a step.

"It's all right."

She set the basket on the ground and walked slowly over to him.

"Good." He used the same reassuring tone with her that he used with the mare. "First, hold your hand under her nose and let her smell you. Like so."

He demonstrated with his palm up, and Prissy dipped her head, her nostrils flaring as she took in his scent.

Muscles snapping tight, Susannah held out her hand. When the mare leaned down, she reflexively jerked back.

"It's all right," Riley said quietly. "Just take your time."

She nodded, extended her hand again. The mare sniffed, her velvety muzzle brushing Susannah's palm. The horse stared at her.

Susannah glanced at Riley.

"Very good. Now, why don't you touch her?"

"Where?"

"Her neck." He stroked a hand down the mare's sleek black hair. "Like this."

Susannah's stomach was barely settled from the henhouse, and standing this close to the horse threatened to unsettle it again. But she replayed the image of eggs crashing to the ground, Cora's money gone. She took a deep breath, reached out.

The horse shifted, muscles rolling beneath silky flesh.

Susannah's hand hovered inches away, trembling. "I'm sorry."

"No need. We can stop if you want."

If she did, she was afraid she might not try again. "I'll do it."

Her hand still shook and she clenched it into a fist, trying to calm herself.

"She can feel your fear."

"Can't *you?*"

A smile tugged at the corners of his mouth. "It might help to close your eyes. Just think of her as a soft, warm pet."

"The size of St. Louis," she muttered, but she closed her eyes as he suggested. She moved her hand closer, close enough to feel the mare's heat, but she couldn't bring herself to touch the animal.

A big, work-roughened hand closed over hers. Her eyes flew open and she stared at Riley's hand dwarfing hers. He placed their joined hands against the horse's firm, warm neck. Susannah's fingers brushed a coarse black mane as he began moving their hands in a slow, stroking motion.

Her discomfort faded somewhat when she saw the mare standing calmly beneath Riley's touch. Susannah could feel his chest at her back, his warmth comforting. She tried to keep her mind on the horse. "She's soft."

"Yes."

"She's letting me touch her," she said with both wonder and uncertainty.

"Just keep your touch easy. That's good." His breath washed against her temple.

Her hand molded to his as they stroked the mare's sleek, firm flesh, and the slow sinuous movement lulled her. For the first time since the Santos mare had bolted, Susannah felt herself calm completely. Riley's strength wrapped around her.

She found her gaze fixed on him, not the mare. Did the strength and power affecting her sensibilities belong to the horse or the man? Riley's jaw was slightly stubbled with end-of-the-day growth. Her gaze skimmed up his corded neck, lingered on his lips.

He turned his head then, looking straight at her as their hands continued to move over the horse. Raw desire shimmered in his blue eyes, and Susannah felt her stomach clench in response.

He looked as if he wanted to stroke *her*.

He leaned in and his lips covered hers with confident ease. Her breath caught as she turned toward him, met his kiss. The wall of his chest pressed against her breasts. She held on tight to what she fuzzily remembered was the horse. Even as she thought she might melt, Riley's tongue touched hers and stroked. A sharp, sheer bliss pierced her.

He lifted his head, eyes blazing and breathing heavy. Her heart thundered in her chest and she prayed her legs would hold her.

Through the fog of her senses, an inner voice told her to step away, but a wild urging for more had her easing closer.

Riley's eyes went dark; he dipped his head.

A door slammed and Susannah heard voices. Cora. And Davis Lee!

Riley dropped his hand from hers and looked back at the horse, saying calmly, "Try it by yourself."

Her nerves shimmered, making her feel unsteady and giddy. She stood motionless for a moment, trying to sort through the blur of her thoughts. *Take a breath*. Her hand still rested on the horse.

"Go on."

She moved her hand down the mare's neck, a dim part of her brain recognizing that the horse allowed her touch.

"Susannah, look at you!" Cora exclaimed.

Feeling jittery, fearing Cora and Davis Lee would know that she and Riley had kissed, Susannah jerked her hand away. She hurried to the other woman. "Oh, Cora, I'm so sorry. I gathered the eggs, but when I came out, Prissy frightened me and I dropped them. I ruined them all."

Tears tightened her throat. The mishap with the eggs combined with Riley's staggering kiss stoked the fire of her volatile emotions. "I'll pay for them."

"I won't hear of it," her friend said firmly. "Accidents happen."

"This one wouldn't have if I weren't so scared of horses. You've lost a day's wages because of me."

"Prissy's a pest," the older woman said dismissively. "She likes to nose around for treats. She's certainly startled me a time or two. Are you all right?"

"Yes."

Davis Lee's gaze went suspiciously from Susannah to his brother. "Are you making Susannah do something she doesn't want?"

"Like what?" Riley demanded.

"No, no!" A flush warmed her cheeks and she thought even he sounded guilty. She couldn't look at him, not after that kiss. "Of course not. I was admiring Riley's skill with Prissy—I'm afraid of horses—and he offered to help me try to overcome my fear."

"What a wonderful idea." Cora squeezed Susannah's arm and smiled broadly at Riley. "There's no better horseman around these parts. Will you be coming every day?"

"Well, uh—" Riley began.

"I think that's the key, you know," the woman continued. "Susannah and Prissy need to get familiar with each other."

So far, Susannah had gotten more familiar with Riley, but that couldn't happen again. The man flustered her beyond bearing. "I'm sure Riley doesn't have time to help me."

"I can come." Davis Lee smiled easily. "But not every day."

"Oh, that would be nice—"

"I'll do it," Riley said brusquely, looking at Susannah. "If you want."

She searched his eyes, but could read nothing. "I would feel better knowing a little something."

"There, you see?" Cora reached over and slapped Prissy on the rump. "Wonderful."

"I can teach you some basic things about being around horses," Riley said.

"And maybe how to hitch up the wagon, in case I ever need to get somewhere?"

"Sure. That's probably a good idea."

"Very wise." Cora looked pleased.

Susannah managed a smile. She didn't want her child picking up this fear, and she felt a pressing need to get it under control. She trusted Riley, but she couldn't let him see how much that kiss had affected her. How much even his presence affected her.

Riley Holt made her silly. And now she'd be seeing him every day.

Hell. He had to get Susannah out of his mind. As Riley rode toward Cora's house the next evening, he yanked his hat farther down on his head, as if that could squeeze out thoughts of her. Kissing her had to be one of the most addlepated things he'd ever done.

Now he knew her taste, the silky slide of her lips against his. Kissing wasn't where he'd wanted to stop, either. He'd wanted to put his hands on her and peel those clothes off, pull her beneath him.

His body tightened and he shifted on his horse, trying to ease the sudden snugness of his trousers. Since the day he'd seen that phony ring on her finger, he'd wanted to kiss her. And now he had.

She was as intoxicating as aged whiskey. This craving inside him was something he'd never felt for a woman. Last night, he'd even thought about downing a bottle of liquor to try and drown the taste of her, but he hadn't. The responsibility he felt for Adam's sister had blurred. His reaction now had nothing to do with looking out for her, and he didn't cotton to the change in him.

He wanted her. There was no getting around that. And he liked her, but that didn't alter the fact that he had no intention of getting involved with any woman. Especially Susannah, who was as ill-suited for this country as his wife had been. Something about Susannah Phelps tugged at him, put him in mind of soft evenings and forever. He wouldn't have it. The plain fact was he couldn't survive another loss like that of his wife.

The time he spent with Susannah would be strictly about horses, not the way his blood heated when he got within a foot of her, not the way she'd kissed him back with enough passion to make him throb.

He reined in the thought that she would've kissed him again if they hadn't been interrupted. What he should think about was her lesson with Prissy tonight. Susannah's willingness to take on what she considered a weakness sparked admiration in him. Not many people would do that. The best thing for him—for both of them—would be if they didn't see each other often. But he couldn't go back on his word.

The roofline of Cora's house came into sight, and Riley remembered that Susannah was supposed to begin her school tonight. For her sake, he hoped at least a couple of men had shown up.

He crested the rise that looked down on Cora's house and reined up with a start. Whip tossed his head at Riley's abrupt handling. What the heck? Saddled horses crowded the grass in front of Cora's house. They were rope-hobbled, obviously waiting for their riders. He counted eight animals, recognized nearly all of them.

He urged Whip into a lope across the remaining yards to the house and dismounted, tuning in to the voices—mostly male—coming from inside Cora's little house. Were these people all here for Susannah's school? Were they all *men?* Riley's lips firmed and he stepped up to the porch, peering in the window at the right of the door.

His eyes widened and a low whistle slipped out. Cora's front room was full to bursting. He saw Pete and Creed Carter, Pearl Anderson's young daughter, Violet, and both the Doyle brothers. The Baldwins were in front of the sink, sitting on Cora's nice chairs, which looked likely to break at the slightest movement from the hulking giants. Cora stood next to them, setting aside a stack of dishes. Susannah sat in the center of the room, holding a cup and saucer and demonstrating how to sip.

Riley chuckled. Until he caught sight of Jake Ross. And Tony Santos with Miguel. Riley didn't much care to know that all these men had spent the evening in Susannah's company. Not every man in town was here, but close enough. They all paid rapt attention to Susannah as she sipped daintily from her cup.

She paused, looking around the room. Carefully, the men lifted their cups. The Baldwin brothers' huge paws completely hid the delicate china. As they tried to imitate Susannah's graceful movements, Riley snorted. Jake Ross did the best, spilling only a tiny drop. Susannah's gaze moved carefully over all the students, then her eyes widened in horror. She rose quickly and went to Tony Santos.

A chuckle escaped Riley as he saw the man sipping from his saucer. Susannah spoke to him and he nodded, pouring the coffee from his saucer back into his cup. The cup clattered against the small plate and Susannah winced.

Tony definitely needed help with his manners, but Riley was suspicious of the other men's reasons for being here. He scanned the room once more, relieved to know that at least Davis Lee hadn't taken leave of his senses and shown up.

Susannah returned to the center of the room and, after a few words, the men rose with a grating scrape of chairs across Cora's pine floor. Class was dismissed. Riley backed up just as the front door opened. Pete Carter rushed out as if being chased by a wildcat.

"Hey, Pete."

"Hullo." The saloon owner reached into his overall pocket for a plug of dark tobacco and pinched off a piece, stuffing it between his cheek and gum. "She made me spit out my chaw. I don't know how long I'm gonna last in there."

"*Why* are you going in there, Pete?" Riley noticed the widower's hair was slicked down and he smelled like bay rum. Too much bay rum. The man was fancied up to impress a lady, not for learning. "You need some help on manners?"

The grizzled man glanced back at Susannah and, with a wicked grin, waggled his eyebrows.

Riley gave him a dead stare, a clear warning to watch himself, and Pete's smile faded. He mumbled something and stepped off the porch, spitting a stream of tobacco juice several feet. Riley could well imagine that Susannah had put a quick stop to that.

Jake Ross stepped outside, carrying his hat. "Hey, Riley."

He nodded. The others streamed out except for the Baldwins, who stayed behind to return Cora's chairs to their rightful place.

"Next week, we'll learn our first dance," Susannah said

from the door. She glanced over, her smile turning guarded when she saw Riley. "I didn't know you'd arrived."

"How many dances are we gonna learn?" Tony asked.

"Most gentlemen know at least three."

"Are we gonna get to dance with you, Miz Susannah?" Creed Carter asked.

"Everybody but you," Miguel teased from his place on the back of his uncle's horse.

"I'll teach you, yes," Susannah said. "Thanks so much for coming, gentlemen. You too, Violet."

"Yes, ma'am." The girl's gaze darted shyly toward Miguel Santos.

"I'll walk you back to town, Violet." Jake Ross slid his hat on his head and said goodbye.

Twilight fell across the land, and as everyone left, their shadows blended into the darkness. Finally their voices faded.

Riley watched Susannah, hit with memories of that kiss, the way she'd surrendered to him. It didn't appear she had favored any one of her male students with special attention. Yet.

Her white bodice and dark skirt looked neat and fresh. She'd gathered her silvery hair into a high chignon. She was mighty pretty. The lamplight over her shoulder gilded her smooth skin with pale gold. "Looks like you had a good turnout."

Wrapping one hand around a porch column, she looked at him. The tiny lines of fatigue around her eyes eased with her smile. "It was wonderful, Riley. I didn't expect so many."

He hadn't expected so many men, either. Didn't like it too much, because he figured most of them had come for the same reason as Pete Carter. Still, her obvious excitement caused Riley to smile. "Think they'll all stick it out?"

"I hope so. With Cora's home-baked goods, I think even she will be able to make some extra money."

Riley studied her. "Was that your idea? It sure lessens the sting of losing those eggs."

"I hope it helps a little bit," she said with a shrug.

She might not be suited for this harsh land, but Susannah was kind. That carried weight in Riley's mind.

"Are you ready to go out to the barn?" What he really wanted to ask was if she'd realized the reason these men came had nothing to do with manners and everything to do with her being a woman. A beautiful woman.

Before he walked into memories of that kiss again, he leaned in and said hello to Cora. He stepped off the porch and Susannah followed.

"Have you been out to see Prissy today?"

"Yes." She moved beside him with her hands clasped tightly in front of her. Her skirts made a soft swishing sound against the dirt. "I tried to do as you suggested and take her a treat. I offered her a carrot."

"How did that go?" he asked as they walked out behind Cora's house. Dusky light settled around them. They'd need a lantern once they reached the barn.

She grimaced and looked away. "I'm hoping tonight will be better. What are we going to do?"

"I'll teach you how to brush her down." The memory of that kiss hung between them as awkwardly as a slap. "After you ride a horse and unsaddle it, it needs to be brushed."

She nodded.

They stepped inside the barn and the mare whinnied. The scents of hay and dirt and animals swirled around them. Beside him, Riley felt Susannah tense up.

"It's okay. Prissy's just saying hello."

"All right." Still she dropped a step behind him, warily approaching the mare's stall.

"I'll tie her up." Prissy didn't need restraining, but Riley figured Susannah would feel better.

After lighting a lantern and placing it atop the stall's door post, he took a rope from the barn wall. One end went over the mare's neck and he tied the other around one of the stall slats.

"Maybe I should just pet her? Like I did last night?" Susannah suggested hopefully.

"Brushing is like a different version of petting." Riley refused to allow himself any thoughts of petting Susannah. "It's something you need to learn, plus it's a good way for you and Prissy to get acquainted."

"Very well," she said primly.

Riley liked it better when Susannah was at ease with him, but he needed to be concerned about how she felt with the horse. "Don't forget she can sense what you're feeling."

Uncertainty shimmered in Susannah's blue eyes.

"She knows you're uneasy," he said. "Brushing will help relax her and maybe give you some confidence."

She let out a shuddery breath and closed her eyes for a moment. When she opened them, he saw the same determination he'd seen there last night when she had approached the mare for the first time.

"I'm ready," she said.

"Good." He sidestepped another memory of her lips on his, the teasing brush of her breasts against his chest. "Put your hands on her. Talk to her."

She placed her hand on the mare's neck. After a few strokes, she said, "Remember me? We got along well last night, didn't we?"

Riley bit back a smile. He hadn't meant for her to carry on a conversation with the animal, but if it worked to help ease Susannah's fears, all the better.

"I think we can be friends," she continued. "You're big, but…pretty."

Prissy edged closer.

Susannah glanced questioningly at him.

"That means she likes what you're doing. She's getting to know your touch and your scent."

He certainly knew both better than he wanted; her clean, soft scent was branded on his brain. But at least the smell of her wouldn't heat up the mare's blood the way it did his. His gaze trailed down the elegant nape of Susannah's neck, exposed by her upswept hair. He wanted to press his lips to the tender patch of skin below her ear.

He dragged his thoughts back to what they were doing. "If you take care of your animal, it'll take care of you."

"Really?" She seemed to relax a bit. "I just don't know much—oh!"

She froze, her eyes going wide.

"What? What is it?" Riley stepped closer, his gaze going to the dirt floor to see if the horse had stepped on Susannah's foot.

She put a hand on her stomach and smiled. "There it is again. That was a hard one. Just surprised me."

"A kick?" he asked, relief and surprise tangling inside him.

"Yes." She smoothed a hand down her skirt, pulling the fabric taut, and for the first time, he saw the swell of her belly. "She's been doing that for a couple of months."

"She? What if it's a he?"

"You're right, it could be. But for some reason, I think it's a girl."

"It would be nice to have a pretty little girl around," he said.

Pleasure heated Susannah's eyes. In the soft lantern light, her face took on a creamy glow. A vulnerable expression of naked love stole across her features and made Riley's chest tighten. He wanted her to look at him that way, wanted to lay claim to her in the most primal, elemental way he knew. The urge to take her rocked him, and then in a dousing, cold rush, he remembered that the baby was why she'd come to Whirlwind. To him.

He stared at her hand on her stomach, questions rolling through his mind. Was that why she'd kissed him last night? Because she still hoped he might be a father to her baby and not because she'd wanted him the way he'd wanted her—with lightning heat? It didn't matter. He wasn't marrying again, certainly not a fluffy tenderfoot who might fall apart at the first howl of a coyote.

She resumed stroking the horse. "What should I do next?"

After a second, he grasped her question and handed her a curry brush. "Here, take this and start at her neck. Use long strokes down to her rump."

"This won't bother her?"

"She'll love it." He'd known he and Susannah would have to address what had happened between them last night. Might as well get it over with.

Susannah began, touching the horse tentatively with the brush.

"Brace one hand on her like this." He demonstrated by placing a palm on the mare's withers, the slope where her neck met her back. "It tells her where you are. Follow her lines with the brush. You won't hurt her."

"All right." She replaced his hand with hers at the base of Prissy's neck and tentatively drew the brush down the mare's back.

Riley dropped his hand, wishing she were touching him, dragging her hand down his back. Or front. *No.* There could be nothing between them. "Use a little more pressure," he said huskily.

She looked at him questioningly, but did as he suggested. The mare turned her head and looked at Susannah with soft, dark eyes.

"I think she likes it," she said softly.

"Yeah."

She glanced at him with a small frown. Riley could smell the faint scent of her beneath those of horseflesh, hay and dirt. He recalled in excruciating detail that she'd tasted exactly like fresh cream.

He shifted away from the temptation of her warmth, bound and determined not to put his hands on her.

He cleared his throat. "Susannah, I wanted to talk to you about last night."

Moving the brush now with more firmness and confidence, she said, "Last night?"

"I was out of line. I shouldn't have kissed you."

She stopped brushing and glanced at him, eyes wide with horror. Or surprise. He couldn't decide which before she turned her face away. "I don't think we should talk about that."

"I don't want you to get the wrong idea."

"I don't want *you* to get the wrong idea."

He stiffened. "What does that mean?"

"I'm not interested in you that way."

"Well, darlin'." He leaned in close enough for his breath to stir the wisps of hair teasing her neck. "That kiss sure felt like interest to me."

She stepped back and planted one hand on her hip. "Is this your idea of sweet-talking me, Riley Holt? You need practice."

She resumed grooming, her strokes growing more brisk.

"We can't do it again," he said flatly.

"Of course not!" Her gaze swung to his and he saw her flush in the pale light. "You surprised me is all. I didn't expect…anything like that."

"Was kissing me back your way of being polite?" The woman astounded him. "Because if so, you need to be real careful who you're polite to around here. Other men might not be as understanding as I am."

"Do tell," she murmured dryly.

Irritated, he said, "So, we're in agreement?" They hadn't even finished this discussion and already he hated the outcome.

"Yes. And if helping me with the horse is going to be a problem for you," she said regally, "I can find someone else."

For some reason, the thought of someone else standing so close to her every night, instructing her about *anything,* was enough to set his teeth on edge. "It isn't going to be a problem."

"So, we can be friends?" she asked brightly. "If not, continuing my lessons wouldn't be a good idea."

Friends? "We can be great friends." He nearly choked on the words, wanted to choke her.

Wasn't *he* supposed to be telling her how things were going to be between them?

He wanted her to have no illusions about him, about them. Evidently, she didn't. Good.

Watching the slender line of her back, the graceful movements of her arm as she brushed the horse, he clenched a fist against his thigh and tried to squelch an unexpected burn of anger. Dadgum woman.

Chapter Seven

She had kissed him back because she wanted to, but she had her wits about her now. A week had passed, after all. Of course, she still had to see him every day because of her lessons with Prissy, but she had shored up her defenses and resolved to listen to her head, not her emotions.

After Riley's little declaration that there would be no more kissing, he'd kept his distance and so had she. They were both polite and friendly; Susannah felt they could continue that way. She was no longer a young girl with foolish ideas. She wouldn't make the same mistake with Riley that she'd made with Paul. And if she did find a man suitable to be her baby's father, she'd be clear from the onset that it was a convenient arrangement for both, not a one-sided love match.

The sight of Riley might cause a funny feeling in her stomach, like she got after the first sip of sarsaparilla, but she wouldn't dwell on it. He was helping her to overcome her fear of horses, and she wanted to continue. He thought she was ready to move on to something new, so tonight he was going to teach her how to put a bridle on Prissy and check her hooves. Even though Susannah had to brace herself each day to work with the mare, she was coming to feel more at ease around the animal. Probably because Prissy hadn't so much as looked cross-eyed at her. Riley made the horse calm, regardless of how he turned Susannah's knees to wax.

Thank goodness she had no such trouble with any of the men in her class, she thought as she led the students out to the barn that Monday evening. As cramped as they'd been last week, the limited space in Cora's house would prove much too confining for learning the waltz.

While the older woman lit and hung the lantern, several of the men rolled the wagon out of the barn, leaving a space in front of the stalls big enough for several couples. Violet Anderson stood close to Cora. Miguel and Andrew Donnelly, a new student sent by his sickly mother, leaned the pitchfork and shovel against one of the stalls. Andrew was twelve, the same age as both Miguel and Creed Carter.

Creed carefully picked up a wooden crate containing Ollie's belongings and placed it in a corner. A straight-edge and shaving soap sat atop neatly folded clothes, along with Ollie's comb, hair pomade and black boots. Susannah's heart squeezed as she caught Cora's sad expression. The widow didn't want to keep her husband's things in the house, but she couldn't bear to put them away yet, either.

Susannah moved to the center of the barn and smoothed her navy serge skirt. "This evening we're going to learn the waltz. It's a slow, elegant dance."

"We cain't all dance with you at the same time, Miz Phelps," Creed Carter said.

"That's right. First, I'll explain the steps to you, then we'll try it."

The men formed a half circle in front of her and watched as she drew marks on the hay-packed dirt floor.

"This is one of the more simple dances," she said, "but

you'll be on the balls of your feet quite a lot and it can be hard on your knees. Is everyone okay to continue?"

Pete Carter raised his hand tentatively. "Miz Susannah, my knee swells up sometimes, but I'd like to try, anyway."

"If it starts to hurt, you should probably stop, Pete. All right?"

He nodded.

"Good. Now, I've marked three places here to show a waltz step. Four complete steps will make a full circle."

"I don't see a circle," Miguel complained.

Creed elbowed him. "There ain't no circle there. She said it'll make a circle after you dance the steps."

"This will be easier to understand once you see someone do it. Who will volunteer?"

All hands except Jake Ross's shot up.

"I will!"

"Me."

"I will."

"Jake, maybe you could help me?"

The quiet man hesitated, then came forward.

"Thank you." She faced the class. "I'll demonstrate the steps, then Jake will repeat them before we all try."

The men moved closer as the last thread of sunlight disappeared. Their shadows flickered and blurred in the lantern light.

Susannah pointed to the first mark on the hard floor. "From here, you and the lady will take a large first step together. Follow with the other foot, covering about three-quarters the distance of the first step."

She glanced around to see if they were listening. After several nods, she continued, "As you step, raise up gently on the balls of your feet. Your third step is small, in the same direction. Lower yourself as the step is completed. That constitutes one step."

"Gol-ly, Miz Phelps," Miguel said. "That sounds like a bunch of hopping around."

Others murmured their agreement.

She laughed, exchanging a smile with Cora. "No, it's not hopping, just a smooth, upward motion. And small, very small. Watch."

She demonstrated, then asked Jake, "Ready to try?"

It took the big man a couple of attempts to get the motion of raising up on the balls of his feet while he moved, but he soon had it, although he moved a bit awkwardly.

"Very good." Susannah applauded lightly, pleased things were going so well.

"Miz Cora, did you make some of that bread this week?" Russ Baldwin asked.

"No, but I have cake, which I'll be happy to cut after your lessons."

Susannah gestured at the men and Violet. "Spread out so you'll have room. Once the four steps are completed, you should have made a full circle."

"Do you just go around in this little circle all night?" Matt Baldwin asked.

"We will at first, but after you have the idea, you'll learn that the small circles will form a much larger circle that takes you and your partner around the outside of a room."

"What the devil? How can we make two circles at the same time?"

"Once we start, you'll see what I mean."

"I hope so. Right now, I'm thinking I cain't do this," Tony Santos said.

"Me, either," Pete Carter admitted.

"Just do it one step at a time," Cora said. "Follow Miz Susannah and she'll soon have you all looking like you came from some fancy dancing school."

Susannah didn't know if she had that much talent. Or

patience. "Jake, demonstrate the steps again. Let's all try it this time."

The others watched intently as Jake carefully repeated the steps he'd made before, then, one by one, the others joined in. There was a lot of jostling as they all scooted and shuffled across the dirt, but after a few moments, they seemed to grasp the steps.

"You're all doing wonderfully." Susannah walked among them, smiling. "Now, let's put the whole thing together. When you dance with a lady, you'll lead with your left foot. Your right hand goes on her waist, your left hand in her right, with your arms extended."

Since Jake was standing closest to her, Susannah curtsied to him. "Jake and I will try it first."

A movement at the door caught her eye and she looked over to see Riley standing there. Her stomach dipped and for a moment, her mind went blank.

He looked hard and rugged, with a shadow of whiskers stubbling his jaw. His blue gaze found hers across the barn and locked on. Jake dropped his arm, which he'd been holding out to her. She snapped her thoughts back to the dance she was supposed to be teaching.

"Hello, Riley," Cora said. "Why don't you join in?"

"I think I'll just watch from over here." He leaned one shoulder against the door and hooked a thumb into the waist of his trousers.

Susannah didn't relish the thought of that steady blue gaze fixed on her, but she would make do. Irritated that Riley's presence affected her as strongly as if he was the one whose hand rested at her waist, she fiddled with the top button of her high-necked white blouse. "Ready, Jake?"

The man nodded, his gray eyes earnest. "I just want to say I'm sorry beforehand, Miz Susannah. For whatever I do."

"Nonsense, you'll do fine. Since you'll lead with your left

foot, let's trade places.'' With her back to Riley, she'd be able to concentrate better. She put her right hand in Jake's left, her other hand on his shoulder. "Keep your elbows slightly bent. There. Ready?''

She gently tugged him into the first step. His brows snapped together as he stared at his feet, concentrating intently.

"Once you find your rhythm, try to look into your partner's eyes.''

"Dang, Miz Susannah, you mean we cain't even watch what we're doing?'' Miguel exclaimed.

She bit back a smile. "You'll soon come to know the dance so well that you won't need to look.''

"In a pig's eye," Tony snorted.

Jake's next steps were a little more certain, and Susannah encouraged him, fighting the urge to look at Riley. After she and Jake made a complete circle, she said, "Let's do it again, and this time we'll connect the steps as one movement.''

"I'll try, ma'am.''

Her neck prickled with the weight of Riley's gaze, and she struggled to ignore it. She wasn't going to give in to the tingly warmth he sparked in her. This time, when her partner took his first step, Susannah began to count out loud in three-quarter time.

He faltered, his foot crashing down on hers.

"Oomph.'' She managed to swallow her surprised yelp.

"Oh, hell! I mean, heck. I'm sorry.''

"Land sakes, Ross!'' Russ Baldwin bellowed.

"It's all right,'' Susannah said. "Let's go on.''

"But I stepped on you.''

"I won't break, Jake. As you can see, I'm fine.'' She smiled encouragingly, so he gave her an apologetic smile and began again.

Just when she thought they would make a full circle without a fault, he stepped on her foot again. Susannah urged him to keep going, but by the time they'd waltzed around the space a second time, her toes were curled inside her kid boots in an attempt to escape Jake's feet.

"I'm stomping all over you, Miz Susannah." The man looked miserable. "I think someone else better try before you can't walk at all."

"All right."

"Here, I'll do it." Matt Baldwin strode up and took Jake's place. "I think I understand the whole thing."

"Wonderful." Susannah felt Riley's intense interest, but refused to acknowledge him. She smiled up at Matt as his big hand closed around hers.

They started off smoothly and he grinned. "Is this pretty good?"

"Yes, it is." She glanced at the class. "Matthew and I will dance around the barn so you can see the larger circle I told you about."

"Here we go." He enthusiastically swung her into the dance, and she hurried to keep up.

His steps were large and so widely spaced that she had to nearly hop a couple of times. He swung her round, faster and faster. The faces became a blur, Riley's blue eyes the only point she recognized in the crowd.

"You don't have to go at it full chisel, Matt Baldwin!" Cora admonished loudly.

His giant steps were fairly smooth, but Susannah felt as if she were flying.

Then his foot hit something. An object whizzed past in a blur and a collective gasp went up. A crash sounded as the dancers stumbled to a stop. Susannah saw the pitchfork bounce off the wall.

"I de-clare!" Cora exclaimed.

"Are you all right, ma'am?" Russ Baldwin rushed up, elbowing his brother out of the way.

"Yes, I'm fine." Susannah's heart pounded wildly and she put a hand to her chest. The baby kicked in protest.

"I'm sorry, Miz Susannah." Matt gave her a sheepish smile. "I guess I got too full of myself."

"It's all right, Matthew."

"If you're willing to give it another go," Russ offered, "I think I can do it. And I promise not to let fly any pitchforks."

She laughed softly. "Certainly."

Maybe teaching these men to dance wasn't a good idea. After all, they were much more likely to spend time with cattle than be required to know the social graces. But she'd offered the classes; she wouldn't back out now. Still, she took Russ Baldwin's hand with a slight trepidation.

They started off smoothly, made a complete circle, and Susannah smiled up at him. Perhaps she'd found a star pupil. "Very fine, Russ."

He beamed. And began to move faster.

"Remember this is a slower dance, Russ. Elegant and measured."

"Maybe we need something to speed things up." He whirled her around in so many circles that Susannah became dizzy.

Before she could react, he caught her around the waist and lifted her off the ground!

Reflex had her digging her nails into his shoulder. "Wh-what are you doing?"

"I think this is easier. You don't weigh any more than a feather pillow, and this way you don't get your feet stepped on."

"Russ, you must put me down."

He continued to twirl her round and round.

"If I'm not dancing *with* you," she said, "how do I know if you're doing it right?"

"Why, you can just take my word for it, ma'am." His eyes twinkled.

She laughed and patted his massive arm. "Put me down now. We've got to learn to do this properly."

Russ complied, slowing, then setting her on the ground carefully.

Cora stepped up beside Susannah. "You boys are never gonna learn if you don't stop acting so silly. No offense to you, Jake."

"None taken."

"Y'all need to watch how it's really done. Riley, why don't you come show 'em?"

Susannah shot a surprised look toward the door. Riley danced?

"This isn't my party, Cora."

"You afraid to show us what you're made of, Holt?" Matt said. "Or could we actually be better dancers than you?"

He shrugged, a grin playing at the corners of his mouth.

"C'mon, Riley." Cora motioned him over. "Susannah's gonna be plumb worn out by the time this bunch figures things out. Besides, I've got chores tomorrow. I can't be here all night."

The men laughed and Susannah watched Riley carefully. He wouldn't do it. A waltz would put him in closer proximity to her than he'd been in seven days. Neither of them wanted that.

She turned to the class. "I'll pair you up with each other."

"Each other?" Creed squeaked.

"I ain't dancin' with no boy," Pete grumbled.

"I'll dance with some of you," Cora offered.

"And there's Violet." Susannah motioned to the young girl, who watched avidly.

"All right." Riley pushed away from the door. "I'll show you yahoos how it's done."

No! Susannah swallowed hard, her gaze locked on the hollow of his throat as he moved easily toward her. His shoulders were broad enough to block out the lantern's flame, and his hips rolled with a lazy grace.

His gaze dark and challenging, he put his hand at her waist. His other hand covered hers. Points of heat fired her nerves.

This was not a good idea, but she forced a smile and curled her hand in his, hoping he'd think her damp palms were from her previous exertion.

At her count, he began to move, and she found herself following him. Smooth, graceful, practiced. She smiled in surprise. "I didn't know you danced. You're very good."

"My ma made sure both Davis Lee and I knew how." Amusement twinkled in his eyes. "It's like riding a horse. You just have to find the rhythm."

"Maybe there's hope for me yet," she murmured, looking away.

At the moment, riding sounded a lot safer than dancing with Riley. The strong hand at her waist stirred the memory of that kiss. She squared her shoulders and struggled to keep her thoughts on the dance only.

"Look at your partner, Miz Phelps." His voice was low, his breath teasing her ear.

She raised her gaze, her hand tightening involuntarily in his. They glided, the scents of dirt and animals fading. Riley smelled of soap and leather. His gaze dropped to her lips, then moved back to her eyes, the secret of their kiss plain in the blue depths.

A flush heated her neck and she became keenly aware of the leashed strength in his arms, the gentleness of his hands.

"Should you be dancing in your condition?'' he asked quietly.

"I don't think it's a problem. Neither does Cora.''

"Okay.'' Matt Baldwin's voice boomed through the barn. "I think we understand. You don't have to make us look like a bunch of clumsy oxen, Holt.''

Riley grinned and stopped, his gaze touching hers briefly as she stepped out of his arms.

She curtsied, her heart pumping harder than it had during the rapid whirling Matt had given her.

"It looks purty, but I don't see how you can dance thata way without stepping on somebody's feet,'' Pete Carter said.

"Or forgetting what you're doing,'' Tony Santos added.

"You'll get it with practice,'' she said breathlessly. "I certainly didn't learn in one lesson, and I doubt Riley did, either.''

"That's right.'' He stood at her shoulder, close enough for her to inhale the nice masculine smell of him.

She moved away, trying to settle the giddiness in her stomach.

"Let's go to the house for that cake.'' Cora started out of the barn, motioning for the others to follow.

The Baldwin brothers hung back, each offering Susannah an arm.

She glanced at Riley. "Thanks for helping me.''

"Happy to do it.''

He didn't look happy. He looked gruff and intense. And a raw hunger burned in his eyes. "I'll wait for you out here. We can start our lesson in a few minutes, unless you'd rather do it another time. Or stop altogether.''

She frowned. "No, I don't want to stop. I thought you said I was making progress.''

"You are.''

She took a step toward him. "Do *you* want to stop?''

He hesitated for a moment, then shook his head. "No."

Something close to relief squeezed her chest, and Susannah smiled. "Good."

She turned to the Baldwins and took their arms.

As they walked toward the house, Matt asked, "What are you learning from Riley?"

Things I probably shouldn't be. "How to be around a horse."

She felt his gaze burning into her and it took considerable willpower not to turn around.

Going inside for a few minutes would give her time to recover her equilibrium. Riley's touch had sparked a desire in her for more, and she refused to yield to it. All she had to do was recall how Paul had gotten past her defenses, then cruelly turned his back on her. She'd been a fool once, but not again.

Certain men addled her brain, and she'd learned she couldn't trust her judgment about them. She had no intention of getting involved like that again. Ever.

Chapter Eight

For the next two Mondays, Riley purposely went late to Susannah's lessons. After holding her in his arms for that waltz, he had no desire to watch her dance with Matt Baldwin. Or Jake Ross. Or any of the other men in her charm school.

Whatever ground he'd gained in being able to treat her strictly as a friend had disappeared when they began to move together. The brush of her body against his, the feel of her slender back beneath his hand, had inspired all kinds of images in Riley's head, none of them Christian. And *all* of them about lust and sweat and her pale naked flesh against his.

He'd made sure to see her only for the lessons with Prissy, with Cora just feet away in the house.

He liked the way Susannah had felt against him, liked the blush that pinkened her cheeks when he'd told her to look at him. He liked too damn much about her. Which was why he kept that memory locked tightly away during their time together. And why he planned to do the same during their trip to Abilene for the last horse race before winter set in. It would be easier, since Cora would be with them.

Early Saturday morning, he drove his buckboard to pick up her and Susannah, as he'd agreed when the older woman had asked.

He braked the wagon in front of Cora's house and climbed down, rearranging several blankets over a bed of hay in the wagon bed. The pallet would be comfortable enough for Cora's older bones or Susannah's delicate state.

Behind him, the door creaked open and he turned. Susannah stood in the doorway, her brow furrowed, her eyes dark with concern. Her moss-green day dress showed her advancing condition. "Cora's hurt."

Riley took both porch steps at once and strode past Susannah into the house. Her full skirts brushed his boots. "What happened?"

The older woman gave him a wan smile from a ladder-backed kitchen chair. She had her left leg stretched out, propped on another chair in front of her. "I twisted my ankle coming down out of the loft in the barn."

"How bad is it? I'd better have a look." He knelt and pulled off his gloves, reaching for her ankle.

Cora smacked him on the shoulder, her eyes teasing. "Don't get fresh with me, young man. I'm fine."

He thumbed his hat back on his head. "I can ride to Fort Greer for the doctor."

"I just need to stay off of it for a while. That's all he'll say."

Still kneeling, Riley looked up at her. "Are you sure, Cora? I can wrap it, if need be."

"I'll be fine. You two go on to Abilene."

"I can stay with you," Susannah said.

"Nonsense." The other woman waved a dismissive hand. "There's no need for that. You two go on and have a good time."

"I don't feel right about leaving," Susannah said to Riley as he rose to his feet.

"And I'll feel guilty as sin if you two change your plans. Please go. The best thing you can do for me is go and have fun."

Susannah looked doubtful. Riley wondered if Cora's ankle really was twisted. He had no reason to doubt her, except that she wouldn't look him full in the face. He wouldn't put it past her to do some matchmaking, get him and Susannah alone. But the sooner she saw that was like spitting into a high wind, the better for all of them.

He turned to Susannah. "I'm willing to go if you are."

"Well…"

"I'd feel ever so much better," the other woman urged. "Besides, you're both widowed. There won't be any fuss about you not being chaperoned."

Susannah exchanged a look with Riley. They both knew she was nowhere near widowed. "Very well."

She arranged a wool wrap over her head and ears, then took her cloak from the hook behind the door. "Can we do something for you before we leave?"

Cora shook her head. "I'm going to rest. I don't need anything."

Susannah threw an uncertain look at Riley and he shrugged.

As he tugged on his gloves, he walked over to the stove, then wrapped a cloth around the handle of the warming pan. "I'll put this down by your feet and you should be warm enough on the way to Abilene."

They bid Cora goodbye, and Riley settled Susannah in the wagon seat, tucking a heavy wool blanket around her and setting the warming pan at her feet. They headed toward Abilene, the sun glistening like gold off the short grass, the flat prairie broken by the occasional mesquite tree. Sporadic bursts of a brisk November wind chafed his cheeks.

Riley searched his mind for something to say, but all that came to mind was how pretty Susannah looked in the green dress, which made her eyes look even more blue. The gold of her silky, upswept hair peeked out from beneath her wrap. She nervously adjusted her black gloves.

He pulled his hat lower on his head.

After a long, awkward silence, she asked, "Are you sure you don't mind taking me?"

"I'm sure." If she could make an effort, so could he. "Are you warm enough?"

"Yes, thank you."

The twenty-five miles to Abilene promised to be the longest of his life. Susannah grew quiet, huddled away from him, the blanket tucked tightly around her legs. She kept her hands clasped in her lap.

He leaned forward, elbows resting on his knees as he stared at his gloved hands. The silence was thick and uneasy. Riley didn't reckon he could ride all the way like this.

He slid a look at her. "You've done well with Prissy this week."

"Thank you." Her eyes warmed with pleasure.

The smoky blue reminded Riley of the way she'd looked after he kissed her. The way she'd surrendered. He cautioned himself against such thoughts. They would get him in trouble quicker than Davis Lee ever had. "Would you like to try driving?"

Her gaze shot to his and she grimaced. "I don't know."

Even though the idea had just come to him, Riley warmed to it. "Pru is as gentle as Cora's mare. Besides, I'll be here the whole time."

Susannah looked skeptically at the horse, then back at him. "Do you think I can?"

"Yes, and this is a good time to try. The way is flat. We've got plenty of time."

She hesitated.

"I won't let anything happen."

After another moment, she nodded. "All right."

He grinned, relieved to have something besides her to occupy his mind.

He pulled Pru to a stop and handed the reins to Susannah. "Just hold them loosely in your hands for a minute, get a feel for them."

She nodded, doubt clouding her blue eyes.

"You have to apply a certain amount of pressure to get her to obey, but not too much. You're light, so you'll need to let her know you're back here. Use both reins so that you don't saw on the bit. The hardest part is keeping equal pressure on them. You'll be able to feel what I mean once you get under way."

"I don't know about this, Riley. I don't want to hurt her. Or you."

He grinned. "You won't."

"What if she sees a snake, like Tony's horse did?"

"I'll be right here to take the reins."

"All right."

"It's easier with one horse, but you still want to be careful when you rein to a stop. Your command has to travel up to her bit, so her response won't be immediate. You want to slow her down, rather than yank her to a stop."

"I think I understand."

"To get her going, slap the reins against her rump, like so." Riley reached over to cover Susannah's gloved hands with his, and gave the leather lines a sharp snap.

At his touch, Susannah stiffened.

His jaw clenched. "I had to touch you so I could show you how it's done."

"I know. That's all right." She smiled brightly, but it did nothing to ease the tension that had arced between them since they'd left Cora's.

Tension that still bowed Riley's shoulders. "Give it a try whenever you're ready."

She smiled halfheartedly, then focused on the mare. She gave the reins a flick, but too much slack in the lines caused the leather to flop uselessly against the horse's rump.

"Try again," he urged. "Pull your arms closer to your sides."

He barely grazed her elbow to guide her, but felt her jerk as tight as a spring. Frustrated, he chewed the inside of his cheek. Did she think he was going to jump on her?

She did as he suggested, and this time when she popped the reins, the leather landed smartly on Pru's rump and the horse lurched into motion.

"Oh!" Susannah looked at him, excitement and uncertainty flashing across her face.

"Try to keep a steady pressure," he reminded her, touching her hands again. At least she wore gloves, so he wasn't touching her flesh, which he knew to be creamy soft. "Can you feel how she responds to you? Don't pull on the reins. Guide her by using her neck, not her mouth. Lay the left rein across her neck if you want her to turn right and the right one to make her go left. See how she veers?"

Susannah frowned in concentration. "Like this?"

The mare plodded off at a right angle.

"Yes." Riley found himself smiling.

The wagon moved smoothly and Susannah began to relax beside him. A couple of times he reached out and guided Pru back into a straight line.

"This is a lot more work than it looks," she remarked later, a little breathlessly.

"You'll get it. It's easier once your hands have gotten stronger, too."

She nodded, her brow furrowed as she concentrated on her driving. Riley kept a close eye on her. "You're doing well."

"Thank you." She smiled, but didn't take her gaze from the horse.

Her cheeks were rosy from the cool air, and the tip of her nose was red. "Are you still warm enough?" he asked.

"Oh, yes."

They moved closer to the edge of the road. Grass brushed the wheels and made a shushing sound against the rims, but Riley didn't interfere. Even if they drove into the grass, she wouldn't be hurting anything. He'd had to practice plenty before he could keep a rig on the road.

"Oh!" She flinched suddenly and flung a hand into the air.

"What?" He jerked toward her, his gaze scanning the horse, then her. Both seemed fine.

Susannah bunched the reins in her right hand and began swatting at her hair with the other. "It's in my hair! Ooh, get it out."

"What is it?"

Pru ambled off the road into the grass, and the buckboard bumped over a rut.

Riley grabbed the seat to keep from pitching forward. "Susannah, what's going on?"

"It's a bug! In my hair!" she squealed.

He saw it then, a grasshopper caught just inside her scarf. "Here, let me."

He reached toward it just as she smacked at it, hitting his hand. Her scarf drooped and the bug fell onto her neck. She grabbed for it.

"Where is it? Get it off!"

He chuckled. "I can't see it. It's gone."

She squealed and nearly came off the seat. "No! It fell down my neckline! My cape. It's in my cape!"

She swatted so furiously that he was afraid she'd hit herself in the face. Or hit him. Every time she went for the insect, the reins would pull one way, then another. The horse swung to the right, then the left, then the right.

"Hang on there, Susannah." Laughing, Riley could barely get out the words. "Whoa, Pru. Whoa."

Susannah glared. "Stop laughing and help me!"

"Do you want me to get the bug?" His gaze went to her bodice and he couldn't resist teasing her. "'Cuz I don't think that would be proper."

"Oh, you." She threw the reins at him. "You drive. I'll get the bug."

Riley reined the mare to a stop, and Susannah yanked off her cape, shaking it out. "How disgusting."

The grasshopper, now dead and smashed flat, fell to the floor of the buckboard. She shuddered.

"I thought you were starting a new dance there." Riley grinned, glad she was all right. She hadn't *completely* panicked.

She refastened her cape around her shoulders, then sat down, pulling the garment snugly around her neck. "Ugh, that thing just hopped on me."

"But you're okay."

"Yes." She glanced at the mare, her face falling. "I've probably ruined any progress I made with driving."

"Pru's not that easily untrained. Or spooked."

"Oh, you mean she isn't a ninny about grasshoppers."

Riley started to snap that he hadn't meant that at all, but then he saw a smile tug at the corners of her mouth. "Yeah, Pru's not like most females. Bugs and such don't send her into a swoon."

"A swoon!" Susannah's eyes widened and her chin lifted stubbornly. "Riley Holt, I was nowhere near swooning."

"I don't know," he drawled, enjoying himself. "You looked pretty pekid."

"I certainly did not," she huffed. "Well! Let's just see how you like it."

"What? You gonna throw a grasshopper on me?" He chuckled.

She got a gleam in her eye he'd never seen, a definite streak of mischief. It tickled him silly; he threw back his head and laughed. "You'd have to pick it up, darlin', and I don't think you—hey!"

She lunged at him and stuffed the dead grasshopper down his shirt. He grabbed her wrist.

"Well, *darlin',* I did pick it up and now it's on you." She smiled into his eyes, so pleased with herself that he forgot all about the bug.

He'd never seen her playful and teasing. Her unguarded smile seduced the starch out of him; he could feel her pulse skitter beneath his touch. He lifted his hand to her cheek and she drew in a breath.

Desire hooked into him, hard and fast enough to shake him. Reminding himself that he wasn't going to get involved with her, he pulled away and forced a laugh. "I guess I underestimated you."

"I guess so." Her smile faded and she sank back down in her seat.

He fished the insect out of his shirt and tossed it to the ground. Clearing his throat, he guided Pru back onto the road.

Susannah sat quietly beside him. His muscles strained with the effort not to pull her onto his lap and kiss the sense out of her. "You surprised me."

"I surprised myself. I apologize for getting so excited, but the grasshopper took me off guard."

"No harm done." Except to his raging blood. "You were doing real fine until then."

"Really?" She glanced at him, blushing becomingly when he nodded. "Could I do it again?"

"Sure." He handed her the reins and she settled in, obvious in her attempt to keep the wagon in the middle of the road.

A smile still touched her lips and Riley found himself staring, reliving the taste of her, the satiny feel of her mouth on his. Nope. He steered his thoughts in another direction. "Once we get a good freeze, those grasshoppers will be gone for a while. You've done well since we started with the horses, but I don't think you're all that comfortable. Did something happen to make you afraid of horses?"

"I guess the horses can tell, as well?"

"Yes, but you're coming along and they can sense that, too. Remember that I untied Prissy last week and both of you did fine."

For a moment, he thought she wouldn't answer his question, then she said, "I was nine. We were in town one Saturday, and crossing the street to meet Adam and Father at my father's office. The milk wagon was driving past and a boy threw a rock at the team. They bolted, and when they did, it startled me. I tried to get out of the way, but I tripped. They barely missed running over me, and dragged that wagon to the other end of the street."

"Sounds like the kid who threw the rock needed a good thumping."

Susannah kept her gaze straight ahead, concentrating intensely on working the reins.

"You're lucky you weren't hurt."

"You probably think I'm silly for still being afraid." She

gave him a wobbly smile. "But I could never get up the courage to be around horses after that."

"Until now," he pointed out.

"Yes, until now."

A true smile bloomed and jolted his bloodstream like a swig of whiskey. "There's nothing silly about being cautious. Horses can be as dangerous as anything I've seen. People get stomped on or dragged. I know of one man who was kicked in the head and he hasn't been able to talk or take care of himself since. Nope, you're not silly."

"I wish I had some witnesses to hear you say that," she said smartly.

"Now, c'mon. I don't treat you like you're silly."

She tilted her head and ran a considering gaze over him. "No, I guess not...Mr. Bossy."

She laughed softly, and Riley couldn't take his eyes off her. His gaze traced her delicate profile, dropped to the swell of her breasts, barely visible beneath her cape. Awareness charged the air between them, humming like a twister ready to touch down and do its damage.

Hell.

"Do you think I can actually do this?"

"You *are* doing it."

Her gaze met his. "Yes, I guess so."

After a long moment, she looked away. "I never thought I'd get close to a horse again, let alone groom one or drive or any of the things you've been teaching me. Now I can go anywhere I need to. Thank you."

Though he admitted to a certain pride in her accomplishment, concern pricked at him. He didn't want to see her smile disappear, nor did he want to scare her, but he wanted her to be careful. "You know not to go out alone, don't you? You need more practice."

"But I think if I had to, if something happened, I could handle Prissy."

"It's not the horse I'm worried about," Riley muttered.

"Are you back to thinking I can't take care of myself?" She stiffened beside him.

"No, I'm thinking of things you can't control, like the weather."

She looked around. "It's beautiful."

"Not always. It can be very unpredictable. Deadly," he said in a flat tone. "You've got to be really careful out here. I've seen twisters carry off barns, even livestock. It can be desert dry one minute and a raging flood fifteen minutes later. Blistering cold in the winter. And we have these dust storms…."

An image of his wife's lifeless body flashed through his mind. "Dust so thick and blowing so hard you can't open your eyes. You lose all sense of direction. It can be—"

"Too much for someone like *me*," Susannah finished angrily.

"For anyone," he said gruffly, a hollow ache in his chest. His hands clenched into fists on his thighs.

She studied him for a moment, curiosity burning in her eyes. "Riley?"

"It shouldn't be long now. We'll reach Abilene in plenty of time for the first race."

"Good."

Whatever questions she'd wanted to ask she seemed to think better of. He'd seen a flash of hurt in her eyes at the way he'd changed the subject, but he wouldn't let himself be swayed by that. They didn't need to know such private information about each other. He didn't want to tell her about Maddie, nor did she need to hear how his wife had died. How she was just as unsuited to this harsh country as Maddie had been, regardless of the fact that Susannah was growing more

at ease around horses. And establishing a life for herself in
Whirlwind.

As soon as Adam got things straightened out with his and
Susannah's parents, she'd be on the first stage out of here. As
she should be.

Riley wanted her, but not on the terms she needed. Or
deserved. She was a woman who should be married. And he
wasn't getting hitched again.

Things were best left as they were. He had every intention
of holding to that, despite the fact that every day
with her blurred what he knew to be true: she didn't belong
here, didn't belong with him. Forgetting that would hurt
them both.

Darkness had long settled around them by the time they
returned to Cora's. Susannah was tired and a couple of times
had caught herself nearly falling asleep on Riley's shoulder.
As inviting as the pallet in the back looked, she was reluctant
to move. She liked being in the front where she could see.

She also didn't want the memory of his touch on her cheek
to circle round and round in her mind, as it was doing.

Her heart had nearly stopped when he'd touched her face,
and she'd wanted more. But the moment had shattered when
they'd both realized it shouldn't happen. That touch was all
it had taken to remind her of Paul, allow her to pull back and
clear her thoughts.

But one image she couldn't erase was the way Riley's eyes
had darkened when he'd warned her so urgently about the
dangerous weather here. His voice had gone hoarse when
he'd spoken about dust storms, but why? Emotion had flashed
quickly through his eyes, then disappeared. An emotion she
couldn't quite identify. Pain? Anger? Regret?

She hesitated to pry. She didn't understand it, but a small

part of her feared knowing. And she didn't want to bring that hollowness back into his eyes.

He pulled the buggy up in front of Cora's house and came around to help her down. Susannah gripped the side of the seat to balance herself as she turned to reach for his shoulders. A sharp pain shot through her palm and up her arm. She winced, gasping.

"What is it?" Riley immediately grasped her waist.

"I hurt my hand."

"How?"

She looked down, but, unable to see clearly, she shook her head. "I don't know."

He took her hand and turned it over, causing her to draw in a sharp breath at his touch. In the fall of moonlight, she saw him frown.

"Damn, your gloves are torn. Your hands are probably blistered but good."

"From driving?"

He nodded, gently helping her down, then moving in front of her to open the door. A lamp burned in the middle of Cora's kitchen table, lighting the way as Susannah walked inside.

"Hello! Good trip?" Cora sat in the corner next to the stove. A lantern on the wall behind her gave off a soft light as she embroidered.

"Yes." Susannah smiled at her friend.

"Hi, Cora." Riley shut the door and pulled out a chair at the table for Susannah. "Those gloves are ruined. They're for Sundays, not driving."

"They're all I have." She sank down into the chair, wriggling in discomfort at another hard seat.

"What happened?" Cora paused in her stitching and leaned forward.

"I drove! I drove the wagon." Despite the burning pain in

her hands, excitement rippled through Susannah. She would never have imagined herself doing such a thing.

"You drove? How wonderful."

"She needs some salve," Riley said.

"In the pantry." Cora pointed to the tall wooden cabinet behind the table, and Riley left to retrieve a small round tin.

"How bad is it?" the older woman asked.

"I think just blisters," Susannah said.

"Her gloves are in shreds and her hands are raw."

"I'm sure they'll be fine." She met Riley's gaze as he pulled a chair in front of her and sat down.

"You should've said something," he said quietly.

"They didn't hurt until we arrived home." Over his shoulder, she met Cora's gaze and rolled her eyes.

Her friend grinned.

Riley plucked off his hat and set it on the table before opening the tin. "I'm going to rub in this salve. It will hurt at first, but it will save your hands. Okay?"

"All right." His touch was gentle as he turned her hands palm up, then dabbed on a glob of yellowish cream. Despite his featherlight touch, pain seared her flesh and she bit her lip to keep from crying out.

"I'm sorry." He held her gaze with his.

She focused on the steadiness in his blue eyes, trying to dull her mind to the pain burning her hands.

"Did you enjoy yourselves?" Cora asked.

"Yes, it was fun," Susannah said. Talking would take her mind off her discomfort. And maybe the soft pleasure stealing through her veins at Riley's touch. "That mystery rider won again."

"Again?"

"By quite a handy margin." Riley started working on her other hand. "Every race."

Susannah shook her head. "His horse must be really fast."

"How many races today?" Cora asked.

"Three." Susannah wasn't surprised that her voice trembled. Riley's thumb stroked over the heel of her palm, grazing her wrist where her pulse pounded erratically.

Cora resumed her embroidery. "How much money?"

"Twenty-five dollars for two races," Riley said. "And forty for the last one."

"I de-clare." Cora bit off a length of thread. "And no one knows who he is?"

"No." He grinned, looking over his shoulder at her. "You should've seen Banker Dobies, though. He was just as sour this time as last."

Cora chuckled.

Riley's finger grazed a tender place in the center of Susannah's palm and she sucked in a breath.

"I'll try to hurry," he said.

"I'm all right." Her voice was hoarse and she knew it was because of Riley's touch, not because of any pain she felt. The concern in his eyes drew her in, generated a warmth inside her that melted her bones. "How are you, Cora?"

"I'll be good as new in a day or two. What did you think of driving the buckboard?"

"I don't know how well I did, but I think I can get the hang of it."

"She did a fine job." Riley continued to stroke salve on her hands. "She got all cocky, driving like a madwoman, then found this grasshopper and dropped it down my shirt."

"I never did!" she exclaimed. "Riley Holt, you tell the truth right now."

"I am. I swear." He grinned.

Cora laughed softly. "Yes, I can just imagine who's telling the truth here. What really happened, Susannah?"

She smirked at Riley. "A grasshopper jumped into my dress and I had to get it out."

"While hopping around like a jackrabbit."

She sniffed. "I didn't. And you weren't much help."

"You killed it dead without any help from me."

"Yes, I'm wicked with insects."

Cora laughed. "I guess I missed out on quite a bit."

"I'm sure Susannah would be glad to show you just how she finally got that grasshopper. She kinda flung her arms out and whacked at everything, including me."

"Oh, you." She tried to look stern, but couldn't.

Cora laughed, putting her embroidery in her lap as she leaned her head against the back of her rocker. "Susannah, before I forget, Evelyn Donnelly paid you a visit today."

"Andrew's mother?"

"Didn't he show up for your charm school?" Riley asked.

Susannah nodded.

"She said she'd sent money with Andrew to pay for the classes, but she found it in the pocket of his jacket. He told her you must've put it back in there."

"I couldn't take his money. I don't think she can afford it. He said she was ill."

"She is. Some kind of consumption, I think." Cora clucked her tongue sympathetically.

"I want him to be able to attend class."

"She gave me the money again," Cora said.

Riley dabbed a layer of salve on her other palm. "She wants to pay, Susannah. It's a matter of pride."

"I didn't mean to insult her. I'll go talk to her."

"She's a seamstress. Maybe you could work out a trade with her," Cora suggested.

"That's a wonderful idea." She shifted, bothered by the sensation working from her arms to her breasts, her legs. Was

Riley almost finished? She felt his touch clear to her core. "I have some clothing I need to let out again. Maybe Mrs. Donnelly would be willing to do that."

"That's a good idea." Riley smiled into her eyes.

Part of her wished he'd never stop touching her, but it was too stimulating. Too distracting. Every time his fingers stroked her palm, her nerve endings drew tight. Liquid heat streamed through her body, between her legs. It was dangerous, the pleasure seducing her into feeling instead of thinking. And she'd made up her mind about that.

No matter how handsome he looked with the lamplight gilding his hair, the strong column of his throat revealed by the barely opened neck of his shirt. His powerful thighs bracketed hers in a slyly sensual way. She could easily forget about Cora being in the room, just as she'd forgotten everyone else when she and Riley had danced in the barn two weeks ago.

She felt herself getting lost in the deep blue of his eyes and realized he'd stopped applying salve. She blinked.

Staring into her eyes, he held her hand for a second longer, then rose. He put the lid back on the tin and placed it on the table. "You should use this two or three times a day for about a week. It will help the blisters."

She nodded, not understanding the ache in her heart, the yearning for something more. "Thank you."

"You're welcome." He turned to Cora, his voice rusty. "Need anything before I go? Wood?"

"Maybe some wood," the older woman said with a smile.

He picked up his hat and settled it on his head. "I'll stack it up here on the porch and see you ladies on Monday evening for horse lessons."

"Good night," Cora called as he walked out and closed the door.

"Good night." Susannah rose from the chair and unfastened

her cloak, hanging it up. Removing the scarf, which had slipped off her head and hung around her shoulders, she placed it on top of her cloak.

"Aren't you glad you went?" Cora asked. "It sounds like you had a nice time."

She hesitated a moment. "I did."

"Are you surprised?"

Susannah shrugged. "I guess I am."

Riley's boots thudded heavily across the porch, then she heard a muffled thunk as he stacked wood outside the door.

"Because you enjoyed Riley's company? Or for some other reason?" Cora's voice was gentle, but it stirred up questions Susannah didn't want to answer.

She said cautiously, "The races were exciting."

She wouldn't voice the secret pleasure she'd felt with him today. It would do no good to contemplate it. Because while laughing with him and feeling his strong, gentle touch on her hands, she'd realized Riley Holt could do more damage to her common sense than Paul ever had.

Chapter Nine

A week later, with Cora's help, Susannah rolled out biscuits on the kitchen table. She'd seen how much Riley enjoyed Cora's biscuits, and had asked Cora to teach her how to make them.

"This is thoughtful of you," the other woman said. "Riley really likes these biscuits."

"I hope he'll like the ones I make." Susannah grimaced. "I want to thank him for driving into town every evening for my lessons. I've never cooked much and I appreciate you taking the time to teach me."

"Didn't your mother cook?"

"She knew how, but preferred for Minnie, our cook, to prepare the meals. I never had much interest in learning until now."

Curiosity burned in Cora's eyes. "And you didn't have to learn when you ran your husband's house?"

"No." Susannah mentally caught herself. Sometimes she forgot she was supposed to be widowed.

Cora's slight frown made it plain she thought it odd that Susannah hadn't learned to cook even then. "What was your life like in St. Louis?"

"Well…" She could remember only a procession of parties, dances and picnics. Surely she'd done something other than pursue entertainment, something productive. "It was different than it is here. I don't know how to do much of anything, which I imagine is obvious."

"Well, life is just a series of lessons in how to make do. Don't you think?"

Yes, she did. Look at her now, making a life for herself and her baby. She didn't know anything about that, either. "Coming here has made me stand on my own for the first time. I hope I'm doing all right."

"You've got a lot of guts. That will serve you well."

"I do?"

"I think so. Just look at how you're trying to get over your fear of horses. You started a charm school, which had to be a bit daunting around here." Cora grinned. "And you're taking care of the chickens. You probably didn't think you'd ever do that."

She laughed. "No, I didn't."

They worked for a moment in silence with Susannah following Cora's lead as she floured the table, then plopped a thick ball of dough onto the surface.

Susannah took the rolling pin and rolled the dough to about a quarter-inch thickness, then began to cut circles with a tin cup. Though she enjoyed her growing friendship with Cora, she was nagged by an uncertainty that had been building, one she'd been ignoring. "Cora, I'm nervous about the baby. What if I'm not a good mother?"

Her friend stopped coating biscuits with melted grease and turned to her. "Do you love this baby?"

"Yes." She put a protective hand over her belly. "More than I ever thought you could love another person."

"You'll do just fine then." The other woman smiled. "I

don't know if anyone ever feels they know exactly how to raise a child."

"I've never asked about your children. Do you have any?"

Cora's eyes misted and she glanced away before answering reluctantly, "We had one, a boy. He's way out behind the house with Ollie. He was stillborn."

"I'm so sorry." Susannah squeezed Cora's hand. "I shouldn't have asked. I didn't think."

"It's fine that you did. I still miss him sometimes." She dabbed at her eyes with her apron. "I only hesitated to tell you because I don't want you to worry. It's not good for the baby."

Susannah's throat tightened at the other woman's pain. "I'll try."

"You think about nice things. Your health is good and you're young. Things will be fine."

She nodded, taking Cora's advice and refusing to consider that something could happen to her baby. But the dark pain in her friend's eyes reminded Susannah of something similar she'd seen in Riley's eyes on their way to Abilene. Had he lost a child, too?

In the days since that trip, she hadn't been able to stop thinking about his raw look when he'd discussed the weather. Was it because of a loss like Cora's? Susannah realized her curiosity about him was becoming insatiable and quite insistent. She knew from Adam that Riley had been married. What had happened to his wife? Had they had children?

"My brother told me Riley's been married before. Did you know his wife?"

"Maddie? Yes, sure did. She was from back East, too."

"Where?"

"Philadelphia, I think. He met her while he was in university."

"And then they were married?"

"Uh-huh. Maddie was a sweet girl, very pretty."

"What did she look like?"

"Light brown hair, brown eyes, a little thing."

Susannah's gaze dropped to her protruding belly. She hadn't felt little in quite some time. "What happened to her?"

"Has he mentioned her?"

"No. I just wondered."

Cora was silent for a moment, then said, "I don't want to speak out of turn, but I will say she passed away. It was sudden and it really knocked Riley off his stride. That boy seemed lost for almost two years."

Susannah nodded, hardly able to imagine anything making Riley seem lost.

"There was a dust storm. Maddie went to the barn to put up her horse and the milk cow. She wasn't that far from the house, but she lost her way and tripped in a rut, broke her neck."

Riley's flat-voiced explanation about dust storms rushed back into Susannah's mind. "Where was Riley?"

"In Abilene with his father. He thought Maddie knew not to go out in the storm. When those things hit, it turns almost as black as night. You can't see a thing. But I think she believed she could take care of the animals quickly."

"How horrible!"

"I think he blamed himself for a while."

"But why?"

"For bringing her here. She was a city girl, though she tried hard to make things work."

Riley's wife had been an outsider, just like Susannah. Was that why he was so convinced she didn't belong here? "Does he ever talk about her?"

"Not to me."

"Do you think…" She tried to keep her voice steady. "Does he still love her?"

"I'm sure he'll always have a special place for her in his heart. Just like you do for your husband."

Susannah's hands froze on the biscuit dough. She couldn't continue lying, not to Cora. "I didn't have a husband," she said quietly.

The woman turned with a frown. "What do you mean? Of course you did."

"No. I'm not a widow. I've never been married."

"But why tell people—" Cora broke off, her gaze dropping to Susannah's protruding stomach.

Heat flooded her face. "I don't want you to think poorly of me, Cora, but I can't lie to you. You've become a good friend and I want you to know the truth. I wear this ring so people will think I'm widowed, so that my baby won't be slighted because of a mistake *I* made. I would never want to bring shame to you. If you want me to find another place to live, I will."

"No, honey, I don't." Cora dusted the flour off her hands and put an arm around Susannah's shoulders. "I want you to stay here with me and have that baby. Stay as long as you want."

Tears stung Susannah's eyes and she gave the woman a quick hug. "I disgraced my family. That's really why I'm here."

"What happened?"

"I was swept away. I fell in love and believed we were to be married. He told me that. That's the only reason I allowed his liberties…. It's no excuse. I was a willing participant. When I found out I was expecting, I told Paul. He disappeared, and when my brother's private investigator found him he wasn't interested."

"Does Riley know?"

"Yes." She pulled nervously at her lower lip, shame filling her. She might as well tell it all. "I came here to marry him. My brother told me that Riley wanted a wife, that he wanted *me*."

"I think that's wonderful! So, what happened? Why didn't you two marry?"

"My brother exaggerated—no, he lied. Riley set me straight on that right away."

"Oh, dear."

She told Cora how Riley had found out about her condition and how they'd talked about it. "But it's worked out better this way," Susannah said. "Riley doesn't want a wife and I want someone who will be a good father to my baby."

"Riley would make a good father."

Susannah forced a smile, keeping to herself that she thought he would also make a good husband.

He would never believe she belonged here. No matter what she did.

Three weeks later, Riley sat with Davis Lee in church, two rows behind Susannah and Cora. Thanksgiving had come and gone. Susannah and Cora had attended the town feast and celebration, with Susannah being more sought after than water during a drought. The next night they'd gotten their first good snow, so he'd told her they would stop their lessons with the mare until the weather warmed up. After the baby came.

Because of that, Riley had seen Susannah only at church these last weeks. He'd been busy at the ranch, moving enough hay for the winter into the main barn, herding the cattle to the south pasture and replacing the pump part that had finally arrived.

As church was dismissed, he admitted he'd missed seeing her. Missed the look of surprised pleasure that stole across her features when she mastered each new step he taught her about the mare. She felt comfortable grooming the horse now and checking the animal's hooves. After their trip to Abilene, Susannah had driven a couple more times, but she still needed a lot of practice there.

He and Davis Lee walked out of the church. Gray clouds hung low in the sky and the chilly wind swept unhindered across the plains. The two of them moved down the three steps, joining a small group of men gathered a short distance away from the white clapboard building. From the corner of his eye, Riley caught a flash of silvery-blond hair and knew by the hum in his blood that Susannah had come outside.

He heard J. T. Baldwin speak to her, and she laughed, the sound playing over Riley's nerves like a secret touch down his spine. He had missed her laugh. And even from here, he thought he could smell the soft vanilla of her scent. He glanced over, jamming his hands in the pockets of his trousers as Russ Baldwin tucked her hand in the crook of his arm and carefully helped her down the steps.

Russ left her standing with Cora, Pearl Anderson and May Haskell, before sauntering over to join Riley, Davis Lee, Jake Ross and Miguel Santos. Pete and Creed Carter walked up. They discussed the deer hunting this season and the possibility of more snow. As the boys and men drifted away, Cora and Susannah came over.

"Hello, ladies." Davis Lee doffed his hat, smiling broadly. "How are the two prettiest women in Texas?"

"Oh, you do go on, boy," Cora said with a smile.

"We're fine." Susannah answered Davis Lee, but her gaze met Riley's. "How are you?"

He nodded. "Just fine. Good morning."

"It's a beautiful day," Davis Lee said. "May we walk you ladies home?"

"No, thank you," Cora said. "But we did want to invite y'all to share Christmas dinner with us. It's only a week away."

"We accept," Davis Lee said, before Riley could even blink. "I would never turn down any dinner at your house, Cora."

"Wonderful. We'll plan on it then." Cora glanced at Riley with a secretive smile.

He winked to let her know he was nearly finished with her gift for Susannah. So that Susannah wouldn't catch the silent communication between them, he eased closer to her. "How are your hands?"

"They healed nicely. I don't think I'll have a single callus."

"Good." He couldn't help admiring her dewy skin, the way her blue eyes sparkled. "How's your school going?"

"I'm encouraged. The entire class promises to make passable waltzers."

"Now, that's something I'll have to see." He grinned.

"We'd better let you boys get to your lunch," Cora said.

"Do you need anything done at your place?" Davis Lee asked.

"Not at the moment, but thank you."

"Let us know," Riley said.

"Will do." Cora waved goodbye, then started walking slowly with Susannah toward the other end of town.

Riley walked beside his brother, his gaze on Susannah's gently swaying skirts ahead of them. Remaining just friends with her was the right decision, but it hadn't stopped this ache inside him. An ache that grew and deepened every time he saw her.

A couple of times during their lunch at the Pearl, Riley caught Davis Lee contemplating him as if trying to figure out a puzzle. They forfeited conversation in favor of eating their roast and potatoes. As they finished their apricot pie, Davis Lee took a long sip of coffee, then leaned back in his chair, still studying him.

After a long moment, he said, "I've got something for you at the office."

Riley laid the money for their meal on the table. "Okay."

During their short walk to the jail, he wondered what was on his brother's mind.

Once inside the office, Davis Lee pulled a small brown paper package from his middle desk drawer. "Haskell had to go pick up his mother-in-law and wanted me to give this to you, since the store won't be open until Tuesday morning."

Riley took the package, not liking the knowing look on his brother's face.

"He asked me if you were courting someone."

His grip tightened on the package, the crackle of paper loud in the small space. "Why would he ask that?"

"Because those gloves you ordered are for ladies."

"So what?" Riley unwrapped them and examined the pair carefully. The sturdy tan leather gloves were well-constructed.

"Who are they for?"

"Susannah." He rewrapped them and stuffed them in the pocket of his coat.

Davis Lee cocked his head. "*Are* you courting her?"

"Hell, no. I'm teaching her how to drive the wagon. She tore up her only pair of gloves doing it, so I bought her a pair of driving gloves."

"That was nice," his brother said cautiously.

Riley scowled. "They're for Christmas. She needs them. I'm not declaring intentions or anything. It's just a gift for a friend."

Davis Lee crossed his arms and eased down onto the corner of his desk. "I think there's something going on with you two. I've seen the way she looks at you."

"She doesn't look at me like anything."

"What's the problem? If you say you haven't noticed her, I'll know you're lying."

"I'm not blind, but I'm not stupid, either."

"Stupid? She's a beautiful woman."

It didn't matter that she heated Riley's blood faster than any woman ever had, didn't matter that she ignited a desire so fierce she needed to be protected from *him*. She couldn't be more wrong for him or for life here.

"Neither one of us is interested in anything more than friendship."

Davis Lee shrugged. "Hope she doesn't get the wrong idea about those gloves."

Riley frowned. "She won't."

They had an understanding. Which was none of Davis Lee's business.

"I think she's getting to you."

"She doesn't belong here. She doesn't even know what kind of gloves to wear to drive a wagon."

"That can be learned. And I think she's trying hard to learn all she can. I mean, you said she's really applied herself during her lessons with Cora's mare."

Riley agreed, but he also knew this land, this life could be the death of her. "It would be better for her and the baby if she were back in St. Louis. She knows it."

"Maybe she thinks she belongs *here*," Davis Lee said quietly.

"Then she's a fool."

"She seems to be making a place for herself just fine."

"I imagine her family will want her home with them after the baby comes."

"Or her husband's family," Davis Lee offered offhandedly, then gave Riley a quizzical look. "How can her last name still be the same as her family if she's a widow?"

"Oh. She...married a distant cousin."

"Hmmm." Amusement sparked in the other man's eyes. "I could swear I've noticed something going on with the two of you."

"There's nothing." Restlessness sent him stalking to one end of Davis Lee's desk and back.

His brother raised an eyebrow. "You've been spending time with her. You have to like her a little."

"I like her fine. Doesn't mean I want to marry her."

"Whoa, I didn't say anything about getting married." He chuckled. "Well, well, little brother."

"Shut up." Riley couldn't stop pacing.

"What's the problem? You admire her."

"Doesn't mean I want to stake a claim on her." Which was exactly what he wanted to do right now. "We're friends. That's all."

Davis Lee was silent for a moment. "Is it because of Maddie? Aren't you ready to move on?"

"I might be ready with the right woman. Susannah Phelps isn't the right woman," he said flatly, his shirt collar choking him.

"Well, if you're just friends then you won't mind if I ask her to church next Sunday."

"No, I don't mind." His jaw was clenched so hard he thought his teeth might break.

Davis Lee chuckled and shook his head. "I won't ask her."

"I said I don't mind."

"You're lying. Don't worry, I won't tell anyone."

Riley's temper flared. Davis Lee could get him riled faster than anybody.

"It wouldn't hurt you to think about getting married again."

That cinched it. "You're a fine one to talk. You've never been married at all."

Silence descended like a weight, and Riley bit back a surge of regret. They both knew why his brother hadn't married. During his job as sheriff of Rock River, Davis Lee had fallen in love with a woman who had conned half the townspeople out of their money, then left. It was his ultimate humiliation and had caused him to lose his job there. The brothers never spoke of it.

Davis Lee held up a hand as a gesture of a truce. "All right, I'll mind my own business. But I think there's something going on."

What if Davis Lee was right and she could learn to survive here? No, Riley wouldn't let himself imagine it. Maddie had learned a lot of things, and this land had taken its toll on her. On him. If he didn't watch out, Susannah would have him ass backwards, where he didn't know come 'ere from sic 'em.

"I think she's just lookin' for some cover," he said. "Somebody she doesn't expect anything from. Someone who doesn't expect anything of her."

"Why? Because of what happened to her husband?"

"Yes, because of him." That wasn't a lie. Exactly.

Susannah's interest in Riley had to do with finding a father for her baby, not a man for herself.

Why that should make him want to hit the wall he didn't know. He knew where she stood. She knew the same about him. No expectations, no high hopes. No problems.

Chapter Ten

Susannah wanted Riley's good opinion and it irritated her no end. He wasn't likely to change his mind about her, especially after what had happened to his wife, and Susannah shouldn't care. She'd made her decision to stay in Whirlwind.

Christmas Day dawned clear and cold. She helped Cora as much as she could with the cooking, mostly by sitting next to the stove and mixing or stirring or paring. She cut the biscuits while Cora tended the stuffed hen roasting in the stove.

As she helped the older woman move food to the table, she found her thoughts drifting. In the week since she'd seen Riley at church and Cora had invited the Holt brothers to Christmas dinner, Susannah had done her best to forget about him. It was as difficult to do as if she'd tried to forget about the babe she carried.

Learning the details of Riley's wife's death only made Susannah more curious about him. She remembered Adam saying it had been a love match. Did Riley still mourn his wife? Was the holiday as hard for him as it was for her? Would he ever marry again? When Susannah had first met him, he'd said no.

Just after noon, the jingle of harness and rattle of wagon wheels sounded outside.

"Oh, good, the boys are here. Since Davis Lee spends Christmas Eve at the ranch with Riley, I thought they'd come together." Cora pulled the bird from the stove and set it on top.

A quick double knock came on the door and Davis Lee stuck his head inside. "Merry Christmas, ladies."

Riley appeared in the doorway beside him. "Merry Christmas."

Cora and Susannah echoed the sentiment. Conscious of her appearance, Susannah refrained from smoothing a hand over her hair or checking the red ribbon in her chignon.

Smiling, Cora walked to the door. "Come in, come in. Dinner's nearly on the table."

Davis Lee stepped inside, looking up as he did so at the cluster of mistletoe hanging there. "Hey, little brother, lookee here."

Riley ducked through the doorway and grinned. "Can't let that go to waste."

The elder Holt brother grabbed Cora on one side and Riley grabbed her on the other. Both men gave her a loud kiss on the cheek.

"You two." She batted at them, obviously pleased.

Susannah laughed, pushing away the wistful thought of she and Riley sharing the traditional Christmas kiss. "Cora looked and looked for a clump with berries."

"And I found one, too," the other woman said proudly. "Even if it is only one berry."

"Come outside," Davis Lee urged. "We've got something for you."

She looked from one to the other. "What have you boys done?"

"Come see." Riley grinned.

Susannah moved around the table and Riley motioned for her to precede him outside. "How are you today?"

"Very well." She patted her protruding belly. "Large, but well."

"You look pretty." His gaze flickered over her, dark and intense, sending a tingle under her skin.

"Thank you." Standing under the mistletoe with him made her nervous. Hopeful. Which she didn't like. She pointed at the cluster of greenery. "I tried to talk Cora out of hanging that."

"I probably would've had the same luck you did," he said in a low voice. "We know she's not hanging it for herself."

"No, she's not." Susannah slid him a look, but found him watching Cora as she approached his wagon with Davis Lee and looked over the side.

"Oh, my goodness!" the older woman exclaimed. "Boys, this is too much."

"It's from Davis Lee," Riley said.

Susannah walked to the edge of the porch and saw a canvas-covered lump in the back of Riley's wagon. She turned to him with a questioning look.

"Venison," he explained. "Half the buck Davis Lee got yesterday. Ever had venison?"

"No, but I'd like to try it."

Cora beamed as if the meat were gold. "Susannah, this means we can eat something besides beans and salt pork all winter."

"Thank you, Davis Lee," Susannah said.

"What a Christmas this is turning out to be." The older woman fingered the soft blue shawl around her shoulders. "Look what Susannah gave me."

"And Cora made a blanket for the baby." Susannah turned to Riley. "She *made* it!"

"Well, you can sure use that."

"She amazes me. Especially that she made it right under my nose."

He chuckled.

Susannah relaxed a bit. All morning, nerves had had her uneasily anticipating dinner with Riley today. She knew it was because she wanted him to believe she belonged here, to accept that she was staying.

She seemed to worry about that a lot where he was concerned, she told herself wryly. She'd taken great pains with her appearance, piling her hair up in a simple twist with a red ribbon that matched the thin stripes in her white wool dress. Thanks to Evelyn Donnelly, who'd let out the skirts again, Susannah would be able to wear this favorite dress until the baby came.

The frigid air bit at her cheeks, and Riley lightly touched her elbow. "Let's get these ladies back inside, Davis Lee."

"Yes, y'all go in," the elder Holt said. "Riley and I will take this meat to the cellar."

Cora thanked them again and followed Susannah into the house. Together, they dished up the hen, potatoes, biscuits and gravy. While Cora strained coffee, Susannah poured a cup of milk for herself. She wasn't able to stomach coffee these days.

The door opened and the men stepped inside, bringing a chill with them. But one look into Riley's blue eyes warmed Susannah to her toes.

She looked away, easing down into the chair that backed up to the stove. Because of the baby, Cora insisted she sit in the warmest spot.

The meal passed in a blur of conversation, laughter and good food. Cora, Riley and Davis Lee reminisced about past Christmases. Susannah enjoyed the talk, but couldn't discount the twinge of homesickness she felt. Anger at her parents and determination to prove that she could survive without them had kept her going since arriving in Whirlwind, but today she missed her family, especially since receiving the letter from Adam two days ago.

She'd reread it ten times, each time searching hard for sentiments that weren't there.

Riley pushed back in his chair, groaning. "Cora, as usual you've outdone yourself. Those biscuits were the best yet."

Susannah agreed, anxious for the day she would master baking the bread. Though she'd finally gotten the right mixture of ingredients, she couldn't seem to determine the exact amount of time in the stove. They were either undercooked and doughy or burned to a crisp. Duplicating Cora's baking time never worked for her. The fire was either too hot or not hot enough.

"I can hardly move." Davis Lee patted his flat stomach. "I'll barely be able to fit in a piece of that apple pie I smelled."

Cora chuckled, glancing at Susannah. "Did you get enough?"

"Oh, yes, more than I needed."

"And you're feeling okay?"

"Yes." Her lower back ached slightly, but it usually did by the middle of the day.

Concern passed across the other woman's face, but Susannah smiled to reassure her. Cora flicked a look at Riley, then rose from her chair. "Davis Lee, could you give me a hand outside? My cow's milk was low today and I'm wondering if she's getting croupy."

"I'll clean up," Susannah said quickly.

"Be happy to look at your cow, Cora." Riley's brother stood and put on his coat and hat, then went outside with their hostess.

As the door closed behind them, Riley snorted. "Davis Lee doesn't know that much about milk cows. I think Cora's got something up her sleeve."

Susannah smiled. Her friend's request had been an obvious ruse to leave her alone with Riley. First the mistletoe and now this. She busied herself scraping plates while Riley stoked the fire and poured water into the kettle. Several minutes later, he dumped the warm water into the sink so she could wash the dishes.

"Have you heard from Adam?" Riley took a pot from her and dried it.

"I had a letter two days ago."

"Is he wanting you to come home?"

"No," she said shortly. Riley always seemed to want her to leave.

He glanced over his shoulder as if to make sure they were still alone. "Did he say anything about your folks? About… you know."

Sadness pierced her, but she forced a smile. "He's not having any luck getting them to soften about my situation." She shrugged, but couldn't stop a sudden burn of tears. "They don't want to correspond, either. At least not yet."

"You're missing them a lot."

"Yes. Or at least happier times."

"How does your family spend the holiday?"

She handed him the skillet. "We exchange gifts in the morning, then have a big dinner, usually turkey with chestnut stuffing. Or a duck. Lots of cakes. We go caroling or perhaps to a ball in the evening."

"Sounds nice."

"Yes." She stared blankly at the pan she was scrubbing.

Riley reached over to put his hand on top of hers. "I'm sorry."

Her gaze met his, drawn in by the tenderness there. The moment stretched between them, taut and expectant. Pulsing with anticipation.

He leaned toward her slightly and Susannah found herself doing the same, wanting to kiss him.

"Oh!" Startled by her thought, she drew back. "What are we doing?"

"Uh. Well." He blinked. For a long minute, he looked nonplussed, then jabbed a thumb toward the front door. "Uh, mistletoe."

"But it's over there."

"So it is." He grinned.

She shook her head, smiling, too. They went back to their chore and after a moment, Susannah tried to ease past the awkwardness. "I'm sorry for your loss, too."

He froze. "What loss?"

Her hand slowed on the plate she washed. "Adam and Cora told me you lost your wife. I imagine days like today are difficult for you, too."

He rubbed hard at the bowl he'd already dried.

Susannah wondered what he was thinking. Was he still in love with his wife? Was her loss too painful for him to discuss?

When he spoke, it was in a low voice. "I think about her more on days like this. I think about my folks, too."

She murmured agreement, wishing he would talk to her about his wife. But he remained silent. After a long moment, she awkwardly changed the subject, trying not to be hurt that he hadn't wanted to tell her more.

"I feel like I have another family here. I adore Cora. In fact…I told her the truth about the baby and why I came to Whirlwind."

Riley turned his head sharply. "You did?"

She nodded. "I offered to move out if she wanted. I don't want to shame her in any way."

"I bet she wouldn't have any of that."

"No, she wouldn't."

He smiled, warming that place deep inside Susannah that only he seemed able to warm. "You know she's trying to push us together."

"It had crossed my mind."

They shared a laugh, then Riley hefted the kettle and carried the used water outside. Susannah hurried to retrieve the gifts she'd wrapped for him and his brother.

Footsteps sounded on the porch and she looked up to see Davis Lee grinning like a man who'd gotten away with something. "Cora's got one more gift for you."

"But she already gave me the blanket."

He stepped aside to let Cora in. Riley came, too, backing in and carrying something covered with a sheet.

"Cora, you shouldn't have. The blanket is more than enough, and I love it."

"Wait till you see." Excitement brightened the older woman's hazel eyes. She moved next to Davis Lee, giving Riley room to move inside. She closed the door as Riley removed the sheet.

Davis Lee's grin grew broader.

Riley turned, holding a cradle made of dark, fine wood. Highly polished, it curved at the head and foot.

"Oh!" She covered her mouth, tears springing to her eyes. "Oh, my. Where did you get such a thing?"

"It was mine." Cora moved beside her, wrapping an arm around her shoulders. "Mine and Ollie's," she whispered, reminding Susannah of the baby boy Cora had lost.

That her friend would pass this beautiful cradle on to her baby put a lump in Susannah's throat. She hugged Cora tightly. "Thank you. I'll cherish it."

"Come look," Riley urged.

She dabbed at her eyes and walked around the table.

"Riley repaired it and shined it up to look like new," Cora said.

Susannah ran a hand lovingly across the curved top, her gaze lifting to his. "You did?"

"I didn't do much. It only needed a few pieces of wood."

Overwhelmed by their gesture, she flung her arms around him just as she'd done Cora. "Thank you. *Thank you.*"

He rested one hand lightly on her back. "You're welcome."

She made herself let go and step away, though what she wanted was to be enfolded in his arms and held against that solid chest. Still amazed, she examined the cradle carefully as Cora and Riley discussed the parts he'd replaced and the nights he'd worked on it.

She smiled. "I have a gift for you and Davis Lee, too."

"Now, you shouldn't have done that." Riley's brother looked pleased despite the admonition.

"I hope you like them." She retrieved the brown paper packages and gave them to the men.

Davis Lee ripped the paper off. "Well, I'll be! *The Return of the Native* by Thomas Hardy."

He seemed pleased with the novel she'd chosen from among from the few she'd brought to Whirlwind. "Have you read him?"

"No, but I've heard about this book. Thank you."

Riley opened his more slowly, his eyes dark with pleasure as he pulled out the garment. "A shirt."

"I hope you like it." She'd discussed the shirt with Cora before having it made. Her friend hadn't thought the gift of clothing improper.

"It's right nice," Davis Lee admired.

"Yes. Thank you." Riley smiled into her eyes and Susannah felt her feet go numb.

She'd chosen light blue because it reminded her of his eyes. "You've been needin' that," Davis Lee said.

"You shouldn't have spent your money on me," Riley said quietly.

"I wanted to."

"Give her your gift, Riley," his brother urged.

"Not another one!" she exclaimed.

Riley laid his shirt carefully on the table and reached behind him to where his coat hung on the wall. He drew out a small rectangular package wrapped in thin white paper and tied with a pale blue ribbon.

She was surprised to find her hands a bit unsteady as she unwrapped the gift. Inside lay a pair of tan kid leather gloves. "Goodness." She looked at him.

"Driving gloves," he said.

"For the wagon?"

"Yes."

"So, we'll continue our lessons?"

"I said we would." He turned to Cora and Davis Lee. "You two should see how well she's doing."

"They should?" Susannah couldn't stop the slow smile that spread across her face. Riley's giving her these gloves told her that he *believed* she could master driving the wagon. The realization bolstered her confidence. And her courage. "Do you think I could learn to ride?"

"If you want. When you put your mind to something, it seems to get done."

She searched his eyes, looking for any sign of hesitation. "Would you teach me?"

"Sure."

"I love these. Thank you." She hugged them to her, looking around at the people who'd already come to mean so much to her. "I love all my gifts. What a wonderful Christmas."

"Yes," Davis Lee said. "Now I think I'm ready for some of that pie, Cora."

The older woman bustled over to the pantry and took out the pie she'd baked earlier that day.

After enjoying the dessert, the men finally stood to leave.

"We'd better head back before dark." Davis Lee shrugged into his coat. "Looks like it might snow tonight. We could use the moisture."

"Y'all be careful," Cora cautioned. "Thank you for everything. It was wonderful."

"It was the best Christmas we've had in a while." Riley kissed her on the cheek, then walked over to take his coat from the peg behind the door.

Davis Lee said goodbye to Susannah and went out to hitch up the wagon. Cora followed him onto the porch.

Riley turned at the door. "Thanks again for the shirt."

"Thank you for the gloves and the cradle."

He hesitated, then said, "Did you give Davis Lee your own copy of that book?"

She smiled.

"Merry Christmas."

"Merry Christmas."

He glanced up at the mistletoe, then winked at her. "This ought to give Cora something to think about."

He reached up and plucked the lone berry from the middle of the greenery. Tradition held that a man took the berry only after stealing a kiss. Susannah laughed softly at Riley's joke on their friend.

"I'll see ya," he said.

"Goodbye."

She walked to the door and watched as he climbed into the wagon. He and Davis Lee set off with a squeak of wheels, the horse's breath a smoky plume on the air.

Rubbing her hands up and down her arms, she stepped back inside as Cora hurried in, closing the door.

"What a wonderful day." The older woman tugged her shawl tighter around her.

"Yes, it was. Thank you so much for the cradle, Cora. And the blanket. They're both beautiful and the baby needs them so much. I'm overwhelmed."

"Good. I think people should get at least one gift in their life that overwhelms them."

Susannah smiled, moving to the table to pick up her driving gloves.

Cora started around the table, then did a double take, craning her neck to study the mistletoe. She shot a look at Susannah and arched an eyebrow.

Biting her lip to keep from smiling, Susannah fled to her room.

"Susannah Phelps, you get back here!"

She laughed and moved to the bed, picking up the soft white blanket Cora had knitted.

Riley was giving her a chance. Warmth showered through Susannah. None of her wonderful gifts today could compare with the compliment Riley had given her. And sharing confidences with him about her family had eased the pain of their separation somewhat.

She'd been wrong about him. Finally, he seemed to accept that she was going to make a life here. That she could belong. She refused to ask herself why that mattered so much.

Riley didn't think he could choke down this whole biscuit. Susannah looked proud of her efforts, but the bread was hard as wood and tasted like ash.

"Could I get some more of that buttermilk?" he asked on the last Friday night in January.

Davis Lee smothered a cough. "Me, too."

He and his brother had accepted an invitation from Susannah for dinner. She wanted to thank him for helping her overcome her fear of horses and wanted to include Davis Lee. Riley was glad he wasn't enjoying this by himself. She'd told him that she had been learning to make Cora's biscuits and was ready to try out her newly acquired skills.

"I don't see how Cora does it." She poured more buttermilk for the men. "She gets everything cooked just right every time. Each time I thought I had it right, I would burn them or mistake the measurements."

Riley slid a look at Cora, who kept her eyes on her plate.

"Aren't you going to eat any?" he asked Susannah.

"Oh, yes." She sat down and picked up a biscuit.

Riley didn't have the heart to watch her. She made a strangled sound and he glanced up.

Grimacing, she dropped the biscuit onto the plate. "How awful! I am so sorry. Stop eating them this minute."

"They're not that bad, Susannah," Davis Lee said, though he readily put his down.

"You're too kind, but these are horrid." Her face fell. "I really thought I had it."

"I thought so, too," Cora said.

Trying to encourage Susannah, Riley said, "The stew is good."

"Cora made that," she informed him.

"Oh."

"You'll get it, honey," the other woman said.

Susannah rested her chin in her hand. "I'm starting to wonder."

"Well, how important is cooking, anyway?" Davis Lee asked.

"Yeah." Riley wanted to lift the despondency from her delicate features. "You've got Cora, after all."

"And the Pearl."

Susannah laughed. "I guess you're both trying to make me feel better?"

"Yeah," they said in unison.

"Maybe y'all should quit trying," Cora quipped, which got a laugh out of all of them.

A few times since receiving Susannah's invitation for tonight, Riley had wondered if it had been her idea to cook dinner for him or Cora's. Since Christmas, Cora had requested his help with several minor tasks, like moving hay from one end of the barn to the other. Or putting the box containing Ollie's things up into the loft, then moving it back down.

He'd seen Susannah at church, but because they'd postponed their wagon-driving lessons, he hadn't seen her much else. Her charm school still met each week and was evidently a success, but he didn't see any need to check for himself.

Cora stood and retrieved a loaf of bread from the pantry. "We can eat this. There's no harm done."

"Just to my pride," Susannah said, but Riley thought she handled it well. In general, she handled things better than he expected. Except cooking.

He grinned.

"Thank goodness Cora has some bread. Edible bread," she corrected gamely.

They ate their meal, finishing with coffee. Susannah poured and Riley noted that, despite her advanced condition, she moved gracefully. Her skin glowed and her blue eyes sparkled. She grew more beautiful every time he saw her.

Her dark green dress complimented her. She wore her hair pulled back in a loose braid. Riley itched to undo the blond strands and run his hands through the thick silk. The long curls looked like liquid sunshine, and even from across the table he caught a whiff of her soft vanilla scent.

A knock sounded on the door and Cora opened it to admit Jake Ross. Riley wondered what had happened to bring one of Davis Lee's new deputies to Cora's.

His brother stood. "Something going on, Jake?"

The quiet man pulled off his hat and nodded to the women before answering. "There's a Ranger waiting in your office. Said he'd come by to see you. Since you weren't far, I offered to fetch you."

"All right." Davis Lee slipped on his coat and pulled his hat from the peg behind the door. "Susannah, thank you for the meal. It was very nice."

"I appreciate you staying and I hope those biscuits didn't break off any teeth."

He chuckled and started out the door. "Thanks, Cora. I'll talk to y'all later."

"Good night," Cora said.

She, Riley and Susannah walked out to the porch with Davis Lee.

"Let me know if you need help with anything before I go back to the ranch," Riley called after his brother. The sissy. Those hard-as-rock biscuits had sent him skedaddling out of here faster than a husband-hunting woman.

"Will do."

Riley turned, noticing that only Cora stood on the porch. "Where's Susannah?"

"She went out to gather the eggs." Cora hurried back inside. "With all her preparations for dinner, she forgot to do it earlier."

"Should she be out there alone?"

"Probably not." Cora grinned. "Why don't you help her?"

Riley shook his head at her obvious attempt. "Did she take a lantern?"

"Yes. And her wrap."

"Good." He shrugged into his coat and pulled the door shut.

He walked around the house and toward the pale yellow lantern light glowing outside the chicken coop. A light fog drifted through the night, haloing Susannah where she stood at the henhouse. Prissy nickered softly, chewing her way through a patch of brown grass several feet from Susannah.

Susannah lifted the lantern from the hook next to the door and placed it inside, but what happened next was a blur. He saw a low dark shape at the corner of the chicken coop, heard a growl.

Susannah screamed and Prissy lunged into action. The mare barreled around Susannah, grazing her with a shoulder and knocking her down.

The horse slid to a stop, putting herself between Susannah and whatever stood at the corner of the chicken coop.

Heart clenching, Riley bolted for her. He'd left his gun in the wagon, dammit. Was it a dog?

Prissy put her head down and blew sharply, her breath curling into the air. A warning. A challenge. Riley's heart pumped painfully.

Susannah lay unmoving on the ground, not making a sound. Another growl and the mare advanced, shielding Susannah's body with her own.

Riley could now identify the animal in front of Prissy. A coyote. It must've come looking for food. Chickens.

"Are you all right?" he asked in a low voice, easing his way forward.

She nodded. Her breathing was ragged and harsh. Or maybe that was his own.

"Lie still." He neared and reached slowly for the lantern, intending to use it as a weapon. The smells of fear and kerosene and animal flesh were strong in his nostrils.

Prissy reared and struck out with her right foreleg. The coyote wheeled and disappeared into the darkness. Prissy's breath curled into the night.

"Did you see what Prissy did?" Susannah asked in a labored voice. "She protected me."

"Yes." Riley knelt beside her, his gaze sliding over her body, probing the shadows.

"What if that coyote had hurt her?"

"Coyotes won't attack a grown horse or cattle unless they're sick or weak." He couldn't spot any blood and she didn't appear to be in pain. "How's the baby? Are you hurt? How do you feel?"

"I think I'm all right. I had the wind knocked out of me—oh." She sucked in a breath. "Ooh, my stomach."

Panic knifed through him. "I'm going to carry you in."

He scooped her up, her dark skirts billowing. "Can you put your arm around my neck?"

Her face contorted in pain. One arm looped limply over his shoulder and she buried her face in his chest. He felt her body tense, and hurried his steps, trying not to jostle her unnecessarily.

"What happened?" Cora came running around the side of the house. "I heard Prissy."

"It was a coyote," Riley explained as he moved past her and onto the porch.

She hurried around him to push open the front door.

Once inside, he headed for Susannah's bedroom. "She's having some pain. I think we need to get the doctor."

"Yes." The older woman picked up a lamp and followed him.

He ducked through the curtain that served as Susannah's door and laid her carefully on the bed. The candlelight played over her skin, making it look pale and waxy. Her lips were drawn tight with pain.

"Susannah?"

She opened her eyes and looked at him, her hands cradling her stomach protectively. "It hurts, Riley."

Her voice tore at him and he said hoarsely, "I'll get the doctor."

He turned for the door, the candlelight showing the concern on Cora's face. "It shouldn't take me long."

"I'll make her comfortable."

Riley nodded and stepped around her. Cora's indrawn breath had him glancing at her, then following her gaze to his arm. A dark stain smeared his forearm. Blood. Susannah's blood.

Chapter Eleven

Riley barely remembered the cold ride through the night to Fort Greer for Dr. Butler. It wasn't until they returned and the doctor went in to check Susannah that his brain seemed to unseize.

Was she going to be all right? What about the baby? What if Prissy hadn't been out there? What if that coyote had hurt Susannah?

Seeing her lying on the ground motionless had twisted Riley's gut into knots. And he couldn't forget the sight of her blood on his arm.

She'd been conscious, he reminded himself. She'd talked to him. That meant she'd be all right, didn't it?

The doctor was taking his sweet damn time in there. *What* was taking so long?

Cora sat quietly, but Riley's nerves were so raw he couldn't sit still. He paced from one end of the front room to the other.

"She'll be okay," Cora said quietly.

He nodded, but only because he didn't know what else to do. *When* would Dr. Butler come out?

The tall, middle-aged man stepped past Susannah's curtain and let it drop before moving to the kitchen table. "She's suffered some trauma."

"Oh, no." Tears brimmed in Cora's eyes.

"I think the baby's all right, for now," the doctor added quickly, his brown eyes reassuring. "But Susannah *has* to stay in bed until she delivers."

"There was blood." Riley's voice sounded hoarse and harsh, foreign.

"Yes, but it's stopped now. The reason I want her to stay in bed is so the bleeding won't start again. If we can keep that from happening, I think both she and the baby will do fine."

Riley nodded, the crushing band around his chest easing enough to let him get a breath.

"Her pain has subsided, but if it comes back, I need to know."

Both Cora and Riley nodded.

The doctor placed his leather bag on the table and opened it, the lantern light catching the few strands of silver in his dark hair. "I've given her something to help her sleep."

"Will it hurt the baby?" Cora asked.

"No. It's a tea I made from cinnamon, blackberry leaves and a couple of other herbs." He pulled a white cloth pouch from his bag. "My wife drank this when carrying our first child and I've had success with other patients several times since. Susannah needs to drink a half cup to one cup a day. If she can't stand the taste, you can boil some black haw bark. That will also help without harming her or the babe."

Cora took the pouch he offered. "Just steep the tea in water?"

"Yes. Now, I don't want her doing anything until that baby comes. Understood?" He leveled a look at both Riley and Cora.

Riley nodded, though he figured Cora would do just fine keeping Susannah in line.

The doctor walked to the door, buttoning his coat. "I'll check in on her tomorrow."

"Thanks, Doc." Cora gave him a chunk of venison she'd wrapped in cloth, and a loaf of bread. "Let me know if I owe you more than this."

"This is plenty. Enough to pay me for five visits. Thank you."

"Thanks for coming so quick."

Dr. Butler gave a tired smile as he settled his cowboy hat on his head. "You can thank Mr. Holt for that. I thought he was about ready to throw me over his own horse if I didn't move faster."

Riley stuck out his hand. "We appreciate it."

After the doctor left, Riley lifted the curtain and peeked in on Susannah. Her head was turned toward the wall and she appeared to be sleeping.

He walked over to look out the window to the left of the front door.

"I'm so glad you were here," Cora said. "I wouldn't have felt right leaving Susannah to go for the doctor."

Riley murmured agreement, his gaze fixed on the darkness beyond, not searching, not probing, just staring. The relief he'd felt upon hearing the doctor say Susannah was all right and that she hadn't lost the baby retreated behind a frigid blackness, a hollow gnawing in his gut.

He'd cleaned her blood from his arm, but it might as well have still been there. He kept seeing her fall to the ground. The chilling growl of the coyote echoed in his head. Tremors had racked her body as he'd carried her inside, ruthlessly reminding him of how vulnerable she was.

"Riley, do you want some coffee?"

He could tell by the insistent way Cora spoke that she'd asked him more than once. "Got anything stronger?"

"I think there's a little of Ollie's whiskey left."

"That would be good." He rubbed a hand across his neck, recalling the sweat that had broken when he'd spied Susannah's blood on his arm.

He downed the measly two fingers of liquor with a desperate anticipation and yet tasted nothing. Felt only the burn, the warmth. But it wasn't warm enough.

Cora sat at the table and sipped her coffee. The stark concern finally faded from her eyes, but she looked haggard.

"You have to do something," he said flatly, still fighting the chill inside that felt strangely like fear.

"I'll see that she rests, like Doc Butler said."

"I don't mean that." Riley splayed his hands on his hips, then drummed his fingers on the table. "She needs to go home. You can convince her."

"Go home?" Cora set down her cup with a thud.

"To St. Louis."

"I know what you meant. Why would I want to send her home? Not that I could."

"Look at what happened tonight, Cora." Pacing again, he tried to gentle his fierce tone, surprised at the savage emotions boiling inside him.

She frowned.

"Susannah doesn't belong here." He realized then that he'd started to accept that she might. Maybe it had been Davis Lee's urging to give her a chance. Maybe it had been her own determination to fit in. Whatever it was, Riley saw now that even he had started to believe she did belong. "It's too dangerous. She's not prepared to live here."

"Prepared to live here? Just what does that mean? Are you addlepated, boy? Maybe you're the one who fell out there."

"She's from the city. A settled area." He paused in front

of the table, then resumed his measured steps. "She's led a sheltered life."

Cora studied him for a long moment. "What's really going on, Riley?"

"I told you."

"You're frightened for her. So am I. But she's strong, a survivor." The older woman shook a finger at him. "I know one when I see one."

"You can convince her. I'll pay for her ticket back to St. Louis and wire Adam to tell him—"

"No. She's a grown woman. It's her decision, not yours."

"Next time, it could be worse. What if something terrible happens to her? Or the baby?"

"Nothing dangerous happened to me and I lost my baby," Cora reminded him quietly. "There's no way to predict everything in life."

Riley felt as if he'd ripped open her soul. He stopped pacing and looked at his friend. "I'm sorry, Cora. I didn't mean to bring up old hurts, but I know you don't want anything else to happen to Susannah."

"It's not in my hands, and it's not in yours, either."

"Don't you see the sense in her leaving?" Frustration clawed through him.

Cora smiled wanly. "I see you're worried and I don't blame you, but running her off isn't the answer."

He drew back. "I'm not running her off."

"She's going to do just fine. She *is* doing just fine."

"She said she told you the truth." He shoved a hand through his hair. "That you know she came here only out of desperation."

"One other thing I know, Riley, is that girl has guts. She's trying her heart out and I think she can make it. I think you should give her a chance."

He braced his hands on his hips, feeling as if he'd been

penned into a castration chute like one of his bulls. "This isn't about giving her a chance."

"Isn't it?"

"No."

"I think you have other reasons for wanting her to leave."

He snorted. "Like what?"

"You're starting to feel something for her."

He about swallowed his teeth. "I feel *responsible* for her. Her brother is one of my best friends—"

"I think you feel more for her. You were white as chalk when you brought her in here."

"She was bleeding," he growled.

"Yes." Cora rose and stepped over to him, saying gently, "You call it what you want, hon, but I've got eyes. I can see what's going on. I hope you do, too. Before it's too late."

"You're wrong, Cora."

"Give her a chance." She walked over and slipped inside Susannah's room, dismissing Riley as easy as how-do.

Frustration boiled to the surface and he grabbed his hat, stalking out. Cora was right about one thing, he fumed as he swung into the saddle and urged Whip into motion. He felt fear for Susannah and what could happen to her here.

Riley headed for the jail to tell Davis Lee what had occurred tonight. He wished the thoughts would fly out of his head, but he couldn't escape Cora's words.

You're starting to feel something for that girl.

Something deep and reaching and damn scary. Responsibility had nothing to do with it. Riley realized it hadn't for some time now. He'd resisted becoming involved with her, told himself he wasn't involved. But he was.

He was hard-pressed to remember what Whirlwind had been like before she came, what he'd done. Endless days of ranch chores, working with the horses and cattle? He supposed so.

Maybe he couldn't remember much of his life before Susannah, but he could damn sure remember his wife. Her death, his emptiness and the agonizing torture of feeling lost day after day.

The very real possibility that Susannah could've been seriously injured or killed drove through him like a blade. His thoughts froze with sudden clarity. The idea that she could fare here better than Maddie was deceptive and tempting. But he knew the truth. He couldn't let himself get any closer to Susannah Phelps. Whatever was between them must stop now.

Susannah felt the edge of her bed give way with someone's weight, and knew it was Cora.

"Are you awake?" her friend asked softly.

"Yes." She tried to breathe past the disappointment that stabbed through her chest.

"How are you feeling?"

"The pain's gone." She'd heard more than the fevered urging in Riley's voice when he spoke to Cora moments ago. She'd heard every word about sending her back to St. Louis. "I heard you two arguing."

"Well, I wouldn't say we were arguing. Exactly."

Susannah gave her a look.

Cora smoothed a hand over her hair.

Why did it hurt so badly? Knowing that Riley didn't want her here was nothing new, but she couldn't deny the ragged pain in her heart. "He wants me to leave."

The other woman muttered, "I knew I should've had a door put on your room."

Susannah shook her head.

"He's worried about you. You gave us both quite a scare. He'll come around."

"I don't think so. You heard him."

"I also know he's gun-shy about some things. And stubborn as an overfed mule. It takes him awhile to admit he's wrong, but he will." Cora looked at her meaningfully, but Susannah didn't respond.

It was time she faced facts. Ever since she'd come to Whirlwind, to *him,* ever since he'd told her he wouldn't marry again, she'd believed he would change his mind.

"Want me to brush your hair?"

She worked up a smile. Thank goodness she had this woman, whose friendship seemed as steadfast as the sunrise. "That would be nice."

Cora helped ease her up in bed and took down her hair, pulling the brush through the strands with slow, soothing strokes. Susannah's brother believed Riley was the man to give her baby love and security. Maybe if she'd been someone else, that would have worked out. She saw now it never would.

On Sunday afternoon, Riley sat across from Davis Lee at a table in the Pearl for their usual weekly lunch. It had only been a day and a half since he'd seen Susannah, but the time had marked him. He hadn't slept, there was an ache in his right shoulder that wouldn't go away, and his boots didn't feel right.

He still had flashes of seeing her on the ground, and he hadn't been able to shake the sight of her blood on his arm. The ever-livin' hell had been scared out of him. That Cora didn't agree Susannah should leave Whirlwind stuck in his craw, so he hadn't paid a visit yesterday. He wasn't proud of the fact.

He didn't know what to do about Susannah. He didn't feel right staying away and he didn't feel right calling on her.

"It was good to see Jericho."

"Yeah," Davis Lee said. "He appreciated the bed you offered him and his partner Friday night. They got on the trail again yesterday, didn't want the McDougal gang to have much of a lead on them."

Their cousin, Jericho Blue, was a Texas Ranger tracking the McDougal gang. He was the one who'd shown up at the jail looking for Davis Lee on Friday night during their dinner with Susannah. Jericho had wanted to say hello to his cousins, but he'd also wanted Davis Lee to know that he and his partner had been following the McDougal gang from Indian Territory and up through Dodge City before tracking them back down into Texas toward Abilene.

He and his partner had spent the night at the ranch, then come into town with Davis Lee to see if he had received any further notices about the McDougal gang. The two Rangers had headed out midmorning yesterday.

Davis Lee pushed away his empty plate and tugged over a saucer holding a piece of apricot pie. "So, how's Susannah doing? She was a little quiet yesterday when I saw her."

Riley shoved a forkful of mashed potatoes in his mouth.

Davis Lee sipped at his coffee. "Little brother?"

Riley swallowed, the potatoes tasting like paste. "I haven't seen her. Today."

If he thought his brother wouldn't notice the pause between his words, he was wrong. Davis Lee's eyes narrowed speculatively. "When *did* you see her?"

He lifted a bite of roast.

"Riley?"

He put it down, stared flatly at his brother. "On Friday night, after the doctor left."

"Not since?"

"No."

"Why not?"

Riley hesitated, not because he didn't know how to tell Davis Lee that he wanted some distance between him and Susannah, but because he didn't plan to tell him at all. He needed some space, certainly more than the few miles between his ranch and Cora's house.

"Why are you staying away? You were the one to help her out after that coyote showed up. She cooked a nice dinner for you—"

"I know what happened. I was there, remember?"

"So why are you being so unneighborly?"

"I'm not." Riley pushed his plate away, not interested in the rest of his food.

"Mother would say you are. I say you're being an ass. Whatever your problems are with Susannah, she doesn't deserve for you to ignore her, especially not with what she's going through." Davis Lee's fork stabbed the air. "As Mother used to say, she would be mortified."

Riley gave a brief smile at the memory of his mother. Lorelai Holt had taught her boys manners, to the point of excruciation sometimes. Their mother wouldn't hold with Riley not being neighborly to Susannah, especially when they were supposed to be friends.

Which was the problem. He didn't know how to be around her without wanting more than friendship.

Simply going by to check on her didn't constitute any declarations on his part. "I'll go see her."

"Today?"

Riley's gaze met his brother's. "Yes, today."

"Good." Davis Lee wiped his mouth with a napkin. "Head on over there. I'll pay for lunch."

Riley scowled. "All right."

His brother reached over and picked up Riley's cup, draining the last of his coffee. "See ya later."

"Why don't you just throw me out?"

"Will it get you moving any faster?"

Riley glared at him, pushed his chair back. It wasn't just

frustration gnawing at him, but also a gut-twisting fear at her close call on Friday night.

Still, Davis Lee was right. He should be ashamed of his reluctance to go see her, but he couldn't seem to sidestep it. He shouldn't ignore Susannah just because he wasn't sure how to act around her.

"Tell her I asked after her," Davis Lee said cheerily.

Riley slammed his hat down on his head and stalked out of the Pearl. He could walk to Cora's, but he might as well take Whip.

For several minutes he stood in the street next to the paint, then finally swung into the saddle. Putting off the visit wouldn't make it any easier. The other night, he hadn't been able to breathe, but he had some distance now.

She didn't have to know anything had changed.

He tied Whip to one of Cora's porch columns and knocked on the door.

After a few seconds, it opened, and Cora smiled brightly at him. "Hello, Riley. Come in."

He stepped inside, hearing voices coming from the direction of Susannah's room. Male voices. Taking off his coat, he glanced at the older woman. "How many visitors does she have?"

"Three or four." Cora's hazel eyes looked clear today, the shadows of concern gone.

"How's she doing?"

"Okay. She gets tired of lying abed, but she knows it's the best thing."

His feet seemed nailed to the floor. "What about the tea Dr. Butler left?"

"She's drinking it faithfully, and it seems to help." Cora stood nearly at eye level with him. "I thought sure we'd see you yesterday."

"Was she expecting me? I hope not."

"No, she didn't say a word, but I was surprised you didn't stop by."

Riley ignored the twinge of irritation that Susannah hadn't seemed to mind his absence. "Got caught up in some things at the ranch."

"Hmm." Cora's gaze probed right through him, but she didn't call him on the lie. "Come in and say hello."

The woman turned and started toward Susannah's room. The curtain was tucked behind a nail, out of the way. Riley stuck his head inside and found Susannah's bed surrounded by men. All three of the Baldwins, plus Jake Ross and Tony Santos. Miguel would probably visit after school. Riley managed to squeeze behind J. T. Baldwin's shoulder.

Susannah glanced from Russ to him. "Hello," she said.

"Hey, Riley," the men chorused.

She looked pale and beautiful in a blue wrapper that rose high on her elegant neck. Her hair was up and a blanket spread over her lap. The total lack of privacy and Cora's watchful presence kept everything proper.

Her voice was friendly enough, but her eyes, the same color blue as her wrapper, were cool. Distant.

"I hear we have you to thank for rescuing Miz Susannah," J.T. said.

"How are you feeling today?" The room seemed to press in on Riley. His gaze roamed her face as he tried to reassure himself she was fine.

"Already tired of being an invalid, but other than that, I'm all right."

"It's lucky Riley was here when that coyote showed up," J.T. added.

Riley felt uncomfortable taking the credit for saving her when all he'd done was carry her inside. "Cora's mare wasn't about to let that animal get close to Susannah."

"I saw a horse do that once. Dernedest thing I ever saw," Jake Ross stated in his quiet voice.

"Riley told me coyotes won't attack adult horses or cattle unless they're sick," Susannah said.

"That's true," J.T. confirmed. "And we're thankful for it."

"They can sure scare the heck out of you," Tony said. "When I was about Miguel's age, my cousin and I were walking in Mexico one night. We thought we heard a noise in a stand of trees and looked up to see two coyotes running straight at us. Almost as if they were racing to see which one could reach us first."

Susannah gasped.

Riley rolled his eyes.

Russ Baldwin barked out a laugh. "Tony, that's the biggest I've ever heard."

"It happened, Russ!" Tony exclaimed.

"Did they decide you were too scrawny to eat?" Matt elbowed the swarthy, barrel-shaped man.

Tony grinned. "I guess so. They got about fifty feet away and veered off. Disappeared into the dark."

Cora shook her head. "I didn't know you were such a big yarn spinner, Tony."

"I swear it's true, Miz Cora."

J. T. Baldwin rubbed his hands together. "Well, then you'll want to hear my story."

"No, Pa," Matt said.

"Don't tell it," Russ echoed before glancing at Susannah. "You're the only one who can stop him."

She smiled, though Riley saw it didn't quite reach her eyes. Maybe she still didn't feel well. "I want to hear it, J.T. Go ahead."

The older man grinned, hooking a thumb toward his sons. "These two were just little fellas. I was riding home late one night from Abilene and kept thinking I saw something out of the corner of my eye. I finally spied a coyote loping along with me, several yards away. He didn't seem inclined to attack, just to run. I hurried my mount on a little and the coyote kept up, so I gave the gelding free rein. That coyote ran apace with us for a while, then about the time I thought my horse might be winded, that flea-bitten critter charged ahead as if he hadn't even been trying!"

"So you were racing a coyote, J.T.?" Riley asked wryly.

"Yep." The big man crossed his arms and grinned at Susannah. "Now, that's a story, ain't it?"

"Yes, it certainly is."

"Maybe you should change your story, Susannah." Riley tried not to care that she wouldn't direct any of her warmth toward him. "You heard *Prissy* cry out and saved her from the coyote."

"That could've really happened," Matt said. "She needs something that sounds exaggerated. Like Pa's."

Susannah nailed Riley with a look that said not everyone shared his opinion of her inability to get along here.

Cora rose from her chair beside the bed. "Don't want to be unsociable, gents, but it's probably time for Susannah to rest now."

"We'll be back to see you, Miz Susannah," Russ said.

The others nodded in agreement.

"Thank you all for coming. You brightened my day."

"Not as much as you brightened ours." J. T. Baldwin pressed a light kiss to her hand. "We're mighty glad you're all right, little lady."

"Thank you."

Cora stepped around Riley and gave him a meaningful poke in the back, then herded the other men out. After one last look from the doorway, she disappeared.

"You don't have to stay." Susannah rearranged the blanket across her lap.

"I wanted to check on you."

"I'm fine, as you can see." She aimed a brittle smile his way.

Her color was better and she didn't appear to be in pain. "How's the tea from Dr. Butler?"

"I think it's working. I rest a lot, but haven't had any more pain."

"Good."

The silence stretched into an awkward moment. Susannah stared up at him with clear blue eyes, studying him.

Riley fought a sudden urge to squirm. Was she upset that he hadn't come by yesterday? "The man who stopped by Davis Lee's office on Friday night was our cousin, Jericho Blue. He's a Texas Ranger."

"Yes, Davis Lee told me when *he* stopped by yesterday. Your cousin is tracking the McDougal gang."

Riley nodded, glancing around the small room. The scent of woman and vanilla drifted around him. Two dresses hung neatly on the wall pegs; the lacy edge of a shift peeked out from behind them. A pair of tiny black kid shoes sat next to the wall. "Do you need anything? A newspaper? Some apricot pie from Pearl's? Would you like to play checkers?"

She stared hard at him. "I'm surprised to see you."

"Why?"

She looked down, her lips firming. He noticed that her body stiffened, and he could feel irritation pouring off her.

"Davis Lee asked after you. He hopes you're doing well."

She played with her fingers, still not looking at him. "Your *brother* is wonderful."

Riley didn't really care for the enthusiastic way she talked about Davis Lee. "Are you sure I can't get you something?"

"I heard what you said. The other night right in that room."

She tilted her chin, looking him in the eye. "And don't pretend you don't know what I'm talking about."

He chewed on the inside of his cheek. "I didn't mean for you to overhear."

"But you're not sorry?"

"I'm sorry if I hurt your feelings."

"Why won't you give me a chance?"

"Susannah—"

"I know about your wife. I know that's why you think I can't make a life here, but I'm not her, Riley."

His jaw set. "Did Adam and Cora tell you everything about Maddie?"

"Yes, but I spoke to Cora again after you and I went to Abilene that day. You acted so strange when I said I'd soon be able to drive myself. You became so adamant when you talked about the weather, and I wanted to know why."

"So now you know?"

"Yes."

"Then why can't you understand? There are just too many things that can happen."

She sighed. "Don't you think I know that?"

"Then why won't you go home? This has to be very difficult for you, being away from your family, coming to a land that's far from tamed."

"Maybe I like it, Riley. Maybe I like being on my own for the first time in my life. Maybe I want my child to grow up in a place where he or she will be accepted, not shunned because of a foolish mistake. Why can't *you* understand?"

He couldn't tell her that his heart had all but stopped when he'd seen that blood on his arm. Couldn't tell her that he wanted her to live to see her children's children.

The bright flash of pain in her eyes grabbed at his throat. "Maybe when we're old and gray, you can say you were wrong about me."

"I hope so." With everything in him, he hoped she was right, but he didn't believe it.

And he could see she knew.

Chapter Twelve

Susannah had wanted Riley to say he hadn't meant those things, that he was wrong and she belonged there, but he hadn't.

After a month spent in bed, she realized that he wouldn't. And it was for the best. Susannah focused on what she did have. A growing friendship with Cora. Several women from town had been by to see her, including May Haskell and Pearl Anderson, as well as Evelyn Donnelly. All the men in her class had visited, as had Davis Lee. Riley's brother had been by every bit as often as Riley, always telling Susannah an entertaining story or bringing her a treat. If this baby didn't come soon, she'd be as big as Cora's barn.

Riley's opinion of her hurt, but she told herself she could forget about him quicker than she could snap her fingers. As her time neared, her fear about the actual birth and what kind of mother she would prove overshadowed her frustration with Riley. Thank goodness she had Cora. The older woman had promised Susannah she would attend the birth along with the doctor, that there was absolutely nothing to worry about.

Susannah believed that even though her nerves still quivered with uncertainty and anticipation. On the last Sunday in February, on a sunny, cold morning, she leaned against the wall in her room, biting down on the pain that threatened to rip her apart. Her back had ached all day yesterday and she'd been walking in her room since the early hours of the morning.

Cora jerked on her coat. "I'll be back quick as I can. I'm taking Prissy and I can get to Doc Butler in less than fifteen minutes. Just hold on. If you feel the need to push, get back in that bed."

"Yes, okay." Susannah's voice was slightly labored, her hair already plastered to her head. "The contractions aren't coming so fast—oh!"

She bent double, sliding one arm around her stomach, bracing herself against the wall with the other.

Cora rushed over and pressed a damp cloth to her slick forehead. "Breathe, hon. It will pass."

After a few seconds, the pain dulled. Susannah drew in a deep breath, her stomach feeling swollen and stretched to bursting.

"I'll hurry. If walking doesn't help, then get back in bed."

"It's still helping," she said breathlessly. "Do you think it will be long now?"

"No." Cora smiled and patted her forehead again with the cloth. "We'll have a baby by this evening, I reckon."

Her face felt as tired as the rest of her, but she smiled. "Go, I'm okay. But hurry."

"I will."

Susannah turned her head against the wall, listening for the sound of Prissy's hooves as her friend rode out. When she heard them, relief washed through her body. "Hurry, Cora," she whispered.

Another contraction seized her, this one more violent than the last. She cried out and her knees went weak. She sagged against the wall, wishing for something to grab on to. For long seconds, she couldn't move. When the sharpness across her lower abdomen eased, she hobbled over to the bed.

Her lower body felt as if it were about to split open. Just as she reached the bed, another pain hit her, gripping her tight and twisting mercilessly. She screamed and grabbed the foot of the bed, burying her face in the bedcovers.

"What the hell! Susannah!"

Riley. What was he doing here? She lifted her head, her vision swimming. "Wh-what are you doing?"

"I think the question is what are *you* doing?" He picked her up and carefully laid her in bed. "Why are you on your feet?"

"Cora said it's time for the baby. I can't get any relief in this bed so I got up to walk."

"Where is Cora?" He frowned, looking around.

"She's gone for the doctor." Susannah grabbed his hand. "It's time, Riley."

"Now?" His eyes went as wide as silver dollars.

She nodded. "She thought she would have time to get Dr. Butler, but I don't think so."

"It won't take her long."

"I don't have long! I need to push."

"Whoa, wait!"

"I can't wait! Go get her!"

He let go of her hand and started out of the room. Another pain struck and Susannah tried to bite back a moan.

"Darlin', I don't think there's time for me to get anybody."

She couldn't bear to think about him seeing her in her nightgown, with sweat plastering the linen to her body, her hair stuck to her head. "I need her!"

"I'm afraid we're gonna have to be the ones to do this." He looked as uncertain as she felt.

She groaned. "You can't see me like this. It isn't proper."

"I guess I could've gone for Cora in the time it's taking us to argue about it."

She opened her mouth to snap at him, but another pain rolled through her. She drew in a sharp breath.

Riley rushed to the bed, leaning over. "What do you want me to do?"

She grabbed his hand and squeezed so tightly he grimaced. "I'm hurting you," she noted.

"No. It's okay. C'mon, push if you need to."

"I…am…pushing." She wanted to slap him away, but another contraction gripped her and she clutched at him with both hands.

He was sweating as much as she was.

"Riley, please," she panted. "What if something's wrong?"

"Nothing's wrong." He stroked her head. "It's just time for this baby to come."

"What am I going to do—ooh!"

"We're gonna have this baby."

"We?" She raised her head and glared. "You're not the one getting ripped apart— It's coming!" she screamed.

"Hell!" Riley disentangled his hands from hers and moved to the foot of the bed, reaching for the sheet.

"You can't look at me!"

"I have to. I can't bring this baby into the world with my eyes closed."

"My mother will die of shame."

"I don't give a damn about her right now." He rolled up his sleeves, his face set. "All I care about is you and this baby."

"Can't you leave the sheet down and just…catch it?" Heat burned her cheeks at even saying such a delicate thing, but Riley didn't seem the least embarrassed.

"I've never done this before, but I don't think so. Childbirth is a natural thing, Susannah. There's nothing to be ashamed about."

"We're not married—it's coming! It's coming. Get it!"

Riley's head disappeared from sight.

Ripped in two by the pain, Susannah no longer cared how immodest she was. "Can you see the baby? Is it okay?" she panted. Sweat slicked her scalp, her chest.

"I can see the head!"

She'd never heard him so excited. "Tell me—aargh!" Sharp, excruciating pressure stretched across her abdomen. "What do I do?"

"Another push, darlin'," he said.

She tried.

"Another one."

"You said that already! How many?" she snapped. Sweat dripped in her eyes and she felt as if she were being torn apart. "I can see a shoulder! C'mon, Susannah. Try."

She felt as if she couldn't lift her hand, let alone push out a baby, but she tried one last time, and Riley laughed.

"I got you, little one. I got you."

She could see only the top of his bent head. "Riley, tell me. Is the baby okay?"

Pain rippled across her belly, her back, between her legs. "Riley?"

He stood, his face slack with awe and disbelief. His hands messy with life, he held her squalling child. "It's a girl, Susannah. A girl."

"A girl?" she whispered.

He laughed, cutting the cord then gently cleaning the baby with one of the linens Cora had left beside the bed. She cried her lungs out as Riley wrapped her in another linen before handing her to Susannah.

As Riley disposed of the afterbirth, the baby quieted. A love so strong it hurt her chest filled Susannah. At first she could only stare, gingerly touching her child. A finger to her cheek, down her chubby arm. "She doesn't have any hair."

"She does. It's just real fine and light." Riley draped an arm around Susannah's shoulder and leaned down so he could run a finger lightly across the baby's head. "See? She'll be blond like you."

"She's beautiful." Susannah hugged the babe close, counting fingers and toes. All there. Perfect upturned nose. Tiny eyelashes and a puckered rosebud mouth.

"What's her name?"

"I don't know yet." Susannah couldn't take her eyes off her daughter. The babe nuzzled her breast, causing sensations to curl from her nipple to her core.

She looked up at Riley, eyes brimming with tears. "I don't know what I would've done if you hadn't been here."

"You would've done just fine."

She slipped her finger inside the baby's curled-up hand. Her throat burned with emotion. "I wish my mother were here. Both my parents."

"Do you want me to wire them about the baby?"

"I'll wire Adam and he'll tell them." She glanced up, struggling with the emotions washing through her. Joy, love, pain. "I've wired them several times, but they haven't responded."

"At all?"

"No." She saw anger flare in his eyes, and added quickly, "They're hurt."

"So are you."

She looked down, preferring to think about her baby. Riley's arm circled her and she wanted to lean into his warmth, his strength.

He nuzzled her hair, then dropped a kiss on her head.

She looked up in surprise. Though she was exhausted, she didn't think she had imagined what he'd just done.

"She's gorgeous. Just like her mama."

"We probably both need some cleaning up."

"We all do."

They smiled at each other, their eyes warm with the shared bond they felt.

"Are you telling me you had that baby?" Cora demanded from the doorway.

Susannah tore her gaze from Riley's. "Yes, Cora! It's a girl."

"She wouldn't wait." Riley straightened.

Dr. Butler appeared right behind Cora. "Babies do things at their own pace."

"What happened?" The older woman came to Susannah's bed, standing across from Riley.

"It was time, I guess. Riley got here right after you left."

"And she was ready," he interjected.

"I'd say so." The doctor smiled, peering over Cora's shoulder. "Looks like you both did a fine job."

Susannah held the baby so he could see her. "Does she look all right, Doctor?"

"I'll take a closer look at her, then I'll want to examine you, too."

Riley smoothed a finger over the baby's head. "I'll warm up some water. She probably wants a bath, and so does Susannah."

"Thank you."

He nodded, his eyes soft as he watched Susannah pass the linen-wrapped bundle—her daughter—to the doctor.

As Riley stepped away from the bed, she caught his hand. "I'm glad you were here. I was in complete panic."

He smiled. "And still you managed to boss me around."

"Oh, you, get out of here."

"I'll be just outside."

She nodded. Happiness overruled the fatigue pulling at her

body. All the embarrassment she'd felt at Riley seeing her in such an immodest state was swept away in the euphoria of having her daughter safely born. The wonder of the life she'd created. The relief that the babe seemed fine.

"You're a pretty one, aren't you?" Cora cooed over the doctor's shoulder. "What's her name?"

"I don't know yet. How is she, Dr. Butler?"

"Fine and dandy, it appears." He rewrapped the baby in the linen and handed her back to Susannah. "When she wants to nurse, go ahead and try. It might take some practice for both of you."

"All right."

Cora stroked the baby's head. "May I hold her?"

"Of course."

Cora took the baby, nestling her easily against her ample bosom.

After the doctor examined Susannah, Riley stepped back into the room.

She smiled at him. "She's really here. I can't believe it."

"I can't, either. How are you feeling?"

"Sore. Wonderful."

"I want to go tell Davis Lee."

"Okay." Drowsy now, Susannah felt as if she were floating, more content than she'd ever been. "I can never repay you, Riley. I'm sorry I was mad at you."

He grinned. "I'm glad I was here. She's a beauty and you did just fine."

She smiled, lifting a hand in farewell when he said goodbye. Cora put the babe in the cradle next to Susannah's bed and went out to talk to the doctor.

Susannah pulled the cradle close and studied her daughter, filled with so much love she thought her heart would burst. Looking at her babe's sweet face, she knew she'd done the right thing by coming to Whirlwind. She fell asleep with her hand on the cradle.

The afternoon following the birth of her daughter, Susannah forced herself to get out of bed, using muscles that screamed in protest. She didn't want to be very far from the baby, who had nursed well this morning, then fallen asleep.

Susannah stood over the cradle, her heart aching with a love deeper than any she'd ever felt. How could her own mother have let her leave St. Louis? Susannah didn't think she would ever be able to let her child go, regardless of what she did.

Where had the day gone? She eased down gingerly onto her bed. The sun sank lower in the sky. She'd slept off and on, waking when the baby did, drifting off when the infant did as well. She was sore and uncomfortable, but looking at her daughter made the pain dim.

Cora had cared for the baby while Susannah bathed, then braided her hair and changed into a dress that now hung loose on her. Just that little bit of activity made her aware all over again of her sore muscles. In the back of her mind all day had been fleeting images of Riley in here with her, bringing her baby into the world, seeing her in ways only a husband should.

Despite her embarrassment, she was grateful. If he hadn't been here, she didn't know how she would've managed.

She heard a muffled knock on the door, then the hinges creaking as Cora opened it. Low, masculine voices drifted from the other room. When Susannah recognized Riley's, she couldn't stop the jump in her pulse.

The curtain at her doorway parted and Cora looked in. "Riley and Davis Lee are here. You up to seeing them?"

"Yes, that would be nice."

Cora smiled. "C'mon in, boys. But keep it down. The little one's asleep."

Susannah pushed herself up from the bed, one hand curled

around the footboard as much out of nervousness as to steady herself.

Cora moved inside, followed by Riley and Davis Lee. Riley's smile was intimate and warm. "Hi."

"Hi," she said, chiding herself for the flutter of sensation in her belly.

Davis Lee grinned. "How are you, little mother?"

"Fine, Davis Lee." She smiled back. "Come see her."

She turned slowly and walked the few steps to the cradle. Both men followed.

"She sure is little." Davis Lee squinted at the infant.

"She's supposed to be." Riley studied the baby, grasping the foot of the cradle and tugging firmly, as if testing it.

"Do you want to hold her?" she asked.

"Will I wake her?"

"I don't think so."

He leaned down and gently picked up the baby. She squirmed and made a whimpering noise, then nuzzled into a spot on his shoulder. His lips curved and warmth flooded Susannah.

Davis Lee reached out with one finger and touched her back. "Riley said she doesn't have a name yet."

"I named her this morning. This is Lorelai."

"Lorelai?" Riley's gaze shot to hers.

She smiled.

Davis Lee looked at his brother, then at her, a broad smile forming. "Our mother was named Lorelai."

"I know," Susannah said quietly. "I asked Cora. I thought it would be nice for her to have a namesake, since one of her sons helped bring a new life into the world. I hope it's all right."

"Hell—I mean heck, yes, it's all right." Davis Lee beamed at his brother. "Isn't it?"

Riley's blue gaze fixed on Susannah, deep and dark with the bond they shared.

That look made her feel as if he'd wrapped his arms around her.

"Yes, it's more than all right," he said in a husky voice. "Naming her after our mother is real fine, Susannah. Real fine."

"I'm glad you think so."

"I think I should hold Lorelai." Davis Lee held out his arms.

Riley hesitated. "You might wake her up."

"You didn't."

Riley glanced down at the sleeping baby, then carefully handed her over. Davis Lee held her awkwardly, his arms stiff and bent away from his body.

"She's not a foal," Riley said. "Cradle her with your arm and hold her next to you. Be careful with her head."

"Had a lot of practice, have ya?" Davis Lee grumbled, but he did as Riley instructed. The baby mewed and the big man froze, his gaze shooting to Susannah's.

"It's all right. She's fine."

He held the baby as if balancing a piece of glass. "She's pretty. She doesn't have much hair."

Susannah laughed softly. "That's what I said."

"That's not all you said," Riley murmured dryly.

"Did she try to whack you again, Riley?" Cora chuckled. "Just about."

"I did not." Susannah shook her head, grinning.

"She was pretty much cussin' and hollerin' her lungs out. I figured everybody in town could hear her."

"And you were so calm," she retorted. "He nearly swooned when I told him Cora was gone."

Cora and Davis Lee laughed. Even Riley cracked a smile.

He reached for the baby again. "Let me see her."

Davis Lee surrendered the tiny bundle and Riley gently laid her in the cradle. "You don't look much like your ma yet, Button, but you will."

Susannah's bemused gaze met Cora's across the room.

"Button?" Cora mouthed.

Susannah shrugged, warmed by the caring in his voice.

"We'll have to teach her to ride horses," Davis Lee said.

"And to fish," Riley added.

"And shoot."

"Why don't y'all wait until she can at least walk?" Cora laughed. "Susannah probably has some things *she* wants to teach her."

The brothers grinned. "I guess so," Riley said.

He leaned down and stroked a hand over the baby's head. "She's even prettier than when she got here."

"You'll have to watch all the fellas around her," Davis Lee advised Susannah.

"I will." Their affection for her daughter touched off a bittersweet pang inside her. Her daughter would grow up loved here, accepted without the stigma of her illegitimacy.

But Riley's and Davis Lee's obvious tenderness for Lorelai reminded Susannah of why she'd originally come to Whirlwind. The father she'd sworn to find for her baby. The father her child now needed more than ever.

Her gaze moved from Davis Lee to Riley, then swung back to Davis Lee, tracing his strong features. He was a good man, well-respected here, and the sheriff to boot. He was handsome, with a winning way about him. Why, he was everything she could want in a father for Lorelai. In a husband for herself.

But Davis Lee wasn't Riley. Her gaze shifted to the big man who'd helped bring her daughter into the world. Riley was who she wanted, who she loved— No! Not loved.

She'd fancied herself in love with Paul, too, and look where that had gotten her. The youngest, pampered child of a wealthy family, who'd been sheltered and too naive to recognize his worldliness. He'd been different from any other man she'd known, well-traveled, mysterious and charming, and she'd let her heart overrule her head. Now those emotions were gone, shriveled to ashes.

How could she trust that these feelings she had for Riley wouldn't disappear the same way? They were friends and would be *only* friends; he'd made that clear. And Susannah, as much as she struggled against the idea, agreed with him.

She'd come to Whirlwind to find security, not love. The small, helpless person lying in the cradle next to her bed brought back that fact with a rush. Susannah's decision wouldn't be based on who she wanted, but on who would be the perfect father for her baby.

And the time had come to find him.

Chapter Thirteen

His intention not to get any closer to Susannah was shot to hell. He'd never been this close to a woman, never shared anything as wondrous as the birth of a child. Not even with Maddie. Because she hadn't been around long enough, he reminded himself ruthlessly.

Remembering how this land had destroyed his wife should've helped him keep a clear head about Susannah, but the bond he now had with her made it increasingly difficult to think of her only as a friend.

Ever since little Lorelai had been born, Riley had been consumed by this savage need to claim Susannah, possess her in every way he could. It frustrated him no end. He knew she was a marrying kind of woman, knew that was why she'd come to Whirlwind, and he wasn't dancing that dance. Still, it became more difficult to walk away each time he saw her.

In the six days since the birth of the baby, he'd seen her daily. He'd given up trying to stay away; he wanted to see the new life he'd helped bring into the world. The baby looked different every day.

His time with the little girl spawned some new hope in him,

a warmth he hadn't known was missing. And helped suppress the raging desire in him to get her mother in a dark place and peel off her clothes. What he felt for Susannah—*all* he felt for her—was lust. It would pass.

As far as Riley was concerned, sharing the birth of a child was nearly as intimate as sharing the marriage bed. And as happy as the occasion had been, it complicated the sense of responsibility he felt for her.

Still, it was his sense of obligation that drove him into town on Saturday night. He'd promised Cora he would check in on Susannah and the baby while the older woman was in Abilene today and tomorrow.

Just after dark, he reined his horse in front of Cora's house as a shadow moved across the front windows. Crying sounded from inside, insistent and hard and aching. Riley dismounted, quickly looping his reins around the porch column.

Pale yellow lamplight slid around the edges of the calico curtains to dapple the porch. He stepped up to the door and knocked. The baby cried harder. He could hear Susannah murmuring, an edge of desperation in her voice.

He knocked again, pressing his ear to the door. Lorelai wailed her lungs out. "Susannah? It's me."

The baby cried hard enough to make Riley grimace. He thought he heard Susannah say something, and stepped inside, shutting the door behind him.

Hell's bells. His breath whooshed out.

Susannah was naked. Or close enough. Her white bodice was unbuttoned to the waist, her chemise untied and spread open. She held the baby close to her, but he glimpsed one pale rose nipple and full, creamy breasts.

Her eyes widened and her mouth dropped open.

As if Lorelai felt the jolt of heat that jumped from her mother to Riley, the baby took a breath. Instant quiet descended. Riley could hear his blood pounding in his veins. Thought he could hear Susannah's hammering, too. She was beautiful, perfect. Her breasts spilled out, pale and full and now slightly pink from the blush staining her skin.

"R-Riley, what are you doing?" She clutched one edge of her chemise, lifting the baby in an effort to cover herself. Lorelai started wailing again, as if Susannah had given a signal.

"Damnation, I am sorry." He stood completely frozen, unable to take his eyes off her. Her breasts strained the edges of the linen. He'd never hurt so badly in his life.

"Well?" she demanded.

"Well?" he repeated stupidly. This was not good, especially after he'd spent so much time trying *not* to imagine her naked. The raw desire he'd been fighting erupted in a white-hot flare.

"Turn around!"

"Oh." His feet felt weighted with rocks, but he turned, the baby's cries finally snapping him back to his senses. "I knocked. I thought you told me to come in."

"I couldn't hear a thing."

He wanted to look over his shoulder, but stared straight ahead at the back of the door. She would fit perfectly in his hands. Her skin was just as velvety and pale as the rest of her. Hell.

"Cora's not here," she said nervously. "She had to meet with Banker Dobies."

"I know. She asked me to stop by." He cleared his throat. "What's wrong with Button?"

"I don't know." Susannah's voice was strained with frustration. "I've tried everything. She doesn't want to eat. I fixed her a sugar teat. She wasn't interested. I've rubbed her tummy and her back, but it just made her cry harder."

"Did you rub her gums?"

"Cora said to rub her gums when her teeth were coming in. You can turn around now."

He did, unable to stem the disappointment he felt when he saw that Susannah's bodice was completely closed. His fists clenched at his sides. "Maybe it would help."

Susannah tried it, but Lorelai turned her head away, squalling just as loudly.

"I don't know what to do for her." Emotion thickened her voice. "Aren't I supposed to know?"

"I don't think you're supposed to always know," he said over the baby's cries. "Want me to try?"

"Yes." Her eyes bright with tears, she handed him the infant.

His knuckles brushed against the pale, creamy breast he'd seen. That he wanted to stroke, to taste. Her eyes went dark and she looked away. Her pulse fluttered rapidly in her throat. She wanted it, too.

Adrenaline rushed through his body. All he had to do was reach out, skim one finger over that magnolia smooth flesh. "No," he said hoarsely.

"The baby," Susannah said in a choked voice, her blush deepening.

He looked down. Lorelai blinked up at him and stopped crying, tears wetting her face.

He grinned. "She just wanted to see Riley."

The baby opened her mouth and wailed.

He frowned at Susannah.

Her hand flattened against her bodice as if to make sure it was completely fastened. "I don't know what else to do. I've walked, I've rocked. I even sang."

"Well, I won't torture her with my voice," he said. "Let me try this." He bundled her up in a soft blanket hanging over a kitchen chair, trying to shush her sobbing. "Let me have another blanket. I'm going to take her outside."

Susannah handed him the soft white covering Cora had made. Riley wrapped the baby tightly, then laid her against his shoulder.

"We'll be right out here."

Susannah opened the door for him and watched as he walked slowly to the end of the porch, then back, bouncing the little girl gently. Lorelai cried just as hard, her racking cries small and pitiful in the dark prairie night.

After several measured trips back and forth across the porch, Riley stopped.

Susannah stepped outside. "Do you think she's getting sick?"

"I don't feel a fever. Let me try something else." He walked over and unlooped Whip's reins from the porch column.

"What are you doing?" she asked sharply. As unlikely as it was, the thought that he might take Lorelai flashed through her mind.

"Pa said he used to do this with me and Davis Lee. Is it all right if I take her on the horse?"

No! Susannah bit back her first reaction. She reminded herself that one of the reasons she'd worked so hard with Cora's mare was so her daughter wouldn't fear horses the way she did. But Lorelai was so tiny.

Riley waited next to Whip, who stood as still as a statue. Susannah knew he wouldn't let anything happen to her baby, and if he felt getting her up there was the least bit dangerous, he wouldn't have even considered it.

"All right."

"I'll be careful," he said, loudly enough to be heard over the baby's cries. "Here, you hold her while I mount up."

Susannah handed the baby to him once Riley was in the saddle.

"We're just going to walk around the yard. Maybe this will work."

"Maybe." She had her doubts, but her poor baby was going to make herself ill if they couldn't stop her crying.

Susannah gripped the porch column, her nails digging into the weathered wood as she watched the paint gelding step away from the house. The cold night air barely registered.

Riley held Lorelai against his chest, bent over so that his hat and shoulder protected her from the wind that occasionally swept around the side of the house. He guided Whip with his knees. The horse walked slowly and smoothly around the yard. Before they'd made a complete circle, Lorelai's sobbing diminished to a whimper. One more sob, than a breath shuddered out of her. A contented sigh.

Susannah moved to the edge of the porch. Silence. Her baby had stopped crying.

A smile curved her lips as Riley and the baby passed in front of her. The lamplight from the open doorway caught the grin on his face. The man would think he hung the moon now.

"Now, look at this," he whispered.

"I don't understand it."

"Pa said we liked the rhythm of the motion. It's soothing. There are still times when I fall asleep in the saddle."

Susannah couldn't imagine being relaxed enough to sleep on a horse, but she loved that her daughter could.

After another few minutes of riding, Riley halted the horse in front of the porch and handed Lorelai down to her. She cuddled the baby close.

"Thank you," she whispered. "I'll go put her down."

He nodded, dismounting and looping the reins around the porch column again. He had no defenses against that baby, he thought with a grin. Or her mother, either. His grin faded as his mind flashed back to the image of her undone chemise, the bare breasts he'd been close enough to touch. And he *had* wanted to touch. To taste.

His body hardened and he fought the savage craving that rose inside him like a dark sweetness. He wanted her. There was no getting around that.

He hesitated in the open doorway, cool March air swirling around him. Now was the time to leave. She and the baby were fine.

Susannah stepped out of her room, looking away as she moved to the far side of the table. "I appreciate your help."

"You're welcome." He wanted to kiss her, so badly his lips burned. "I'm glad it worked."

She wouldn't meet his gaze. "That's a trick I'll remember. I guess I'll have to learn to ride horses now. Can't expect you to run over here every time she cries like that."

"I'll come anytime you want." Hell, he wished *he* didn't want it so badly. "You gonna be all right here by yourself tonight? 'Cuz I can sleep in the barn."

"I think we'll be fine."

He wanted her to look at him. The need to apologize again was strong, even though his walking in on her that way had been unintentional. "I'm sorry. For…what happened earlier."

"I know it was an accident."

Even in the dancing lamplight, he could see her flush again. "I should've waited until I knew you heard me."

She chewed at her lip, trying for a nonchalant smile. "Well, there's no redoing it, so I can forget it if you can."

Forget it? Maybe in a hundred years. "Sure."

"Good." She looked uncertain and nervous.

Something had passed between them, something hot and jolting and purely physical that Riley knew wouldn't go away. Something that shifted the invisible line between them. Something he had to put behind him. He knew that would be like spitting into a high wind.

* * *

How was she supposed to forget about him when he looked at her as if he had to have her or die?

Susannah hadn't thought she could ever feel such searing desire again, especially before a man even touched her, but Riley set off a low-burning flame inside her that melted her bones to wax.

She wanted him, but she knew he'd never change his mind about her. How could anything good come of them being together?

He wanted her, too. She'd seen it in his eyes, in the blazing intensity of his gaze on her body. But she had an obligation to her baby to find the best father she could. She and Riley both knew that wasn't him.

She had to forget about him and the wanton feelings he triggered inside her. Feelings she'd sworn she would never surrender to again.

Desire had sawed a hole through Riley's gut since he'd walked in on Susannah bared to the waist last night.

The sight of her luscious breasts had unleashed something inside him, and now he couldn't corral it. He'd been trying to put her out of his mind, but the image of her stayed stubbornly rooted in his head, even as he took a seat in church the next morning.

Just after the sermon began, he slipped into the back pew. Several rows ahead, he saw Susannah's blond ringlets tamed into a loose chignon. She sat between Cora and Davis Lee. Riley had never known his brother to arrive much earlier than he did. Fighting the brisk March wind had cost Whip a little speed, so he had been late.

His gaze rested on her and so did his mind. The hymns didn't penetrate the very unchristian thoughts he was having about the woman who had somehow gotten under his skin.

He tried to direct his attention to Reverend Scoggins's message, but he was too aware of Susannah. Her hair looked like silk piled on her head, a stray tendril teasing her neck. A wedge of satiny skin showed above the collar of her light green dress.

A baby fussed and Riley recognized the sound as coming from Lorelai. Susannah lifted the child to her shoulder and gently jiggled her. The little girl quieted back to sleep.

Telling himself Susannah didn't belong in Whirlwind had done nothing to douse the wildfire she'd lit inside him last night. In fact, he didn't care anymore whether she belonged here or not. What he had to worry about was getting this craving for her under control.

He could not get her out of his mind, whether he was awake or asleep.

Church passed in a blur, and he was surprised when the service was dismissed.

He stepped out into the aisle and saw Davis Lee bend his head to speak to Susannah, stepping aside so she could move to the aisle, also. Several women and young girls crowded around her, admiring the baby. Riley started toward them, wanting to see Lorelai.

The knot of chattering women held fast no matter how he tried to get through, so he moved next to his brother.

Davis Lee grinned. "She's mighty pretty, isn't she?"

"Yes, she is."

"She's a little thing. I don't think I realized just how little."

Riley frowned at the way his brother's voice had dropped admiringly. They both had held Lorelai just a day after her birth. Why wouldn't he know how small she was?

"And she really has a way with that baby."

Riley looked sharply at his brother. "Are you talking about Susannah?"

"Yes." Davis Lee glanced at him. "Who are *you* talking about?"

"You're admiring Susannah?"

"Of course. I tend to admire the women I call on."

Riley barely kept his jaw from dropping. He glanced at Susannah, then back at his brother. "Did you bring her to church?"

"Yes."

"Why?" A strange unwelcome heat moved through his chest.

"Why?" Davis Lee laughed. "Well, I've been thinking about what you said, and you were right."

"What I said?"

"That it's time I thought about settling down."

"Not with Susannah. She's not interested in you," Riley said incredulously.

His brother shrugged, his gaze moving to the subject of their conversation. "She accepted my invitation to church. I'd call that interest."

Susannah had come with Davis Lee to church. They had come together. As a couple.

Riley couldn't fathom it. And he'd seen that *gotcha* look in his brother's eyes before. He didn't like it. "Why are you interested in her? You didn't seem too interested before."

"Do you have eyes in your head, little brother? She's a beautiful woman and seems to be a good mother."

Riley stared. Was Davis Lee joshing? Since when had he heeded any advice Riley had given?

His brother stared back, his eyes clear and sincere.

"You're lyin', aren't you? Just trying to get me riled up?"

"Why would that rile you up?" Davis Lee rocked back on his heels and crossed his arms. "I thought you said y'all were just friends."

"We are."

"Well, then?"

Susannah walked up with the baby and smiled at Riley. "Good morning."

"Morning." He leaned over to look at the sleeping babe. "How's Button today?"

"She's doing well." She was wrapped tightly in the blanket Cora had made, and wore a tiny blue ribbon in her hair. The baby's sweet, innocent face tugged a smile from Riley.

"She looks pretty." Riley's gaze was on Susannah, not her daughter. He couldn't keep his eyes from sliding over her breasts. Their fullness was covered by the light green wool of her bodice, but he knew what lay beneath.

His pulse hammered harder in his groin. He glanced away, tried again to dismiss the image that seemed branded on his brain.

A flush pinkened Susannah's neck and she hugged the baby closer to her, her gaze skittering away from him and going to Davis Lee. "She'll be waking up soon and ready to eat."

His brother clapped him on the back. "I'd better get these two ladies to dinner before they starve."

"Sure." Riley tried to keep his voice easy. It was none of his business who called on Susannah. Or who Davis Lee called on, for that matter.

His brother had paid one call on Susannah. That was probably the end of it.

Church was not the end of Davis Lee's keeping company with Susannah, Riley found out two nights later when he stopped by Cora's.

His brother rode up right behind him and dismounted. "Hey, little brother. What brings you out here?"

"I'm here to see the baby." Riley stepped onto the porch. "What are you doing?"

"I'm here to see Susannah." He grinned. "We had a real

nice time at church the other day. I thought she might like to go to a picnic over at Eishen's pecan grove."

Riley gave him a sharp look. "Picnicking is not what people do at Eishen's pecan grove."

"Sure it is." Davis Lee grinned again and squeezed Riley's shoulder. "Sometimes, anyway."

Riley's eyes narrowed. How often had Davis Lee been over here? Just how many times had he and Susannah gone out together? Were they courting? Wouldn't he know if they were?

He stepped to the side as his brother reached over and knocked.

Cora opened the door. "Hi, boys. Good to see you." As they stepped inside, she called over her shoulder, "Susannah, Davis Lee is here. And Riley, too."

Susannah came out of her room with the baby. Davis Lee met her, tickling the baby under the chin. "Hey, little one."

She blinked up at him with wide blue eyes.

Susannah smiled, handing her to Cora. "We're just taking a short walk. We won't be long. Hi, Riley."

She smiled and walked toward him and the door. When his brother solicitously draped her shawl around her shoulders, Riley's jaw set.

As they left, Cora passed him the baby. "I bet you came to see our little doll."

"Yes." Cradling Lorelai, he looked down into the baby's guileless blue eyes, and his heart melted. She smelled sweet and clean. "How are you today, Button?"

As if in answer, she squirmed in his hands. Riley chuckled, trying to push away the thought of Susannah out with his brother.

Cora walked over to the stove. "Care for some coffee?"

"That would be nice." He took a chair at the table. "What

have you been up to today, Button? Read all your mama's books yet?''

The older woman laughed. "Your brother seems to like Lorelai, too. He brought her a little pretty the other day."

Riley's head came up. "When was that?"

"Yesterday. Or, well, maybe the day before."

He frowned. "Just how often is Davis Lee coming by?"

"About as often as you, always to see Susannah."

"What do you think about that?"

"I love your brother, you know that. He and Susannah would make a fine match." She slid a look at him. "What do *you* think about it?"

"I guess it's all right, if it's what Susannah wants."

"Seems to be. Davis Lee has come more than those other fellas, at least so far."

"What other fellas?" Riley didn't take his gaze from the sweet baby in his arms, but he paid close attention.

Cora lifted the lid on the coffeepot, then settled it back into place. "Well, Matt Baldwin took her to dinner at the Pearl. She's been on a buggy ride with Russ. Tony Santos and Jake Ross have both paid calls. Susannah thought they might lose interest after the baby was born, but I don't think they have. They all love our little doll."

More likely they wanted her mama, Riley thought savagely. He'd seen the way they all looked at Susannah. Hell, *he* looked at her that way. "Is she going to continue her school?"

"Yes. She started back last week."

Why hadn't he known that? Susannah hadn't mentioned it to him. Of course, he hadn't asked. Did Davis Lee know? Probably, Riley thought with a jolt of possessiveness. Was his brother still looking to settle down? With Susannah? Was she of a like mind?

Trying to unclench his jaw, Riley stared down into little Lorelai's eyes. "What's the matter with your mama, Button?

You'd think she was trying to get herself hitched." The thought struck him like a blow to the chest.

Cora said slyly, "If you wanted to do something about it, now would be the time."

"What would I want to do about it?" Hadn't he decided to steer clear of Susannah's business?

Cora brought his coffee and a cup for herself, sitting down at the table. He lifted the baby until she was at eye level. "Your mama's not a silly woman, Button. She won't do anything foolish, like run off and get married."

The idea stopped him cold and he looked at Cora. "Will she?"

"You'd have to ask her." The older woman smiled.

He frowned, tucking the baby into his shoulder and gently patting her back. His gaze slid to the door. "Will they be gone long?"

"Oh, I expect as long as usual. About an hour or so."

"An hour! Where are they walking to? My ranch?"

Cora chuckled.

Just exactly what *was* Susannah doing with Davis Lee? Riley didn't like to think about it, but he couldn't stop.

Susannah felt perfectly comfortable and calm with Davis Lee. That was the last thing she felt around his brother. As they walked through town and he spoke to everyone they passed, she thought what a fine man Davis Lee was. He would make a good father and husband. But was he interested in a commitment? During the calls he'd paid, they hadn't discussed it.

They had talked about their families, and he told her he'd once been the sheriff in Rock River, a town about a hundred miles south. He hadn't said why he'd left, but from the tightness in his voice, she got the impression it had been under bad circumstances. Susannah liked Davis Lee, but her pulse didn't race when she saw him. Her heart didn't pound out of her chest. Still, she'd made the decision to follow her head, not her heart. A man like Davis Lee was what she needed.

He was gentle and affectionate with Lorelai. He was handsome and clean, responsible and dependable. His brother was all those things, too, and Susannah had given up trying to keep thoughts of Riley out of her head. Since the night he'd walked in on her with her bodice open, she'd been unable to think of anything but him. His hands on her, his mouth. Wild, reckless thoughts that completely drove logic out of her head. She'd been destroyed once by heeding such emotion. She couldn't do it again, not when her child stood to be hurt by such a decision.

She and Davis Lee walked into Cora's yard. Riley's horse was still tethered there. She stepped onto the porch, stopping when Davis Lee caught her gloved hand.

"Do you enjoy our walks, Susannah?"

"Yes, very much." She tilted her head, nearly eye level with him, since he had remained a step below her. "Do you?"

"Yes." Moonlight dappled his handsome features, which were somewhat sharper than Riley's, and gilded his brown hair. "I enjoy any time I spend with you."

"You're very kind."

"I admire you a great deal, Susannah. Surely you know that."

Her breath caught. She hadn't expected him to turn serious, certainly not with his brother inside. He wasn't about to declare himself, was he?

Earnest eyes searched her face. She smiled, uncertain and curious about what he would say next.

He leaned toward her and she realized he meant to kiss her. She thought she might like to kiss Davis Lee, and turned her face up, closed her eyes.

His breath brushed her lips and she stiffened involuntarily.

She hoped he hadn't felt that. He was such a nice man. He moved closer, his breath feathering across her cheek. Then he kissed her forehead.

Her eyes flew open and she stared at him. *Her forehead?*

He laughed shortly, sounding sheepish. "Hell, Susannah, I just don't think I can kiss you. At least not the way you should be kissed."

Relief rolled through her, so strong it nearly buckled her knees. "Really?"

"I think we're going to have to be just friends. I must be crazy, but I don't feel romantic about you."

"You don't?" She curled one hand around the porch column. "I thought it was just me."

"You feel the same?"

She nodded.

"Good." He chuckled. "Here we are, glad we don't fancy each other. Aren't we a pair?"

"I guess so."

"Maybe you ought to think about that," he said lightly. "Surely you feel romantic about someone?"

She didn't want to explain why she couldn't take such a chance again. "I do enjoy spending time with you, though. You're a good friend to me."

"And you to me." Davis Lee smiled, his teeth flashing white in the dim light. "Listen to us. We're saying goodbye as if we're taking off on a long journey. I'll still see you and the baby."

"Yes, I'd like that."

"And I'd still like to take you to the Founder's Day dance."

She'd agreed over a week ago. "I'd like that, too."

He kissed her hand. "I'll say good-night then. Thank you for a lovely evening."

"Thank you." She squeezed his hand.

"You're a fine lady, Susannah Phelps. I'm glad to know you."

She stood on the porch until he'd disappeared into the darkness, then she turned to go in. If she was relieved that a wonderful man like Davis Lee hadn't kissed her on the mouth, how was she going to settle for any other man she didn't love when that man would have the right to do much more than kiss her?

Closing the door behind her, she took off her wrap and hung it on the peg behind the door. Riley stepped out of her bedroom.

"Button's asleep," he whispered, coming over to her.

She smiled and went in to check on her daughter. Lorelai slept peacefully in her cradle, the moonlight skimming across one chubby cheek and tiny ear. Susannah's heart swelled with love and she brushed a light kiss on her daughter's soft head.

She walked back out to the front room, where Riley stood in front of the stove facing her, his hands behind his back.

His shoulders seemed broader than usual. His shadow stretched across the back wall, hiding the sink and part of the pantry. His blue eyes seemed black in the lantern light and his gaze moved over her slowly, deliberately.

Awareness skipped across her nerves and she felt the need to keep something between them. Staying on the opposite side of the table, she asked, "Where's Cora?"

"She went on to bed. I told her I'd put Button down."

"Thank you." She glanced around, suddenly very aware that they were alone. "I don't mean to keep you. It's late."

"Did you have a nice walk with Davis Lee?"

There was an edge to his voice, enough that she narrowed her eyes. "Yes, I did," she said almost defiantly. She had no intention of telling him that she and Davis Lee had probably shared their last walk.

"Are you still interested in those riding lessons?"

"Yes." She curled her hands over the back of a chair, inexplicably feeling as if she needed to be careful of this conversation. "When do we start?"

"You don't think your social engagements will interfere with your lessons?" His words held a definite bite.

"I'm sure I can manage," she said coolly.

"Really?" He stepped away from the stove and moved to the edge of the table, leaving a few feet between them. "You've been accepting a lot of invitations from a lot of different men lately."

"Yes." Why did he care how many invitations she accepted? How did he even know about them?

"Are you serious about any of them?"

What gall! She lifted her chin. "I'm serious about finding a good father for my baby. I have to think of Lorelai's security and our future."

"You don't have to be in a hurry. You've got a friend in Cora, a place to live, and the baby's happy."

"Well, I did come here to find a good father for Lorelai." Susannah felt uncomfortable talking about this with Riley. "There's no need to put it off."

His eyes turned stormy. "And this is how you're going about it?"

"What would you suggest?" Excitement or anger—she couldn't tell which—rushed through her veins. "I think it's prudent to get to know someone, see if we have interests in common. I have no intention of being a mail-order bride."

"How many times have you been out with Jake Ross?"

She gave a short laugh. "That's none of your business."

He closed the distance between them, his voice soft. Dangerous. "How many?"

"Three or four." She grew still, her gaze moving over his stern jaw, the lips she knew could be generous.

"He's not for you. He never says more than three words at a time."

"Right now, I think that's a good thing," she retorted.

"He's so shy he'd never ask you to marry him."

She could feel Riley's heat and the restless energy that poured off him. "We haven't seemed to run out of things to talk about."

His jaw tightened. "What about Matt Baldwin?"

"Are you going to ask me about all the invitations I've had?"

"Yes."

Irritation shot through her, but Riley looked irritated in turn. "I've accepted two invitations from Matthew."

"And Russ?"

"Two as well."

"If you pick one of them, you'll make the other mad. You sure wouldn't want to live in their house if that happened."

She frowned. "I hardly think things will come to that."

"And haven't you been around with Tony? He's already raising his nephew. What if he doesn't treat Lorelai the same?"

"You seem very sure of your opinions about these men."

"I've known them all a long time. Longer than you have."

Her lips tightened. "You've pointed out faults for every man I've seen lately, except your brother."

He hesitated. "I don't think Davis Lee is serious about settling down."

"Hmm, maybe you should talk to him, too," she said dryly. "Your encouraging words certainly have *me* ready to say 'I do.'"

Riley's nostrils flared and his gaze locked on her lips, instantly reviving the memory of their one kiss. "I'm just trying to help you make a good decision."

She felt that treacherous stirring for him in her body. "None of these men are perfect, but at least they all think I belong here. You don't."

"We're not talking about me."

"Why not?" She shouldn't push, but his prodding and criticism vexed her. "You certainly have an opinion about me."

His gaze lifted to search her face. He picked up his hat and settled it on his head. "I'm concerned for you, is all."

Then why don't you call on me? "I think you don't want me here, so you're trying to convince me to leave."

"That's not true. I care what happens to you."

"Is that why you wired Adam and asked him if my parents were ready to forgive me?" She hadn't planned to mention what her brother had told her in the telegram he'd sent last week, but she was tired of Riley hiding behind his concern.

His eyes narrowed. "Those weren't my exact words. I knew you missed your parents. I wired him to see if he'd made any headway in patching relations between you all."

"Then I'm sure you learned he hasn't." Her voice nearly cracked, but not due to the emotion she felt over her estranged family. It was all due to the lean cowboy standing in front of her. "I appreciate your concern, but as you can see, I'm doing just fine without your help. Lorelai and I both are."

"I won't butt in again then." He pulled on his coat and opened the door. "Just watch yourself. That's all I'm saying."

Long after he'd gone, she sat at the table staring at the smoldering red flames in the stove. Because she was his best friend's sister, concern was probably the most of what he felt for her.

She closed her eyes, refusing to dwell on the disappointment. He wasn't the man for her. Why couldn't she accept that?

Chapter Fourteen

He knew Susannah meant what she said about finding a father for her baby. After all, that was why she'd come to Whirlwind in the first place. She'd already faced fear and scandal for her child, left her home and friends and family, made a job for herself here. There was nothing she wouldn't do for Lorelai.

Riley felt the same himself, and the child wasn't even his blood. Still, just the thought that some other man would raise Lorelai and sleep in Susannah's bed set off a deep-reaching anger inside him. He had no right to tell her what to do, and she was the wrong woman for him.

But since they'd talked last week about her suitors, discontent had risen in him like a cresting river. It edged into a flutter of panic, then grew, grabbing him around the throat and choking him.

Two days ago, April had come in on a storm, but the weather for tonight's Founder's Day dance held at the Pearl was clear and calm, with only a slight nip in the air. Riley hadn't come to town for all the festivities, like the box social or the horseshoe competition. Two calves had gotten stuck in a bog and he'd spent the day pulling them out and getting them back to their mamas. Then he'd cleaned up and headed for the dance.

He knew Susannah would be here on some man's arm. This past week, he had purposely kept his conversation with her limited to the baby or Cora's mare. She'd made it clear that she didn't want his opinion on anything else.

Pearl Anderson had moved all the tables against the walls in her restaurant and cleared a large area for dancing. Cal Doyle sat at the piano, brought over from Pete Carter's saloon. Jed Doyle stood next to him, playing the fiddle. Couples already whirled around the pine floor to the lively turn of "Turkey in the Straw."

Riley spotted Susannah right off...dancing with his brother. His gut started to churn. And when Davis Lee and Susannah glided past, and Riley got a good look at her blue satin dress, he nearly cussed.

It was cut low on her bosom, so low that one wrong step could send her tumbling out of it. The ice-blue color matched her eyes, and the lace kerchief tucked into her neckline for modesty dipped so deeply between her breasts, fuller since Lorelai's birth, that it only teased a man with what he couldn't have.

The fair, lustrous hair piled atop her head drew Riley's eye to her elegant neck and shoulders, down to the swell of her breasts. What the hell was she thinking, wearing something that daring? Every man in here would pounce on her like a fox on a chicken.

Riley's hands curled into fists and he went looking for something to drink, hoping Pete Carter had sneaked in his usual bottle of whiskey to slip into the punch. Riley downed two cupfuls of the liquor-laced brew, restlessness boiling inside him.

Between dances, Davis Lee fetched Susannah some of

Pearl's untouched punch. He said something to her and she laughed, the joyful sound clutching deep at Riley's gut. He decided he'd better dance before he did something stupid, like drag her out of there.

An hour later, he'd danced with every widow in the place, except Cora, who'd stayed home with the baby. Every *true* widow, he amended as his gaze once again found Susannah. She was now partnered with Jake Ross. The Baldwins had already claimed the reels to "Durang's Hornpipe" and "Buffalo Gals." Tony Santos had swept her around the room during the "Blue Danube Waltz."

The sight of her with every one of those men pulled at some darkness inside Riley, a ferocity to protect that he'd never experienced and didn't understand. The worst was seeing her with his own brother, he admitted as Davis Lee once again led Susannah onto the dance floor for another reel.

It hit him then. If Davis Lee hitched up with Susannah, Riley would be her *brother-in-law* and little Lorelai's uncle. He didn't feel brotherly in the least toward the blonde who tied his gut in knots. If she wound up with Davis Lee, Riley would forever have to see her and the baby and know they belonged to another man.

A man whom he had never seen before stepped inside the restaurant, the tin star he wore branding him a lawman. He asked something of Pete Carter, who stood next to the door. What was going on?

Pete pointed toward Davis Lee and Susannah, whirling on the opposite side of the room. The stranger paused next to the fiddler and waited for the song's end.

As Davis Lee led Susannah off the floor, the stranger followed. He caught up to them at the refreshment table set up along one long wall. After a short conversation, Davis Lee nodded and pointed out the door. The man said goodbye to Susannah, his gaze lingering on her exposed bosom so long that Riley took an involuntary step forward before reminding himself she was none of his concern.

Davis Lee tucked her hand in his arm and made his way across the dance floor to Pearl and May Haskell, depositing Susannah with them. Then he walked over to Riley. "Could you take Susannah home tonight?"

"What's going on?"

"That was the sheriff from Waco. He's delivering a prisoner for trial, and I'll be in charge of him until the judge gets to Abilene."

The last thing Riley wanted was to be alone with Susannah, even if it was only for the short walk to Cora's. "Why me?"

Davis Lee's gaze scanned the crowd, stopping to rest on the Baldwins, who had already formed a circle around Susannah. "Well, I sure don't trust her with all those other fellas. Have you seen the way they're looking at her?"

How could he miss it? "All right," he said reluctantly.

"Unless you're willing to let her take her chances in that dress."

Riley stared flatly at his brother. "I said all right."

Davis Lee grinned and slapped him on the back. "I'll tell Susannah. Thanks."

After Davis Lee left, Riley made his way over to her and the older women in her circle. He greeted them all, keenly aware of the rapid rise and fall of Susannah's chest, her skin radiant from all her exertion. Her blue eyes glowed like smoky sapphires, and desire pricked at his already raw nerves like a knife.

Impatience and a sense of urgency streamed through him, but he said to Susannah, "We can stay as long as you like. Just let me know when you're ready to go."

"Thank you." She barely spared him a glance, smiling broadly when J. T. Baldwin bent over her hand and asked for the next dance.

She accepted and they stepped out on the floor for a waltz, this one to the poignant strains of "Silver Threads among the Gold."

She seemed as unwilling to be alone with Riley as he was with her. They were the last ones to walk out the door a couple of hours later, as Pearl said good-night.

All of Susannah's dance partners had tried to convince Riley to let them walk her home, but he'd said no. He would've agreed if he hadn't promised his brother, he told himself, even though he knew it wasn't true.

The two of them walked in silence, which irritated Riley. But he had no inclination to start a conversation, which also irritated him.

She held her shawl loosely about her shoulders, and moonlight slid into the valley of her breasts. Riley swallowed, pulling his gaze away. Didn't she realize what a woman dressing like that did to a man? Hadn't she noticed how every male at the dance had been drooling over her? If they'd ever seen her bare breasts the way he had, she could've been in danger of being ravished. "You had a good time tonight," he said.

"Yes, it was wonderful," she said dreamily. "I don't remember the last time I danced."

"Probably wore your slippers clean out," he groused.

She flicked him a look. "I was so proud of all my students. To a one, they mastered the waltz."

"They sure couldn't wait to show off for you."

She frowned, then looked away from him, humming softly under her breath. They neared Cora's and she turned to him. "You can leave me off here. No need to walk me to the door."

"I told Davis Lee I'd see you home. That means the door."

"Very well." She looked down her nose at him and quickly covered the several yards to Cora's house.

He didn't know what devil came over him, but he damn

well wasn't having her walk away from him when every other man in town had put his hands on her tonight. "You ought to take care with what you wear. Wouldn't take much for things to get out of control."

She stopped in front of the door, her gaze freezing on him. "Are you saying I tried to entice someone? Tease him?"

"I'm just saying you ought to cover up." He stopped at the edge of the porch. "That dress might be considered indecent by some."

She glanced down, her fingers grazing the swell of her breasts. Right where he wanted *his* fingers. "Davis Lee had no complaints."

Whatever control Riley had exercised tonight snapped like a frayed lead rope. In two steps, he was in front of her. "Neither do I."

He didn't think, just closed one hand around her wrist and hauled her to him.

"What are you—"

His lips covered hers. His hand tightened on her waist, holding her to him. His other hand curled around her neck, which was warm and silky beneath his palm. He expected resistance, kissed her hard and deep in an effort to overcome it.

But she didn't stiffen. She leaned into him, her breasts pressing against his chest. She looped her arms around his neck, opening her mouth to his. Their tongues tangled and she made a soft noise in her throat.

Raging need drove through him and he backed her into the wall, sheltering her body with his as he reached beneath her shawl and pulled down one sleeve of her dress and chemise. He drank her in, deep and sweet and giving every bit as good as she got.

He grew hard, throbbing, the desire quickly overtaking whatever common sense he had left. She framed his face in her hands, her kisses soft and willing. Her tongue played with his. He didn't want to leave her mouth, but a searing need spurred his lips to her ear, down her throat.

She kissed his jaw. Heat sizzled between their bodies. Her skin felt like warm silk beneath his palms and he lifted her to him.

He nipped at her collarbone, aching when she whispered his name and offered herself to him. He trailed his lips down her velvety skin where her breasts swelled over the top of her corset. He tugged her thin chemise down as far as he could and closed his mouth over her nipple. He laved her, drawing the peak into a tight bud that tickled his tongue, nearly drove him over the edge when she moaned and clutched him to her.

His mouth moved to her other breast, and he dragged at the fabric, gently grazing her other nipple with his teeth. She pressed against him, her hips seeking his through the folds of her skirt. She caught at his waistband and tugged him closer; her hand slid down, pressing and kneading.

He was already full and hard, straining for her. His hands moved up her arms to cup her breasts, and he felt goose bumps. Cold. Realized where they were and what they were doing.

He stopped, lifted his head, his blood swirling with black, savage need. She opened her eyes and the sultry invitation there brought him as close to begging as he'd ever been. Heat centered between his legs and he realized she still had her hand on him.

They stared at each other, their breathing labored. Realization dawned for her at the same moment it did for him. Uncertainty flared in her eyes and she dropped her hand. He ached to his very marrow.

"No."

They said it together. She half turned from him, hurriedly adjusting her chemise and corset, then straightening her bodice.

"Susannah…"

"I don't understand, Riley." Her voice thickened as she looked at him with eyes half-dazed from desire and confusion. "You say you want to be friends, then you kiss me like that. What am I supposed to do?"

"You kissed me back."

She caught her bottom lip between her teeth and pulled her shawl tight around her.

He throbbed beneath his trousers, the want carving away self-restraint, common sense. But he'd seen the hurt in her eyes. He couldn't let it remain. "I thought I wanted to be friends, but I don't."

"Very well—"

"Hear me out." He wanted to touch her, but that was the worst thing he could do right now. "I want more than friendship from you, but I don't want to put you in the same position LaFortune did. I don't want to hurt you, Susannah. I don't want your being with me to be a source of shame."

She stared at him for a moment, her breathing still ragged. "You want me?"

"Yes. I know you feel it, too."

Her features were sharp and fragile with desire. "I do, and I want to be with you right now, Riley. Tonight." She reached for his hand, linked her fingers with his. "When you touch me, I want more."

He stroked her cheek, tempted to accept her invitation and forget what she deserved. Which was more than a fast coupling in the dark. "Go inside, darlin'. Before I do something that's wrong for both of us."

"Come with me," she whispered, her voice shaking.

Every part of his body pulsed with the need to go, to say yes. "Susannah, I can't be noble much longer."

Rejection flashed in her eyes. After a long moment, she unlinked their fingers and went inside.

He started off the porch, then hooked an arm around the column and knocked his head against it. He wanted her more than he'd ever wanted any woman, almost enough to deceive himself into believing that she belonged here. With him.

Watching her dance with all those men tonight had torn him up, but claiming her this way wasn't right.

Riley's kisses last night had turned everything upside down. Until then, Susannah thought she'd known where she stood with him.

She'd gone soft and wet when he'd first touched her, and when he'd put his mouth on her breasts, she'd nearly come undone. She wanted to take him to her bed. To her utter mortification, she had asked him to come inside with her.

Remembering that moment, she bit back a groan. It didn't matter how much she told herself to listen to her head. Whenever he was around, her body took over. She knew these feelings would go away in time, but the middle of the next morning, they were still making her ache for him.

Cora stood by the dry sink, mixing up a batch of biscuits, while Susannah gathered up her newest set of flyers. She checked on Lorelai, glad to see the baby had gone to sleep after her recent feeding.

Taking her light shawl from the peg behind the door, Susannah wrapped it around her shoulders. "After I stop at the newspaper office to post this notice, I'm going to tack up some flyers around town."

"I can't tell you how much it means to me that you're willing to help so much."

She went to the woman who had become a surrogate mother, and hugged her. "You gave Lorelai and me a home when we had none, Cora. We'll both be forever grateful. I'll help you any way I can."

"That Banker Dobies has no idea who he's messin' with," Cora said with a strained smile. "We'll show him, won't we?"

"Absolutely." Susannah hoped her smile covered up any uncertainty. The banker had raised Cora's mortgage payments, and last week his threat to foreclose on the house had struck panic into both her and Susannah. But together they had come up with some ideas to make more money.

Susannah had decided she would offer to teach reading. Through her charm school, she'd noticed only three of her students could read. Tony, who operated the telegraph, was literate, as was his nephew, Miguel. Once they read her advertisement, they could tell others. The Baldwins, Pete Carter and Jake Ross all had need of her services. There had to be others, as well.

She opened the front door. "I won't be long."

"All right."

She hurried off the porch, refusing to look at the place where she and Riley had gotten so passionate. But how could she forget about him saying that he didn't want to put her in the same position Paul had? How could she resist him when he said things like that? Ooh, the man made her crazy.

The only thing she knew to do was stay away from him. The mild spring air was just what she needed to try and erase the memory of what they'd done last night. Enjoying the warmth from the bright sunshine, she walked to town. New green grass poked through the red dirt. Birds called cheerily from the tops of the town's buildings.

She stopped first at the newspaper office of the *Prairie Caller* and placed an advertisement, then went next door to the saloon. In deference to her reputation, Pete Carter came outside. She explained why he needed to attend her newest school. After his initial scoffing protests, she saw genuine interest on his rough-hewn features.

She walked back to Haskell's to ask about tacking a flyer outside his store. Just as she finished pinning up the notice, she saw a big man heading purposefully down the walk toward her. Riley.

She practically jumped into the street and headed across to the Pearl.

Embarrassment flamed through her again about what had happened last night, how she'd thrown herself at him. She had learned better from her experience with Paul, so what was wrong with her? A quick glance across her shoulder showed no sign of Riley. Breathing a sigh of relief, she went into the restaurant and left some flyers with Pearl, who was sure some of her customers would be interested in Susannah's new school.

She stepped outside, her gaze darting across the street. No sign of Riley, thank goodness. Intent on tacking up a notice at the post office, she turned right. A strong hand closed around her elbow.

"You're not avoiding me, are you, Miz Phelps?"

Riley's deep voice sent awareness sizzling up her spine. The memory of his hands on her, his mouth, flashed in a rush of heat.

He stepped from behind her. "I went to Cora's looking for you."

His gaze was intense, making her nerves jangle. She could barely meet his eyes. "Here I am."

"What are you doing?" He leaned over her shoulder to look at the paper she held, close enough that she could feel the warmth of his body, smell his too-familiar scent of soap and leather.

"Uh, passing out flyers." She pulled away and took a step to the side. "I'm offering a new school. To teach reading."

"Between your charm school and raising the baby, do you think you have enough time for this?"

"I'll find time. Cora does a lot more than I do and she manages."

"Do you need money?"

"No." She lowered her voice. "I don't think Cora would mind if I told you. Her visit to the banker in Abilene was about the house. He told her if she couldn't make higher payments he would foreclose. She was making the payments in the fall after Ollie died, but now Banker Dobies has increased them. I need to help as much as possible."

"I could give you money."

"I can't take it," she protested with a half laugh.

He hesitated, his gaze steady on her. "We need to talk. About last night."

She glanced around, as if afraid someone was listening. "It shouldn't have happened. And you certainly shouldn't bring it up."

"Well, pardon me, but that's why I came looking for you. It bears talking about and we're gonna talk about it."

She lifted her chin. "I'm busy—"

"This is important, Susannah. Don't make me haul you somewhere. That would set the whole town to talking for sure."

She glanced around, noticing that Charlie Haskell had come to the door of his store and was staring curiously. Susannah felt Pearl behind her, also studying them.

"Let's walk," Riley suggested.

"All right," she said reluctantly.

He jammed his hands in his trousers and she gripped her flyers with both hands, trying not to brush against him as they moved past the post office toward the east end of town.

"I was awake all last night."

She had been, too, reliving the wicked feel of his mouth on her flesh. "Riley, I don't think we should talk about this."

"You really are embarrassed, aren't you?"

She flicked him a look. "Aside from the liberties I allowed, I threw myself at you."

"That's not how I remember it," he said softly.

They reached the Whirlwind Hotel. As they stepped off the planked walk, he glanced around and took her elbow.

"What are you doing?"

"Going somewhere private so we can have this conversation."

He was right to put it to rest. After all, she couldn't avoid him the rest of her life, but she dreaded talking about the recklessness that had taken them both over last night.

He stopped behind the hotel and released her. A quick glance up the alley to her right showed they were alone back here behind the businesses.

He palmed off his hat and slapped it lightly against his thigh.

Why, he was just as unnerved as she was! For some reason, that settled her stomach.

"If we'd made love last night, it would've been no different than what LaFortune did to you. I don't want to have you and leave."

She pressed back into the wall, her breath jammed in her lungs. "What *do* you want?"

His jaw worked. After a long moment, he said, "I want you. More than I've ever wanted any other woman in my life."

She shook her head. "That solves nothing. I know whereof I speak. Paul—"

"Don't talk about him," Riley said fiercely. "This is between you and *me*."

She met his searing gaze, surprised at the ferocity of his words. "All right."

He took the flyers from her and slid them in the back pocket of his Levi's. "I've tried getting you out of my head, but I can't. I have to have you."

Despite the delicious dip in her stomach, she struggled to keep her wits. "You're not asking me to be your mistress? I don't think you'd do that to Lorelai."

"No, I'm not asking you to be my mistress."

Relief and a deep stabbing regret hit her at the same time. "Then what?"

"I want you to be my wife."

A slap couldn't have surprised her more. "Wh-what?"

"You could take my money if you were my wife."

A buzzing sounded in her ears. "Take your money?"

"For Cora." His gaze burned into hers. "Marry me."

"For money? I won't."

"For Lorelai, and for you, too."

"Your offer is very sweet, Riley, but if I marry you, live with you, I won't need the money. Cora will, though. Would you still be willing to help?"

"Of course."

"We don't need to marry for you to do that." Even though she knew this wasn't a proposal out of love, she spoke gently.

"You're right, we don't need to marry for me to help Cora, so forget that. I still want to marry you."

Had he really thought this out? "I thought you believed I didn't belong here. Have you changed your mind?"

"No, but you're obviously not leaving."

"No, I'm not."

"If we're married, I can take care of you."

And that's what it was all about in his mind, she realized. Responsibility, not love. And wasn't responsibility the very reason she'd come to Texas in the first place?

"Susannah, this makes sense."

It did. And it didn't. "You told me you were never going to marry again."

"I love Lorelai like she's my own. I've been there since her first breath and I want to be there for every one that follows. I *will* be there. I pledge that to you."

"I do know you adore her, but what about me, Riley?" Susannah couldn't believe she was asking, but she wanted to have everything out in the open now. "Are you proposing just for the baby?"

She tried to keep her voice from shaking. She needed no proof he adored her child, but after last night, she had to know his full intention.

He studied her. "I know that's what you want."

Yes, she wanted a man who would love her child, who didn't care that Lorelai had been fathered by another.

But could Susannah marry Riley? It would be so easy to fall in love with him—she was afraid she already loved him—but how long would that last? She couldn't make the same mistake she'd made before, and she knew deep in her soul that if she really fell in love with Riley, she'd never recover from it.

The only other thing she knew was that Riley would be there for Lorelai.

"I'm not proposing just for the baby." His voice deepened and his gaze burned over every inch of her.

She shivered and tried to duck under his arm. "I want to know what's expected of me."

He planted his hands against the wall on either side of her, caging her. "I want you to be my wife in every way, Susannah. I want you in my bed. Surely you know any man you choose would want the same thing."

She hadn't let herself think about it, she realized, until the night Davis Lee had tried to kiss her. And Riley was right.

"Can this work, Riley? You won't change your mind about my being here. Don't you think that will cause problems?"

He answered thoughtfully, "I can see you've made a place for yourself. Your charm school and now your reading school show me that you're more resourceful than half the people who come here. That tells me you're determined to succeed."

"But you don't think I will?" Why couldn't she get past wanting his approval?

"I don't know, darlin', but I know you've got grit and that's what it takes to build a life here. I do know I want you. That's worth something."

The desire would fade, but maybe when it did, they would still have genuine liking for each other, and respect. A lot of marriages didn't have even that.

"You fancy me, too, or you couldn't kiss me the way you do."

"How long can that last?" she asked dryly.

"As long as we want it to."

"You're not naive. You know better."

He lowered his head and caught her lower lip between his teeth, tugging gently and causing a burst of sparks in her belly. "It could last a good long time."

She tried to turn her head away.

"It's pretty damn powerful. We can't ignore it, and I won't." He lifted one hand to gently stroke her throat, then trail it down to rest lightly against her breast. "I could've had you last night, Susannah, and you know it."

Her face flamed and she stiffened. "And if you had, would we be having this conversation?"

"I think so. I didn't lie when I said I wouldn't treat you the way LaFortune did. I love that baby. I have feelings for you. And the truth is I can't keep my hands off you."

He leaned down, his lips brushing her cheek, his chest nudging hers. He nuzzled her neck, her jaw, the corners of her lips.

Her legs trembled and she curled her fingers into the front

of his shirt. "But this is fleeting, don't you see? You've felt it before, and so have I."

He kissed her, deep and long and slow.

She slid her hands up to grip his shoulders so she wouldn't sag to the ground. She wanted his hands on her, his mouth, the way they'd been last night. He lifted his head, blue eyes blazing into hers.

"Are you telling me you've responded like that to every man in town who's kissed you?"

"No, I haven't."

"Not even my brother?" His eyes narrowed.

"No." She saw no reason to tell him that Davis Lee was the only one who'd tried to kiss her and the end result had been nowhere near the same.

Riley gripped her shoulders. "You're not in love with him. I'd know it now."

"No."

"You're sure?"

She wanted Riley to kiss her. "We decided we're only cut out to be friends."

"All right." He claimed her lips again, and after a long moment, pulled away. "You haven't said yes yet."

She knew the qualities she wanted in her baby's father, and Riley topped the list. So why did she hesitate? Staring into his eyes, she admitted it was because she feared she might fall in love with him. If he never returned her feelings, that might be the worst thing that could happen for her daughter. But he was a good man, the only man she really wanted as Lorelai's father. She certainly respected and liked him.

"All right," she said.

"Yes?" A light brightened his eyes.

She smiled. "Yes."

"I don't want to wait. I want to do this now. Okay?"

"Right now?"

"How about in three days? Is that too soon?"

"No, I can be ready."

"Good." His arms slid loosely around her waist. "This will work, Susannah. I'll be good for the baby."

"I know." She felt a little dizzy.

"I'll make it good for you, too." He lowered his head. "You can kiss me now. We're engaged."

A thrill raced through her. She inched up on tiptoe and kissed him. His arms tightened and she slipped her tongue inside his mouth. His hands cupped her bottom, sending a shock of sensation through her.

She melted against his hard length, giving herself over to the heat spreading through her like slow-running honey.

"See?" he murmured against her lips.

She nodded, thrusting her fingers into his hair as he took her mouth again.

"Hey, Holt, just what's going on back here?"

Matt Baldwin. Susannah opened her eyes, her dazed mind struggling to recognize his voice. The concern in his words.

"Goodbye, Matt. Susannah and I have business."

Matt peered at her over Riley's shoulder. "Miz Susannah?"

She stared into Riley's eyes, which were hungry and bold with promises. She was barely aware of her words. "'Bye, Matt," she said dreamily.

"All right, then." The big man disappeared around the corner, and Riley kissed her again.

When he lifted his head a long time later, he said, "It's a good thing you agreed to marry me."

"Why?"

"Because the story of how you were having your way with me back here is going to be all over town in about an hour."

"Oh, you." She tried to push him away and he hugged her tightly.

"There you go again," he said against her neck. "I'm just not safe from you, am I?"

She laughed, delighted when he joined in. Oh, she did like him. Very much. This was more than she'd hoped for when she'd left St. Louis six months ago. She just had to hope it was enough.

Riley walked Susannah back to Cora's, and after fifteen minutes of congratulations and hugs, he headed over to see his brother. He left the women discussing how to quickly alter the wedding dress Cora had offered to let Susannah wear.

Riley wanted to ask Davis Lee to stand up with him, and he owed him an apology. Susannah might be his now, but she hadn't been last night when his brother had trusted him to get her safely home and away from the men who would've forgotten all about propriety in the darkness. Just as he had.

Davis Lee heard the news of Riley's engagement with genuine joy, hugging him tightly. He quickly agreed to stand up with them in front of the magistrate in Abilene.

Riley pushed his hat back on his head. "I need to confess something."

"Already?"

"Not that." Riley hoped his brother took this news in such good humor. "Last night, you trusted me to take Susannah home, and I did, but I...kissed her."

Davis Lee stared at him long enough that Riley checked to make sure his brother hadn't doubled his fists.

"Good." Davis Lee slapped him on the back.

"Good?"

"You're one stubborn cuss, Riley Holt. It's about time."

His eyes narrowed as he tried to take in his brother's nonchalant acceptance. "Are you trying to make me think you wanted me to get with Susannah?"

"Yes."

"Oh, c'mon. What about those times you called on her? Am I supposed to believe you weren't really interested in settling down?"

"I wasn't."

"I'm sure Susannah will be flattered to learn that."

Davis Lee grinned. "She agreed that we can only be friends. A blind man could see you two tiptoeing around each other like horses in heat. You just needed a little push."

A suspicion suddenly popped into Riley's mind. "Cora, too?"

His brother laughed. "Cora, too."

"Humph, I don't know about this."

"Why not? You did the work. We just helped a little. You're marrying a beautiful woman."

"It's for the baby," Riley corrected. "I'm not disputing that Susannah is beautiful—"

"Or that you want her," his brother pointed out.

"Or that I want her, but my concern is for the baby. I think I'd be the best father."

"I'm glad for you."

"So you'll come to Abilene with us?"

"You bet." Davis Lee clapped him on the shoulder again. "I wouldn't miss it."

"Thank you." Riley left his brother's office and started for Cora's to get his horse.

Along with the contentment he felt about having things settled, there was also a heaviness inside him. A sense that he came just short of happiness, which was hardly fair to Susannah.

Maybe if she were different, or if he were, he could love her. But he could never suffer again the way he had when Maddie died. He had feelings for Susannah, but she didn't own his heart. No one ever would again.

Chapter Fifteen

$\infty\!\infty\!\infty\!\infty$

The three days before the wedding passed in a blur of preparations, most of the time spent altering Cora's wedding dress to fit Susannah. The hem had to be taken up quite a bit because the other woman was a good six inches taller than Susannah's five foot three. The bust fit well enough. After they nipped in the waist a couple of inches and tucked the full sleeves to lay closer to her arms, Susannah couldn't have asked for anything more perfect.

The first Saturday of April dawned with the sun occasionally peeking out from behind gray clouds, as if mirroring the same uncertainty she felt about her decision. The temperature was mild, and Cora thought the sun would burn off the clouds, saving them from rain. Susannah hoped so.

Cora hitched Prissy to the wagon and Susannah laid her carefully wrapped gown in the bed along with a valise packed with the things they would need for the overnight stay Riley had told them to plan on. He and Davis Lee rode up, helping her and Cora into the wagon before handing Susannah the baby.

It was midmorning before they got on the road, with

the men following on their horses. Even though Susannah would've felt comfortable driving, especially with Cora in the wagon, her thoughts darted in a hundred different directions and she knew her friend's concentration was better.

Riley planned to pay for rooms at the new Texas Crown Hotel so that everyone could enjoy the wedding and celebratory dinner without worrying about starting for home in the dark.

Cora insisted on staying in a room with Lorelai so that Riley and Susannah could have their wedding night alone, and he had readily agreed.

Abilene wasn't much bigger than Whirlwind at this point, but as a stop on the Texas and Pacific Railroad, it was buzzing with activity. As they rode through town, Riley pointed out flyers advertising the upcoming horse races, which took place every weekend beginning in April. He told Susannah that tomorrow people and horses would line both sides of the street. He hoped they could get a room at the new hotel.

Susannah noted the town already had a public school. According to her three traveling companions, Buffalo Gap had been designated the county seat of Taylor County back in 1878, but when the railroad pushed west in 1880, several of the area's ranchers and businessmen arranged to have it bypass Buffalo Gap and instead run through a new town they named Abilene.

After the railroad arrived in '81, several hundred folks arrived and organized a church along with their businesses. That same year, town lots were auctioned and Abilene established. The town's residents had voted in January to incorporate, and an election was scheduled in the fall for a vote to make the bustling town the new county seat.

Whirlwind seemed to have almost as many businesses as Abilene, but not the constant motion or the sense of anticipation that permeated the air, as if something big were about to happen.

Riley secured rooms for them at the Texas Crown, located on First and Cypress. The hotel was so new that the scent of fresh pine greeted them as they walked into the spacious lobby. The long, light green structure faced south to First Street, with a dining room downstairs and hotel rooms upstairs. Inside, a long gallery ran the length of the building's south wall.

After seeing everyone settled, he and Davis Lee left to find the magistrate and make arrangements. Riley kissed the baby and told Susannah he'd be back as soon as he had things worked out.

She couldn't help wishing he'd given her a little kiss or some reassurance that she was doing the right thing. Well, her uncertainty wasn't his fault, she told herself, trying to focus on the here and now.

Lorelai let out a cry and Susannah realized it was time for her afternoon feeding. Once the baby was satisfied, Susannah placed her on the bed and surrounded her with a soft wall of pillows. The baby's gaze followed her mother as she washed off the dust and grime from the ride before putting on her wedding dress with Cora's help.

The sun had finally pushed away the clouds and now shone brightly through the tall plate glass window of their room.

Her friend pulled her in front of a gleaming cheval mirror. "Oh, honey, you are beautiful. That dress never looked so good."

"Nonsense, Cora. I would love to have seen you on your wedding day."

The other woman hugged her tight. "Look at yourself."

Susannah did, her stomach churning nervously. The white satin had aged to a creamy eggshell and glowed warmly against her skin. The square, fitted bodice was cut just above her cleavage, with three-quarter-length sleeves. The full skirt made her waist seem small. Not as small as it had been before Lorelai, but nicely defined. Her eyes glowed bright blue.

She flattened a hand against her stomach, trying to stem the flutters there. It wasn't as if this were a real wedding, but she was nervous nonetheless. Had she done the right thing in accepting Riley's proposal? He was certainly the man she wanted to be her baby's father, but had she made that decision because of the desire she felt for him? Had her feelings clouded her judgment?

She'd always imagined this day would happen in St. Louis, surrounded by her family, attended by her mother. An ache pierced her heart and she dabbed at a tear in the corner of her eye.

"Missing your mama?" Cora asked quietly.

"Yes."

"I'm sorry she isn't here."

Susannah thought back to the stricken look on Ginny Phelps's face when she'd told her parents about their grandchild. "It's probably for the best, but I'm sorry, too." She summoned a smile. "Thank you, Cora, for being such a dear friend."

"I feel the same about you." The older woman stepped back and adjusted Susannah's sleeves. "You really are gorgeous, honey. Riley will be speechless."

"I hope not. At least until the vows are said," she said lightly.

A knock sounded. "You ladies ready?" Davis Lee called.

Cora hurried to the door, exchanging a few words with him before she returned to Susannah. "Let's fix your hair."

"Is everything okay?" She couldn't quite shrug off the anxiety tightening her shoulders. What if Riley had changed his mind? What if *she* couldn't go through with it at the last minute?

"Everything's fine. Riley spoke to the magistrate and he's coming here to perform the ceremony."

"Here? Oh, my." She took in her day dress tossed across the end of the bed, her valise open with her nightdress hanging out, as well as an extra chemise.

"Well, I meant the suite Riley reserved for y'all tonight. It has a sitting room, and Davis Lee said the ceremony would be held there. Won't that be nice?"

A sitting room? Riley had spared no expense. "Very."

Cora unpinned Susannah's chignon and brushed out her hair. Gathering the curls into a loose fall, she secured them with Susannah's pearl hair ornament high on the back of her head so that the heavy mass brushed her shoulders. "You look perfect."

Susannah's mouth was dry, her pulse thudding hard. This *was* the right thing, she told herself. She'd thought it out. She was following her head, not her heart. There was no better father for Lorelai.

Cora picked up the baby and opened the door. "You ready?"

Susannah felt as giddy and uncertain as she had the day she'd first arrived at Riley's ranch.

When she walked into the sitting room, richly appointed with tasteful beige settees and a burgundy floral rug, she couldn't stop a gasp of surprise. From the polished dark wooden floors to the delicate wrought-iron miniature chandelier overhead, the room was beautiful. The heavy brocade drapes at the window had been drawn, throwing candle-soft light through the room.

"Lordy, you're a vision."

She turned toward Davis Lee's voice, coming from a corner behind her. Riley stood beside him, his jaw slack, his gaze coveting her hungrily.

No man had ever looked at her the way he did. A blush heated her cheeks.

Davis Lee elbowed his brother. "Say something, you idiot."

Riley's gaze tracked over her and he shook his head, but the appreciation in his eyes was clear. She admired his broad shoulders covered by the dark cloth of his dress coat, the white shirt that made his bronze skin even darker. Dark trousers fit nicely, but couldn't disguise the massive thighs beneath, the power in his taut body.

She searched his rugged features for any of the uncertainty she felt, but saw only heat and possessiveness. That he was here and still willing sent relief rolling through her.

Davis Lee stepped over and took her hand, brushing a kiss atop her glove. "You're beautiful, Susannah. Maybe I should take Riley's place."

"Thank you." She smoothed her hands down the sleek skirt. "Cora loaned me her dress."

"It didn't look like that on me, I can tell ya." The older woman switched Lorelai to her other arm and adjusted the back of Susannah's skirt.

"Shall we get started, folks?" the magistrate said. "I don't mean to hurry through such a lovely occasion, but I've got to get to a dinner."

"Of course." Susannah slid a look at Riley, wishing he would say something.

He walked over to her, his eyes hot and gleaming like polished steel. "You ready?"

"Yes."

His gaze traced her features and a smile curved his lips. "So am I."

He took her hand and they walked the few steps to the center of the sitting room, to stand in front of the man who would marry them.

Cora took her place on Susannah's left and Davis Lee on Riley's right. The ceremony passed in a blur, with Riley's deep voice guiding her. He kissed her, slow and sure, to seal their vows, and she refused to allow any more doubts. It was done, for better or worse.

After congratulating them, the magistrate left. Davis Lee walked over to a heavy mahogany sideboard and opened a bottle of champagne, then offered a lovely toast. Susannah wished she could register a single one of his words, but her nerves were a jumble of anticipation and uncertainty.

With his arm around her, Riley led them all down for a sumptuous dinner in the hotel's grand dining room. Throughout the meal, Susannah often found his gaze on her, heated and blatantly sensual, which caused a jump in her emotions from hesitance to impatience. Soon, the meal ended.

"I'll say goodbye tonight." Back upstairs, Davis Lee halted outside Riley and Susannah's suite. "I'll be leaving first thing in the morning to get back home."

"Thank you so much for coming, Davis Lee," she murmured.

He kissed her cheek. "Welcome to the family, Susannah. I think you got the better brother."

She smiled at Riley, who shook his brother's hand. Davis Lee pressed a kiss to Lorelai's head, then to Cora's. "Good night, ladies."

Riley's hand curled on Susannah's waist and her nerves fluttered.

"I'll put the baby to bed," Cora offered. "She'll be fine tonight."

Susannah bent to kiss her daughter, her heart clenching when Riley did the same. "If you need me—" she began.

"We'll be fine." The older woman hugged her with her free arm. "And so will you," she whispered.

"Good night, Cora." Riley kissed the woman's cheek, then

told Susannah, "Go in with them if you want. I don't mind waiting."

She thought his offer kind, but wanted to walk into their room with him. The truth was she didn't know if she could go to him alone. It seemed brazen somehow, as if she were offering herself to him out of gratitude for loving her baby. "I'll let Cora put her down."

"Good night, then." Their friend disappeared into the room where Susannah had dressed earlier, leaving her with Riley in the hall.

His lazy half smile traveled through her with the punch of liquor, and a shiver raced up her arms. He opened their door and she started in.

"Hold on, darlin'. We have to do this right." He swept her up into his arms.

She gave a surprised laugh as he stepped across the threshold. He shut the door with his foot and slid her to the floor, her body skimming against his. Their stomachs touched; her breasts pressed to his chest, making her feel winded.

"You smell good," he murmured into her hair as his hands stroked her back.

Her smile was wobbly. His touch burned through the satin of her dress. She might not be pure, but she'd never experienced such a combination of anticipation and apprehension. With everything in her, she hoped Riley wasn't put off that he wasn't her first.

She glanced around the room where they had married. A kerosene lamp burned low on the polished wooden table next to the settee, casting a soft light through the room. A doorway to her right opened into the bedroom, and she slid a sideways look at Riley.

"If you're not ready—"

"I am." She held his gaze. "I want to be your wife. In every way."

A savage light flared in his eyes and he folded his hand into hers, leading her into the bedroom. The ornate headboard and thick mattress drew her eye to the center of the large room. The decor was tasteful, in a pale green and the same beige as the settee in the next room. Bright white sheets were turned down with the thick, pale green coverlet. Fat pillows were plumped at the bed's head.

In here, too, an oil lamp burned. The soft amber light dipped into the creases of the heavy drapes drawn at the tall window, puddled in a warm circle on the wooden floor. A chair sat in front of a large mirror and vanity. She caught a whiff of the light rosewater scent she'd worn today, the deep musk that was Riley. Her pulse throbbed.

"Do you like it?" he asked.

"I love it. You didn't have to do all this."

"I wanted to. It's not every day people get married." He tugged her to him, taking her lips in a dizzying kiss.

Her hands gripped his shoulders as a wildness stirred her blood.

"Mrs. Holt," he murmured against her lips.

"Mmm?" She opened her eyes, quivering at the raw need that drew his features taut.

"I want to see your hair down."

Mesmerized by the dark desire in his eyes, she lifted her hands to accommodate him, but he stopped her.

"Let me." He moved to stand behind her, strong and warm against her back. Delicious heat pooled low in her belly.

Gently, he removed her pearl ornament and her hair tumbled to the middle of her back. He gathered the curls in his hands and buried his face there. "You smell like sunshine and flowers. I've wanted to see you like this for a long time."

"You have?"

Sliding one knuckle along her jaw, he angled her face to his, taking her mouth in an open kiss that quickly edged her from languorous to excited. Still standing behind her, he caressed her breast through the satin of her dress, making her ache to feel his hands on her bare flesh.

She wanted to touch him, undress him, but wasn't sure what to do. She'd never mastered any skills at lovemaking, always following or waiting passively. Urgency burned inside her now and she didn't think she could wait with Riley.

"Do you like that?" His hand kneaded her through the satin, his thumb grazing her nipple.

"Yes, but—"

"Tell me."

Catching her bottom lip between her teeth, she placed her hand over his and moved it across her shoulder so that he pushed her sleeve down.

"You bet, darlin'. If I do anything you don't like, you let me know. Deal?"

"Yes."

"I want this to be good for you."

Her palms damp and itching to touch him, she nodded, wanting him to hurry and yet take his time.

"And if you like something, you can let me know, too." His voice deepened with the same desire simmering inside her.

Lowering his head, he nibbled kisses along her collarbone and down one bare shoulder. She arched her neck, rested her head on his shoulder. His hands busily pushed aside her other sleeve, causing her bodice to pull tight across her breasts and heighten the sensations tickling her nipples. He dipped one finger into the valley between her breasts and she pressed her legs together against the wetness starting there.

His hands moved down the back of her dress and he fumbled the buttons open, sliding the bodice completely off her arms. Her nipples, now peaked, strained at the transparent linen of her low-cut dress chemise.

She had to touch him, tried to turn so she could undo the

buttons on his crisp white shirt, feel the warmth of his skin next to hers.

He stopped her, his eyes blazing blue fire. "One second, darlin'."

"You don't want me to touch you?"

"Oh, yes, I do. But I'm being selfish right now. I want to get my hands on you first. I haven't forgotten how you looked that night," he said in a hoarse whisper, "and I want to see you again. This time with nothing between us."

She flushed, her body aching.

"You're wondrous, Susannah. Wondrous."

Could the awe in his voice be real? And really for her? He may have seen her in the altogether when he'd delivered the baby, but she still had inhibitions.

His hands slid around to rest under her breasts, setting off a hum in her blood that made her light-headed. "Okay?"

"Yes." Her breath lodged under her ribs, stoking the anticipation inside her.

He kissed her neck and she held him to her with one hand on his thigh, the other cupping his head. His hands, callused and tender, reached up and untied the satin ribbon holding her chemise together. The garment parted and he filled his hands with her breasts. Her own hands tightened on him and she drew in a sharp breath.

Watching his thumb graze her nipples had her going wet between her legs. She pressed into him, her hips lifting involuntarily to his arousal, throbbing hard against her bottom.

She couldn't take her gaze from his hands, playing with her, his bronze skin dark against the pale magnolia of hers.

"You're quite somethin', Mrs. Holt."

A restlessness she'd never known filled her. "I want you to kiss me."

"There?" His voice was deep and husky.

"Everywhere." She turned to him, looping her arms around his neck and meeting his kiss.

Even while he ravaged her mouth, he shoved her dress to the floor, then loosened the laces of her corset and pulled the restrictive undergarment from her. Her chemise followed.

Needing a breath, wanting to see all of him as he saw her, she drew back. His eyes burned into hers. Her hands went to the few buttons of his white shirt; he undid the cuffs, helping her pull the garment over his head.

He was magnificent. His broad chest, slightly less bronzed than his hands, rippled with muscle. Golden-brown hair whorled in the center of his chest, then arrowed into a thin line to disappear beneath the waistband of his trousers.

Amazed at the tempered strength in his chest, she touched him. His flat nipple tightened. He toed off his boots, peeled down her stockings and reached for the fastening of his trousers.

She stepped out of her shoes, reaching for his hand. "Let me?"

A muscle in his jaw flexed. He held her waist as she unhooked him and slid down the zipper, pushing down his clothing. His erection strained toward her and she lifted her gaze to his, asking a silent question.

He nodded, the veins on his neck corded. He stood completely still, his muscles quivering. She took him in her hand with a firm gentleness and stroked him, amazed at the steel velvet feel of him.

His eyes flashed and his hand moved between her legs, his finger sliding inside her silky heat. She gasped, her body going soft as she eased closer to him. She needed to touch him, feel him inside her.

With one arm curved around her waist, he lifted her and took her breast into his mouth. She drew in a sharp breath at the pleasure that pricked her like a silken needle. He suckled her, causing a deep-reaching tension inside her to wind tight.

"Susannah, darlin', if we don't move to the bed, I'm gonna fall down."

So was she. He carried her the short distance, laying her gently on the mattress and coming down on top of her. His hand worked her with achingly slow strokes. Pressure built low inside her and she felt the longing shift to need. Restraint quivered in Riley's body. Her hips rose against his, his flesh supple and warm against hers. Running her hands up his oak-hewn arms, she drew him closer, kissing his lips, his jaw.

Shadows played over their bodies. His eyes were blue-black, his features sharp with desire.

"Now?" she whispered.

He nudged her knees apart. "You tell me if I hurt you the slightest bit."

He didn't seem to care that he wasn't her first. Tears stung her eyes and she caught him to her, splaying her hands on his taut buttocks. "I want you."

His mouth took hers as he slid inside. The first thrust, full and stretching, was a shock, but she soon caught his rhythm and met him stroke for stroke.

Their gazes locked as their bodies did the same. She'd never experienced such intense physical pleasure, nor such a connection as she did with Riley. He reached deep into her soul, as if finally finishing some part of her.

The tight knot of pressure inside her strained, and just when she teetered on the edge of coming undone, he slowed, start-ing over with long deliberate strokes. He kissed her lips, her forehead, her eyes. His body moved inside hers, sharpening the pleasure until she thought she might scream. She pressed her mouth to his shoulder, her moans mingling with his.

He stiffened, lifting his head to stare into her eyes. He

matched his rhythm to the first quick ripples deep inside her. All thought crumbled and she existed only on sensation.

Silver flames licked at her from the inside out, splintering everything except Riley's soap and peppermint scent, the solid feel of muscle against her, the incredible wash of color that spilled over her.

He groaned her name and sagged into her, spent.

Her body pulsed with warmth and such raw sensations that her nerves seemed exposed.

He rolled to the side, gathering her close. "Happy wedding, Mrs. Holt."

She smiled and snuggled into him.

She'd been right to marry him, right to choose him for Lorelai. Since she'd arrived in Whirlwind, Riley was the only man she had wanted, the only one she ever would've let touch her this way.

And that's when she knew what she'd done. She'd fallen in love with him.

Chapter Sixteen

He woke to the feel of soft, naked woman against him. Sunshine peeked through an opening in the drapes, and the noise of people moving around outside slipped into his consciousness.

Susannah lay against him, spoon fashion, her arm over his own, which draped over her waist. She slept easily, one hand pillowing her head. The smell of their loving rose around him, and his erection grew rigid against her bottom.

Had it been like this with Maddie? If so, Riley didn't recall it. In fact, he couldn't recall being so caught up in a woman as he was in Susannah, wanting her as much after having her as he had before.

He cared for her and there was a quietness about their situation that he hadn't ever experienced.

Her curls fell in a seductive tangle over her shoulder. He buried his face in her neck, breathing in her sweet womanly scent as he slid a hand to her breast. He played with her, desire building in a pleasurable ache as her pale rose nipple beaded under his touch.

She stirred, moving her legs and pressing against his arousal. She ran a hand down his flank. "Mmm, morning."

"Morning." He turned her toward him, kissing her deeply as his hands covered her breasts.

She opened her legs to him and he slipped inside her, warm and snug. He locked his gaze on hers, wanting to see every reaction. Their lovemaking was slow, their movements deliberate. Her eyes grew sultry with need and she held him to her.

He went deeper, drawing out every stroke until she made little sounds in the back of her throat and convulsed around him.

He moved atop her and her inner muscles clenched him tightly until they both sagged into the mattress. She might not be a virgin, but he knew in his gut that she'd never been this way with any other man.

She scraped her nails lightly across his chest. "Oh, my, Mr. Holt."

He grinned, caressing her bottom. "Not a bad way to wake up."

"No." She smiled lazily, her eyes a misty blue, her lips curving in the smile of a woman who'd been well satisfied.

He slipped his hand between them, only to be interrupted by a knock on the door, then the demanding cry of the baby.

Susannah sighed. "I'd better go."

She slid out of bed and Riley folded his arms behind his head, enjoying the sight of her bare curves before she hid them beneath her cotton wrapper.

After she tended to the baby and they'd all dressed, he took everyone, including Cora, down to the dining room. Once they'd eaten, he carried Button and treated the ladies to a shopping excursion.

He couldn't take his eyes off his wife. Or stop thinking about being buried inside her. He liked how her eyes lit up when Cora said something funny, how her brow furrowed slightly when she studied a piece of fabric or the price on a tin of peaches.

He wanted to buy everyone a little something, but she insisted she didn't need anything. As he slowly sucked on a peppermint stick, he thought he might like to savor Susannah the same way.

When he finally convinced her to spend some of his money, she bought some lawn to make a couple of gowns for the baby and a length of calico for Cora. Riley saw her eyeing a sheer linen nightdress and had the store's owner wrap it up.

After they deposited their purchases at the hotel and Susannah fed and changed the baby, they walked up and down Main Street. Horses of all sizes and colors waited with their riders for the races to start. Cora had begged off for the afternoon, saying she'd developed a headache. Even though the older woman had offered to keep the baby, Riley and Susannah declined. Besides, he wanted Button with him and Susannah. The little darling was already asleep on his shoulder.

He and Susannah studied the horses, making predictions about the fastest ones. Seeing a dainty brown mare hitched in front of the livery, Susannah approached prudently but without fear, reaching out first to stroke the animal's neck as Riley had taught her. The mare turned her head, dark eyes measuring the woman at her side. The horse pressed her nose against Susannah's hand, looking for a treat.

Satisfaction swelled his chest. There was nothing the woman couldn't do. Despite the odds, and his skepticism when she'd arrived, she'd burrowed in and made a cozy little nest for herself in Whirlwind, just as she'd done in his life.

"It's almost time," he told her.

They started toward the other end of town, trying to squeeze in with all the others who wanted to be near the finish line.

"Have you seen the black mare this time?" Susannah

searched the crowd as Riley lightly clasped her elbow, making their way through the throng of people. "The one who beat everyone in the races last winter?"

"No, not hide nor hair. Maybe that mystery rider won enough money from everyone around here."

"Maybe so." She smiled, putting a kink in his gut.

He wanted to kiss her, but knew he wouldn't stop there. As they walked, he noticed he wasn't the only man taken with her. He glared at a cowboy who looked her up and down with obvious intent.

Riley found them a spot at the finish line and situated her in front of him so she could see and so he could keep any overly interested onlookers away from her.

A man at the opposite end of town shouted for the riders to take their marks. Horses pranced at the starting point.

Riley nudged Susannah, pointing to the far right of the starting line. "Look."

He shifted Lorelai to his other shoulder, drawing Susannah close.

She saw the black mare, its rider's face covered by a mask. "That's the mystery rider, isn't it?"

"Yes, I think so."

"This should be interesting."

He chuckled. "I don't think that's the way Banker Dobies sees it."

He watched the bony man, able to tell even at this distance that the banker was displeased.

"If you want to race Whip, we'll be fine," Susannah offered.

"Maybe the next one. If the banker loses, he'll enter again."

"And what if he wins?"

"He might stop the races altogether. Wouldn't want to push

his luck.'' Caught by the way the sun danced on her hair, the softness in her blue eyes, Riley stroked her cheek.

She tucked her arm through his, her breast full and warm against him, tempting him to take her back to the hotel and make love to her until dark. But he'd promised her a nice day out.

The man who'd called for the entrants to take their places raised his pistol and yelled, "Get set!"

Horses stomped, straining at their bits. Riders leaned forward in their saddles.

His gun cracked and the animals exploded into motion.

Lorelai jerked at the noise and Riley cradled her close, hushing her startled cries. Susannah turned, soothing the baby. Lorelai quieted, but kept her wide-eyed gaze trained on Riley.

He kissed her soft head, his own gaze going back to the race. The black mare pulled easily out in front and the banker's bay ran neck and neck with her.

Over the din of people yelling and cheering, Riley said to Susannah, "Today's races will be short ones, so people can enter their mounts more than once if they want. The longer distances are too tiring.''

She nodded, pressing tight to him, but watching avidly as the animals tore past. Dirt flew from their hooves and the scent of warm horseflesh rose in the air. Deafening cheers swelled. After three times up and down the street, they crossed the finish line only feet from Susannah. The stranger's black mare crossed the line first, a neck ahead of the banker.

"I can't believe how fast that horse is!'' Excitement glittered in Susannah's eyes. "I couldn't see anything except a blur of horse and one boot when he crossed the line.''

"I know.'' Riley squeezed her waist. "That mare's a hell of a runner.''

The mystery rider took every one of the five races that

afternoon. Banker Dobies face grew darker and darker, his eyes hard and angry.

Riley kept the tall, thin stranger in sight as the man collected his winnings. "He doesn't look spent at all, and that mare is hardly winded."

"She's a beautiful horse, isn't she?" Susannah exclaimed.

He smiled down at her, noticing that she was watching the winner closely, too. When he looked back, the stranger had disappeared into the crowd.

Susannah stretched up on tiptoe. "I can't see him now, can you?"

"No." He did see the banker, pushing his way through the crowd and obviously looking for the unidentified rider.

After a few minutes, Dobies worked his way back, stopping close to them. Frustration flushed his thin features. "Doesn't anyone know who that is?"

Several people shook their heads; others turned to walk away. The banker approached a stoop-shouldered man standing nearby. "Burl, don't you have to see these people when they enter? They pay you a fee, don't they? I sure paid mine in person."

"Ain't no rule that sez they have to pay it themselves, banker. Now that I recollect, I think a woman paid for him a time or two. I don't know her, though."

"Oh, hell." Dobies sighed. "I mean to find out who this sneaky rider is."

"I don't know if I'd want to know who was beatin' me all the time," a man called out.

Laughter rippled through the crowd.

The banker frowned. "Seems to me there's something wrong when a man won't show his face, win or lose."

"What could be wrong?" Riley asked. "Maybe he doesn't like crowds or feels that staying around would be boastful."

The other man stared flatly at him. "Well, I mean to learn

his identity. I'm establishing a new race, the Grand Turn. Two weeks from today. I'll put up a fifty-dollar pot. It'll be a mile and a half. We'll see who wins then."

"Fifty dollars?" Burl said. "You done lost yore mind!"

"Does anyone want to increase the pot?" Dobies asked.

Riley chuckled. "I'll put in five."

Susannah's fingers curled around his arm and he grinned at the excitement lighting her eyes.

A husky man who was as wide as he was tall stepped out of the crowd. "I'll put in five, too."

"Well, count me in." Another man who stepped forward owned one of the stores Riley and Susannah had visited earlier.

By the time the banker was satisfied, a total of seventy-five dollars made up the grand prize. Riley and Susannah, along with the others who'd tossed in prize money, walked over to the bank to contribute.

"I'll see y'all back here in two weeks." Dobies gave his clerk the cash and the man carefully placed the money in the vault. "Will y'all be entering?"

"Yessir," the big cowboy said. "I shore will."

Riley grinned, already anticipating the run. Watching that one would be as good as riding in it. "I'm not sure yet."

Since it was late afternoon, he and Susannah walked back to the hotel. Lorelai began to cry and Susannah took her, bouncing her gently in an effort to comfort her.

"She hungry?"

"Yes." She smiled up at Riley. "Thank you for a wonderful day. And all the things you bought."

"Glad to do it. You needed them."

"Well." She sent him a flirty look. "I don't really need that nightdress. Not with you around."

"No, you sure don't." Chuckling, he paused inside the hotel and kissed her. "You think Cora might feel up to supper?"

"I'll ask. I want to check on her, anyway."

Lorelai wailed angrily and Riley said, "Maybe I should check on her. Sounds like Button wants immediate attention."

"Thank you."

He opened the door of their suite and watched the gentle sway of Susannah's hips as she went inside. The lingering smell of roses drifted around him. He couldn't wait to get her naked and beneath him again.

Cora answered his knock looking flushed. Her hair was mussed, a state he'd never seen, and she wore her wrapper. Her head wasn't any better, she told him.

He offered to have some food sent up and she thanked him, saying she would enjoy that.

As he walked downstairs to check on Cora's supper, he decided to have a meal sent up for him and Susannah, too. That way, he could get her out of her clothes and keep her out of them. Just thinking about sinking into her tight velvet warmth made his body throb. Oh, yes, he had plans for his wife tonight.

After making the arrangements, he went back upstairs, anticipation building inside him. He opened the door to their suite and paused. Susannah sat on the settee, her bodice undone to feed the baby. Soft gold light from the nearby lamp caressed her breasts, as he had last night, and the sight of her with the baby sparked an unfamiliar warmth in his chest.

He thought back over the day—her ready smile, her ease in touching him. She'd been comfortable with the horses, all unfamiliar to her. He knew she couldn't have gotten near them six months ago. She'd met that challenge with everything in her, the same way she'd given herself to him last night.

She'd turned into a strong, determined woman who could do whatever she set her mind to, and she belonged to him.

The thought sliced like cold steel through his mind,

and he reflexively backed out of the room, silently closing the door.

Laying his head against the wall, he tried to breathe. This… whatever he felt right now…was too much. Was it for Susannah or the little girl who'd claimed his heart with her first cry of life?

Something was going on inside him. Something he didn't understand, and sure as hell didn't like. All he knew was he couldn't breathe.

After a delicious dinner in their room and being sated by her husband's amorous advances, Susannah lay in the darkness listening to Riley's even breathing. She loved him. At first the realization panicked Susannah, because she knew these feelings weren't temporary, as she'd tried to convince herself. After the shock faded, she admitted there was no escaping the truth.

In comparison to what she felt for Riley, she could see now that her feelings for Paul had been immature. She'd yearned to feel the giddiness of love, to believe she was special. Until she had Lorelai, she'd had no idea that true love was deep and so much broader. Unselfish, unconditional, forgiving.

That's how she knew what she felt for Riley was real. It broke her heart that he didn't feel the same, but he was a good man. They could make a good life together. She held out hope that he might someday come to love her.

They returned to Whirlwind after their two-day wedding trip, and Riley moved her things to his ranch. The house, built by his father for his mother, was a spacious two-story frame building with water piped in through some method related to the windmill. Riley explained that he'd put in the windmill just last year because his father, God rest him, had wanted every modern convenience for this house. Susannah loved having an indoor privy and ready water for washing.

Over the next two weeks, they settled in. Susannah's wire

to her brother about her marriage to Riley was met with an immediate reply from Adam that he was well pleased and hoped they would be very happy. But he said nothing about their parents.

She and Riley slept in his room and put the baby in his parents' old room across the hall. Susannah applied herself to being a good wife. Caring for the baby and cleaning the house came easily to her, but cooking gave her fits.

Riley, bless his heart, ate more than one burned meal without complaining. A few times she tried making Cora's biscuits, but had to throw them out after burning them. She didn't know how her friend ran her house with any energy left over.

Susannah fell into bed exhausted, still awake most nights when Riley took her in his arms and loved away all thought of the chores of the day. One night she was asleep before he joined her, and he woke her with his hands and lips.

Just as he kissed his way down her belly, the baby cried out from the corner of the room where Susannah had put her after her feeding.

"I'm sorry," she whispered, her hands pausing on his bare arms.

His eyes glittered in the pale moonlight coming through the window. "It's all right. You want me to check on her?" His voice was gritty from fatigue. He'd left at daybreak this morning to ride fence in the south pasture.

"No, I'll get her." Susannah scooted out of bed and pulled on her wrapper, then bent to pick up the baby from her pallet.

Lorelai lay on her back, kicking her legs and crying angrily. Susannah picked her up, putting the baby to her breast before she realized that she had laid her daughter on her stomach, not her back.

"Riley, Lorelai rolled over! All by herself." Susannah laughed, looking toward the bed. He was sound asleep.

She considered waking him, but he was putting in long days on the ranch, so much so that Susannah saw him only for supper before he went out to care for the milk cows and the horses that stayed in the barn near the house.

"We'll let him sleep," she whispered to the baby, who grabbed one of her own feet, her little mouth working greedily.

When Susannah told him the next morning what he'd missed, he looked disappointed. That evening, he returned to the house before sundown, saying he wanted to spend some time with Button.

Watching them, Susannah smiled, touched in spite of the ache deep inside her as she wished for more time with him herself. They rarely talked about anything except the baby or the ranch. He satisfied her physically in every way she could imagine, but emotionally he'd pulled away. She'd felt it since their return home, but didn't know what to do, if anything. What could she say? "You're a wonderful lover, but I want more"?

Would pressuring him cause him to love her or push him further away? Would he ever feel about her the way she felt about him?

After he put Lorelai to bed across the hall, he came to Susannah, loving the doubts right out of her. And the next day, when he returned at noon and asked if she'd like to have a riding lesson, she accepted with new hope.

He cared for her and loved her baby. She could be patient.

As they walked to the barn, he carried the cradle and gently put Lorelai in it just inside the big double doors, so he or Susannah could hear her if she woke.

He saddled a dapple gray mare named Ghost and led her into the corral for Susannah. Nerves fluttered in her stomach, but they could've been caused by the rugged man in front of her as much as by the thought of getting on the horse.

He brought her to the left side of the horse to mount. "You'll learn to ride straddle."

"But I'm in a dress."

"We're the only ones here. Besides, I don't have a side-saddle."

She felt daring and a little silly, but when he boosted her into the saddle, she swung her right leg over the side.

"Good. Take the reins in your left hand and hold them loosely." His hand sneaked under her skirts to slide up her calf to her thigh.

She clutched at the saddle horn, gasping at his audacity and the jolt of heat his touch generated. "Are you trying to make me fall off?"

"I can honestly say I wasn't thinking that at all."

"You're a bad man." She shook a finger at him. "Focus on my lesson."

His hand moved higher on her leg, drifted inside her thigh. "Maybe I want to teach you something beside horseback riding."

"Maybe you should finish this lesson so you can," she said sweetly, pressing her leg tight against the saddle to prohibit him from reaching farther.

"Hmm, I think I'll just drag you off there right now."

His hands curved on her waist and he lifted her out of the saddle, swinging her into his arms and striding into the barn.

"Riley Holt!" She looped her arms around his neck. "What are you doing?"

"I have need of my wife," he growled.

"It's the middle of the day."

"Close your eyes." He grinned wickedly, taking her to

a dark corner of the barn and setting her down, his hands already working the buttons on her shirtwaist.

She blinked in the murky light, seeing that her daughter still slept in her cradle. "What about the baby?"

"You'll have to be real quiet. Think you can?"

"Try me," she challenged, unfastening his trousers while pressing kisses to his jaw.

Sunlight danced through the door of the barn, and Riley's warm scent blocked out those of dirt, hay and animals. The cradle was in plain sight over his shoulder; a stall door supported Susannah's back as he spread her bodice and pulled the tie on her chemise. Thank goodness she wasn't wearing a corset today.

His hands covered her breasts as his mouth took hers. She gave herself up to the sensations rolling over her like a hot wind, stinging and begging to be soothed.

His mouth moved to her breasts as he slid a hand up her skirts and between her legs, through the opening of her drawers. He cupped her. She was already wet, and the tightness low in her belly had her lifting her hips to his, pushing his trousers down and guiding him to her.

When he entered her in one long stroke, she cried out. Eyes laughing, he quickly covered her mouth with his.

He gripped her hips, pumping into her hard and fast. Her hand closed over the top of the stall door at her back. Susannah felt every inch of him deeper than she ever had.

They moved in perfect rhythm and she couldn't tell where his body separated from hers. He bent his head, his lips toying with her nipple. She swallowed a moan, the attempt to stay quiet sharpening the velvet-rough feel of his tongue on her tender flesh.

His eyes burned into her, reaching deep into her soul, possessing, claiming. He sent her tumbling over the edge before she knew what was happening.

. She clutched at him, wanting him with her as she slid into oblivion. His eyes darkened and she saw him lose control. Her heart was completely conquered.

They shuddered together, and after long minutes, the sound of their ragged breathing slowed. Riley held her close, his head bowed on her shoulder.

She slid her arms around him and he stiffened. If they hadn't still been connected, she wouldn't have felt the small movement at all. Hurt slashed through her and she stared into his eyes, trying to read past the sated desire.

"Hello!"

"Davis Lee!" Recognizing the faint male voice, she shoved at her skirts.

"Shh." Riley withdrew, adjusting his trousers, then helping to button her bodice.

"He's going to find us."

"No, he won't. He'll go in the house first."

Skin still tingling from their lovemaking, she finished her buttons, slapping at Riley's hand when he cupped her breast. "Stop that."

He laughed and dropped a kiss on her nose. "We're married. It's all right."

"Not if your brother sees us," she whispered frantically.

"Riley? Susannah?" Davis Lee's voice sounded just outside the barn.

Riley started toward the open doorway.

"Your shirt," she reminded him quietly, feeling again the way he'd shrunk from her touch.

Was his body all she would ever have of him? He owned her heart and she couldn't seem to steal even a piece of his. She'd known when she accepted his proposal that he didn't love her. But still she hoped.

Chapter Seventeen

Susannah didn't know what to make of Riley flinching away from her when they'd made love in the barn. During the next two days, he didn't react that way at all. He didn't seem repulsed by her, and even sought her out. She tried not to let the incident torture her, and when she watched him with Lorelai, the pain dulled.

They still planned to attend Banker Dobies's big race in Abilene. On Saturday morning, Riley hitched Pru to the wagon and handed Lorelai up to Susannah. He tied Whip to the back, still not sure if he would race in the newly established Grand Turn, but wanting to be ready in case he decided to compete.

The race wasn't scheduled to start until one o'clock, and they left in plenty of time for a leisurely drive, arriving in Abilene around eleven. Riley suggested they have lunch at the Texas Crown, and Susannah agreed. She scanned the crowd of people moving along First Street as they entered town. Cora had arrived in Abilene yesterday, for a meeting with Banker Dobies today.

Susannah hadn't liked hearing that. Cora's last meeting

with the man had been less than a month ago, when he'd decided to raise her mortgage payments.

Riley drove up Cypress Street to Second and left their wagon outside Fulwiler's Livery Stable, since his barn was already full. They walked south to First and had lunch at the hotel. After their meal, Susannah took the baby out to the boardwalk while Riley spoke to the proprietor inside.

He came out, settling his hat on his head and taking the baby from her. "Mr. Brant just told me that Banker Dobies arranged it so that the entry fees have to be paid at the bank."

"Why would he do that?" The impressive, two-story stone building housing Taylor County Bank was over a couple of blocks, at Second and Pine. "Weren't the entry fees paid at one of the general stores last time?"

"Yeah, but this way, the banker can keep an eye on who enters. He's determined to learn the identity of this mystery rider."

"The man may not even show up."

"He probably will," Riley said lightly. "Seventy-five dollars is an awful lot of money. Didn't you say Cora had a meeting at the bank? We have time to find her before the race, if you want."

"Yes, let's."

They walked to Pine and found the bank, its wide steps flanked by wrought-iron rails. The race would start and finish at Pine and First, the course heading west on First out of town and circling back, to constitute a mile and a half.

"Oh, there's Cora." Susannah tugged at Riley's arm, pointing ahead, where their friend approached the bank from the opposite end of Pine Street. "Cora! Hello!"

The older woman saw them and waved, crossing Second to meet them in front of the bank building. "Good day."

She hugged them both, giving the baby a peck on the forehead.

"I'm glad you made it all right." Riley drew the light blanket up to shield Lorelai's face from the sun.

"Yes, no problems." Cora glanced back at the bank. "I hope I don't have any problems with the banker, either."

"Want me to go with you?" Riley asked.

"Oh, hon, thank you, but there's no need." She patted his arm.

"We'll see you at the race, won't we?" Susannah asked.

"I think I'll be finished in time."

"I'd bet on it," Riley said. "There's no way the banker will miss this race. He thinks he's going to win."

"What do y'all think?"

"That he's going to get his pants beat off," Susannah said smartly.

Riley and Cora laughed.

"There sure are a lot of people entering this race," the older woman said. "Well, I'd better go. Can't be late for my meeting."

"You don't think he's going to raise your payments again, do you?" Susannah worried that her friend wouldn't be able to afford much more.

Cora sighed. "I don't know, but don't you worry about it. Things will work out."

"We'll save a place for you." She turned to Riley. "We'd better go or we won't find a good spot to watch the race. Are you sure you don't want to enter?"

"I'd rather watch with you and Button."

Cora lifted her skirts and started for the bank. Susannah waved, noticing as she turned away that the shoes peeking out from under Cora's dress weren't her usual brown everyday shoes, but black boots.

She and Riley made their way down the street, stopping

at few shops as they went. They passed a dry goods store, a saddle shop and as many doctor's and lawyer's offices as one would see in St. Louis. A half hour later, they squeezed as close to the finish line on the east side of Pine as they could. Lorelai lifted her head from Riley's shoulder, watching the people around her with wide eyes.

Susannah smiled at the two of them. Riley might not love her, but he loved her daughter as much as she did.

More people crowded in, packing Susannah tight against him. The sounds of voices, clattering boots and running children swelled around them. The smell of unwashed bodies was strong in the air and she wrinkled her nose.

After several minutes, she pushed up on tiptoe, looking for the mystery rider. The banker was in the forefront of the group of milling riders and horses. "I don't see the masked rider or the black mare."

"I don't, either."

"But Banker Dobies is there, so his meeting with Cora must be over."

Riley looked around. "I don't see her yet."

Susannah glanced back at the bank, identifying the white shirt and black armband of the man in the doorway as belonging to the clerk. Where was Cora? She hadn't said she had other business.

Susannah searched her memory, her thoughts stalling on the moment when she'd seen Cora heading for the bank. She'd worn boots. Not her shoes, but a man's boots. *Ollie's boots.*

Susannah remembered seeing them now, in the box of his things that Cora had moved to the barn.

And not just there! The race two weeks ago flashed through Susannah's head. Those boots were nearly identical to the ones she'd seen on the mystery rider. No!

She recalled the times she'd seen the tall, thin rider. Who

was close to Cora's height. Cora's build. It made perfect sense. The mystery rider had to be her friend.

But what horse did she ride in the races? Why was Banker Dobies here and not Cora?

Crammed together as they were, Susannah squeezed around to face Riley. "Cora still isn't here."

He looked over the heads in the crowd, glanced back toward the bank. "I hope she doesn't miss it."

Susannah tugged him down to her and said in a low voice, "I think Cora is the mystery rider."

Amusement twinkled in his eyes. "What?"

She explained about Cora's boots and how she thought they were the same boots the mystery rider had worn two weeks ago.

He looked skeptical. "Are you sure?"

"I think so."

Realization flashed across his features. "She needs the money for her higher mortgage payments."

"Yes."

"Well, if you're right, she's probably headed over here right now —wait, what the hell horse is she using?"

"I don't know, but the race starts in less than ten minutes. I don't think she'd be this late. Especially since it's obvious her meeting is over."

"You think something's happened?"

Susannah didn't want to believe it. "I think we should try to find her."

"Yes." He took her elbow. "Okay, where do you think we should start?"

"Let's try the bank, just to be sure. We know she was going there."

As they threaded their way through the crowd, he said, "If she is the masked rider, maybe she changed her mind about racing."

"I don't think so. She needs the money too badly. Besides, if she did decide not to race, she certainly would've found us."

"True."

Finally breaking free of the swarm of bodies, they hurried across the street and up to the bank. Once inside, Susannah asked the clerk if he remembered Cora. He did, and had seen her when she arrived for a meeting with the banker.

"Do you know what time they finished?" she asked.

"Probably twenty minutes ago. Mr. Dobies has been gone about fifteen minutes, I guess."

"Did Cora leave when he did?" Riley asked.

The man thought for a moment, then said slowly, "I must've been busy. I don't recall seeing her leave."

"So you didn't happen to see which way she went?" Alarm curled through Susannah.

"No."

"Did you see her talking to anyone else when she was here?"

"No, I'm sorry." He looked from her to Riley. "Is everything all right?"

"I hope so." Susannah smiled, but her concern grew. "If she happens to come back, would you please tell her we're looking for her?"

"Yes."

Anxiety knotted her stomach as she and Riley stepped outside. "Now what should we do?"

"Let's go to the livery. If she *is* the mystery rider, she'll need her horse, and that's probably where it is."

Susannah agreed and they hurried across Second and west to Fulwiler's on the corner.

As they approached the large barn, Riley called out, "Hullo! Is anyone there?"

No answer.

"Everyone's probably at the race," he mused.

Only three horses, a dun gelding, a sorrel and a black mare, occupied the stable.

"That's the mystery rider's horse." Susannah moved toward the midnight-black horse with no markings.

Riley followed. "Wouldn't we know if this was Cora's horse? I think you must be mistaken, Susannah."

"Something is going on. I really think she's the mystery rider."

As Riley had taught her, she approached the black mare, speaking in a low, soothing voice so as not to spook the animal. The mare swung her head around, then lowered her muzzle and nudged Susannah's chest.

"Oh."

"She acts like she knows you." He moved up beside her.

"How can that be…" Susannah stepped back, studying the animal. "No! Is this Prissy?"

The horse snuffled softly and nibbled at Susannah's sleeve, begging for a scratch.

Riley ran a hand along the mare's side and down one flank. He turned her head from side to side, eyes narrowed. "I'll be."

"What?" Susannah was about to jump out of her skin.

"Look." He ran his thumb across the flat spot between the horse's eyes, then held his hand up. They both peered closely at the inky smudge on his skin. "What is that?"

She eyed the horse's forehead, now sporting a pale gray spot where before there had been only black. Some black substance covered Prissy's white star.

Susannah sniffed and drew back, amused. "It's hair pomade."

"What?" Riley smelled his fingers, then rubbed them together, looking at the dark ointment. "And coal dust." He started laughing. "That woman beats all. She's been winning all these races with Prissy."

"And they've both been disguised." Susannah enjoyed the fact that Cora had fooled everyone, plus bested the best horsemen in three counties. But where was she? Why hadn't anyone seen her since she'd left the bank? If Cora was missing and Prissy was here, then something had happened to her friend.

Susannah knew how desperately she needed the prize money. "Riley, there's no way Cora can fetch Prissy and get to the race in time."

"No, I suppose not."

"You'll have to do it."

He swung toward her. "Me? What are you talking about?"

"Cora's been entering these races to get extra money to pay her mortgage."

"I can't ride for her. Everyone will know who I am."

Susannah sighed, catching sight of a dirty bandanna hanging over the stall next to Prissy's. She jerked it down, holding it up to him. "Not if you disguise yourself the way Cora has been."

He shot a look at the bandanna. "This is crazy, Susannah."

"She needs this money or she might lose her farm. She gave Lorelai and me a home when we had none. She's been good to you, too."

"If something has happened, we need to find her."

Susannah hesitated, knowing he was right. Surely the banker wouldn't have done anything dire to their friend. "If the clerk didn't see her leave the bank, maybe she didn't."

"We didn't see her there. She wouldn't be hiding."

"Maybe not by choice."

Riley frowned.

"The race will start soon," Susannah murmured. "I'll go back to the bank and ask around. Look around. Maybe someone else knows something. You can meet me there after the race is over."

"Do you think she paid to enter?"

"I can't be sure, but I think she would. She could've done it before or after her meeting with Dobies. That kind of money could really help her."

"I don't like this."

"We're running out of time, Riley. If you don't race for Cora, she could lose the house."

He searched her eyes, then groaned. "All right."

Susannah took the baby, checking Prissy's bit and looping the bridle over her head while Riley tied on the bandanna so that it covered his nose, mouth and chin.

He pulled his hat low on his head and quickly saddled Prissy with the saddle hanging over her stall door. "If you don't learn anything new at the bank," he said in a muffled voice, "stay there until I arrive. We'll look together."

"All right." She walked with him outside, squeezing his hand before he mounted up. "You've got to win, Riley. Cora needs that money."

"I'll do my best, darlin'."

She checked the watch pinned to her bodice. "Hurry. The race will be starting in three minutes."

He urged Prissy into a canter down Second, turned the corner at Pine, and Susannah lost sight of him.

Mentally crossing her fingers that she could find Cora quickly, Susannah cradled Lorelai close and rushed to the bank. Riley had to win. He just had to. And she had to find her friend.

The clerk stood on the bank's landing, eyes trained on the riders taking their places down the block.

"Hello," she said pleasantly. "Banker Dobies left his pocket watch on his desk and asked me to come retrieve it."

The man frowned. "I thought he had it when he left."

"Oh, so did he," she said breezily, hoping the clerk would just let her into the banker's office. She'd used the first excuse that came to her mind.

He stepped back so she could precede him inside. "His door is open, but I'll have to go with you."

"All right." She followed him into a small, but nicely appointed office.

As soon as they walked in, Susannah went to the well-oiled wooden desk, pretending to search. "I don't see it on top here."

A noise sounded to her right, then a muffled thump. She turned. "What was that?"

She peeped into the small alcove behind the banker's desk, noticed a door in the wall to the right.

"I don't see his watch," the clerk said. "He must have taken it with him. He forgets things sometimes."

The noise sounded again, definitely coming from behind the door in the wall, and Susannah moved across the pine floor. "Is that a closet?"

"Yes, but—"

"Cora?" Susannah called. "Cora?"

The thumping grew louder and Susannah jerked open the door. Her friend lay facedown on the floor. "Cora!"

The clerk gasped and knelt to help the older woman.

She was hog-tied, helpless to move her hands or her feet, and a gag was stuffed in her mouth. Anger fired her eyes as the man fumbled with the rope around her wrists and ankles.

Once free, she allowed him to help her to her feet.

"Where is that skunk?" She stomped out of the closet, turning in a circle.

Susannah reached for Cora's hand, looking at her scraped wrist. "Are you okay?"

"Just madder than a wet hen. When I get my hands on that banker, I'm gonna light him up."

"Madam, I am so sorry," the clerk said. "There must be some mistake. Mr. Dobies would never—"

"No mistake on my part, son, or yours."

"Cora, the race has already started."

Tears sprang to the woman's eyes. "Oh, no! Maybe I can still make it. The banker wants two months' worth of payments by tomorrow. I'll explain everything later."

Susannah took her arm, jiggling Lorelai to try and stop her fussing. "I know what's going on, Cora. Riley and I both do. Let's go. We can talk on the way over."

"Madam, is there anything I can do for you?" the clerk offered, worry clouding his face.

"No, but thank you," Cora said.

As they hurried down the street and turned onto Pine, Susannah said, "Please tell me you paid your entry fee."

"Yes."

"Good." She explained how she'd noticed Cora wearing Ollie's boots and how she'd seen them on the mystery rider.

Cora flushed. "I didn't want to lie to you, honey. The idea to run those races just came to me one day, so I did it."

"It's all right. What matters now is that Riley wins."

"Riley?" Cora spun toward her.

"He's riding for you. In disguise." Susannah told her everything as they elbowed their way through the crowd standing near the finish line.

In a few minutes, a murmur started through the crowd, then grew in intensity. People cheered on their favorites. Susannah heard "mystery rider" and "masked rider" more than once. She and Cora leaned forward.

"Here they come." Cora gripped her hand.

"He'll win," Susannah said. "He has to."

The horses raced into view. Riley, still wearing the bandanna, was in the lead. No, the banker was!

The two women held hands, their grips tightening as the horses thundered toward them. Susannah silently urged Riley on, and Prissy pulled even with the banker's bay.

"C'mon, Priss. You can do it." Cora's grip nearly crushed Susannah's hand.

With only feet to spare, Prissy pulled ahead. She and Riley crossed the finish line a full second ahead of the banker.

"Yahoo!" Cora gave a little hop, startling the baby.

Lorelai started crying, but her wails were hardly audible over the raucous cheers of the crowd.

Susannah watched as Riley slowed Prissy to a walk.

The banker wheeled around and pointed toward them. "The rules clearly state no woman shall enter, and that entrant is a woman. It's a forfeit."

"I didn't read that rule." Cora took a step forward.

Susannah put a hand on her arm, nodding toward Riley. "Wait."

He guided Prissy back to the finish line, the mare dancing in place several feet from the banker.

"Unmask yourself, madam, and stop this charade."

Riley removed his hat with one hand, the bandanna with the other.

The banker gaped. "You!"

Laughter rippled through the crowd.

"I don't much appreciate being called a woman, Banker Dobies."

"It's Holt," someone called out.

"That ain't no woman, Dobies. Or has it been that long for you?" another man hollered.

The banker sputtered. "Wh-what is going on? I know you're not the rider who's been winning these races."

"How do you know that?" Riley dismounted, walking slowly up to grip the banker's bridle.

"I saw who paid that entry fee, and it wasn't you."

"And just what happened to the person who did pay it?" Riley's voice dropped dangerously low.

"Why, here I am." Cora stepped out into the street.

The banker blanched, and Susannah thought he might fall right off his horse. She grinned, bouncing Lorelai, who watched everything with wide eyes.

Cora's gaze swept the crowd. "It's a wonder I made it to this race at all, seeing as how your banker tied me up and locked me in a closet."

"He what?!" Shocked outrage spread through the crowd.

A stocky, serious looking man wearing the circled-star badge of a marshal stepped forward, looking from Cora to the banker. "Is this right, Dobies?"

"She's a woman, Marshal Green. Women can't enter."

"You don't lock them in closets, that's for darn sure." The lawman turned to Cora. "Ma'am, would you like to press charges?"

"I'd like to remove his family jewels," she said hotly.

The crowd roared with laughter. Riley came over to join Susannah, who blushed scarlet, though she smiled broadly.

"But I'll settle for not pressing charges *if* the banker stops pestering me to pay off my mortgage early."

"He's been doing that to me, too." A slight, stooped woman with silver hair stepped up, her voice crackly with age.

"Me, too." An elderly gentleman raised his hand.

"And I want my payments to go back down to where they were when my husband was alive," Cora said.

"What do you say, Dobies?" The marshal tapped the butt of the six-shooter slung low around his waist.

The banker looked from Cora to Riley. Susannah couldn't see her husband's face, but she knew the banker got a silent message because his face paled. Sweat stood out on his upper lip.

Marshal Green smiled at Cora. "Ma'am, I guarantee you the banker will do exactly what you want." He pushed Dobies toward her. "Tell the lady you'll do it, Mr. Dobies."

"Yes, I'll do it." He glanced at Riley. "I swear."

A few hours later, Susannah and the others rocked along in the wagon toward home. Whip and Prissy were both tied to the wagon bed. A south wind blew a pleasant breeze across the prairie. Cora and Lorelai slept in the back. After today's excitement, Susannah was tired, too. Staring into the setting sun made spots dance in front of her eyes, and she tugged the brim of her bonnet a little lower.

Riley squinted into the bright light, his shoulder brushing hers as he worked the reins. He glanced at her. "I'm glad Cora got her money."

"So am I. Thank you so much." Susannah pressed a kiss to his jaw.

"That Prissy is something else. I never knew." He glanced over his shoulder at the mare walking peacefully beside Whip. "Davis Lee is gonna be sorry he missed this race."

"Yes." Susannah smiled, letting her head rest on his shoulder as they reached a smooth patch of trail. Thank goodness things had worked out. Cora was no longer in danger of losing her house, and had a little extra money in hand.

"You sure amazed me, Mrs. Holt," Riley said against her hair.

"I did?" She sat up, smiling into his blue eyes.

"I'm impressed with the way you figured out Cora was the mystery rider."

"All I did was notice her boots."

"It's more than I did."

Pleasure warmed her. "I guess so."

"Yessir, I do admire the way your mind works."

"Really?"

"Well, that's not all." His voice dropped suggestively, as did his gaze.

She laughed softly, her body waking to that anticipation he always sparked in her. "That's not all I admire about you, either."

"Well, I'll be." He pulled Pru to a stop and gathered Susannah in his arms, kissing her long and deeply.

She curved her arms around his shoulders, sinking into the kiss.

He lifted his head and started the wagon again, keeping her close with one arm around her waist. She snuggled against him, content in the moment and refusing to think further ahead.

They stopped at Cora's, where Riley unsaddled and groomed Prissy before turning her out to pasture. Susannah insisted Cora go to bed while she gathered the eggs, then fed the baby. It was well after dark when she and Riley started their last three miles home.

As the wagon passed under the Rocking H sign, Riley reined up suddenly.

Susannah bounced into him at the abrupt motion, holding Lorelai tight in an effort to keep her from being jostled too badly. "What is it?"

"It's me." Davis Lee rode out of the shadows, tipping his hat. "Sorry if I startled you."

"No, we're fine."

"You waitin' on us?" Riley asked, moonlight sliding over his hands, which held the reins loosely between his knees. "You shoulda seen that race today—"

"Something's happened." Davis Lee's voice was curt.

Susannah could make out his features now, strained and sharp in the dim light. "Davis Lee?"

"Don't mean to alarm you, Susannah, but it's serious. The McDougals hit again, this time in Mobeetie."

"Where's that?"

"A cow town north of us." Riley braked the wagon, leaning forward. "Up in the Panhandle. What did they do?"

"Shot up the whole town, killed three bystanders."

"Oh, no!" Susannah covered her mouth in horror.

"Two of them were a husband and wife. I'm putting together a posse. After their last trip through this area, I don't want them anywhere near Whirlwind."

Susannah knew Davis Lee referred to when the McDougals had killed Cora's husband, Ollie.

"We're heading out tonight," he continued. "I know you just returned, but I wanted to let you know."

"Count me in," Riley said. "I need to take Susannah to the house and get a fresh horse."

"Good. I can use every man available. Jake Ross is staying in town as sheriff until I return. All of the Baldwins are waiting for us at Catclaw Creek."

Susannah tried not to panic, but she'd never seen that deadly light in her husband's eyes. Or his brother's. At the house, Riley helped her down from the wagon and walked her inside, kissing the baby gently on the head.

He took Susannah in his arms. "I don't know how long we'll be, but I'll try to wire you if I can."

"Thank you. Please be careful." She blinked against a sting of tears. She wouldn't cling and beg him not to go, though she felt like doing just that.

He cupped her shoulders, his eyes dark and serious. "We don't know where the gang is or where we'll catch up to them. Don't travel alone, all right?"

She nodded. "We'll be fine."

Once Cora heard about what had happened, she knew the

older woman would somehow manage to get out here and check on them.

Riley took Susannah's face in his hands and kissed her softly, savoring her as if he were etching the feel of her on his lips.

He started out the door, then spun and kissed her again, this time hard and desperately. They were both breathless when he walked out. She moved to the door, watching as his shadowy form mounted a fresh horse. Then he and his brother galloped off into the night, the sound of pounding hooves finally fading.

The baby started to cry, as if she sensed danger and her mother's own uncertainty. Susannah cuddled her close, wishing she'd told Riley she loved him.

Chapter Eighteen

Riley had been gone four long days. Everything was fine at the ranch, but Susannah was jumpy and easily distracted. She wondered how women survived the waiting when their men went off to war, especially before the invention of the telegraph. Two days ago, Cora had come out with Jake Ross to check on her and the baby. Jake didn't have any news yet; he'd accompanied Cora as a precaution.

Susannah kept her hands occupied, but her mind worried over Riley. Had the posse found the McDougal gang? Was Riley unharmed?

She determined to make a batch of good biscuits to welcome him home, some he would truly love and not just choke down so as not to hurt her feelings. She resolutely kept a positive frame of mind, though the nights were hard. Alone in their bed, surrounded by his familiar scent, she missed his touch, his warmth. Her heart missed him.

The big bed seemed even bigger without him, but she felt closer to him there. And that strength, garnered in the dark of night, helped her get through the days of uncertainty.

On the afternoon of the fourth day after he and Davis Lee

had ridden out, she received a telegram. Tony Santos drove out personally to deliver it, and she thanked him profusely.

Riley had sent the wire from Mineral Wells, a small town about fifty-five miles northeast of Abilene. His message said only that he expected to be home tomorrow. They must've caught the McDougals, and were bringing them back to Davis Lee's jail.

Susannah wanted to make Riley's homecoming special. The next day, right after noon, she hitched Pru to the wagon and drove Lorelai into town to stay overnight with Cora. She and Riley hadn't had a night all to themselves since the wedding; surely he'd like that. He would be exhausted, and Susannah could focus her entire attention on him for one night.

Pru handled well on the trip and Susannah managed driving with what she considered a fair competence, thankful for the gloves Riley had given her at Christmas. Someday handling the wagon might come as naturally to her as it did to him, she thought with a smile as she spied the squat mesquite tree signaling the last mile before home.

Home. Looking out over the vast prairie, the short grass rippling in the wind, she realized she had made a place here for herself and for her child. Marriage to Riley completed that, but even if she'd remained alone, Whirlwind would always be as much a part of her as St. Louis.

She'd done things here that the city girl she'd been would never have done. Slowly, pride began to fill her with a confidence that had been sorely lacking when she arrived six months ago.

All at once the ground beneath the wheels began to vibrate, as if shaking the wagon. Pru's ears perked up, then flattened to her head.

Alarm swirled through Susannah at the animal's response. Something was wrong. Then she heard a low drumming. She listened hard for a moment before recognizing the sound as hoofbeats—horses thundering over the hill behind her.

The mare broke into a gallop before Susannah could urge her to. She glanced back, fear rushing through her, though she didn't know why. A thin cloud of dust rose at the crest of the hill and a group of horses appeared. Four riders.

What on earth was happening? She tried to turn Pru to the left and get out of their path, but the mare didn't respond. She ran flat out, stretching the reins taut. Susannah could see now that the riders were men, leaning low over their mounts' necks and heading straight for her. She focused all her strength on getting Pru to move off the road.

Finally the horse did so, the men bearing down on them like a human twister. The mare raced through the grass, slowing somewhat, but still bumping and jostling Susannah in the seat. She flew up once, her bottom cracking hard when she landed. She glanced back to make sure she was out of their way, expecting to see them pass her. Instead, a horse leaped over the bed of her wagon.

She screamed, her heart skipping painfully at the shock. Pru jerked hard on the harness, ripping the reins from Susannah's hands.

Shouts and curses rained around them. Susannah fumbled for the reins. They snaked across the floorboard, and she snatched them up, wrapping them twice around her wrists.

Pru was a mass of strength and power. Susannah fought to keep some control despite the burning in her arms and hands.

A horse darted in front of Pru, two more behind. The mare shied away, tipping the wagon. Susannah grabbed for the footboard, screaming.

Another horse jumped the bed, its hoof striking the side with a resounding crack. Pru veered right and hit a hole, throwing Susannah high into the air.

The reins were yanked from her hands; the sky spun round and round. She thought she screamed before she hit the ground and everything went black.

Riley lay low over the dun's neck, keeping pace with his brother. The three Baldwins fanned out behind them as they chased the McDougals up the hill and onto a flat stretch of land only a mile from Riley's ranch.

The bastards had gone south, as Davis Lee had said four days ago, then headed east. They'd holed up somewhere around Cleburne. The posse had picked up their trail again, following it north to Mineral Wells before the McDougals disappeared.

Riley had wired Susannah from there yesterday before putting in twelve hours of riding a trail that was cold and dead. That he and the other men had picked up the outlaws' trail going west this morning had surprised them all. Four hours from home, they'd followed the trail of broken grass and two cold campfire remains, realizing the McDougal gang was heading for Abilene. Or Whirlwind.

Though they were tired and angry, the threat to their homes and loved ones gave the posse renewed energy—at least it did Riley—and they had managed to pressure the outlaws into riding past both towns. They'd finally caught sight of the bastards about a mile back.

Just as they'd closed in on them, the McDougals topped a hill. The posse charged behind them, in time for Riley to see a wagon in the distance. The gang rode straight for it.

As one, the posse picked up speed, pushing their mounts harder. The sound of pounding hooves rolled across the prairie. The McDougals had shown more than once that they had no qualms about hurting innocent citizens. The four outlaws neared the wagon at a full-out gallop.

"They're trying to put the wagon between us and them," Riley yelled as he and Davis Lee flew across the ground.

"They think they'll buy some time," his brother answered.

One of the outlaw's horses jumped the wagon. It toppled, skittered several feet, then collapsed.

"No!" Riley yelled. "Hell!"

The horse tumbled, struggling against the harness. The outlaws' laughter could be faintly heard above the crashing noises, the felled horse's scream.

Riley urged his dun faster, dread tightening his gut.

Matt Baldwin reached the scene first. "There's a woman here, dammit."

The five of them reined up near the wagon. The horse lay beneath the heavy weight, its sides heaving and slicked with sweat.

From the saddle, Riley saw a glint of blond hair in the grass beyond. Blond curls. He threw himself off before his mount even stopped. "Susannah!"

His wife lay on the ground motionless, her hair tangled around her shoulders. That was *his* wagon on its side, *his* horse down.

Cold fear like he'd never known sliced through him. "Susannah?"

He rushed through the grass and knelt beside her, afraid to touch her. Blood smeared her temple, marring her pale forehead. Hardly able to breathe, he bent and put his ear to her chest, finally hearing a faint heartbeat.

Fear and panic crowded out reason. He forced himself to check her limbs carefully, then gently gathered her to him. "Susannah, wake up, darlin'."

She moaned, her eyes fluttering open.

The baby! Riley's heart stopped. Where in the hell was Lorelai?

* * *

He thought he might be sick. Matt Baldwin knelt beside him and spoke, but Riley didn't comprehend a single word.

He stroked Susannah's hair from her face, his hand trembling. "Can you hear me?"

"Yes," she croaked.

"Where's Lorelai, darlin'?" He turned blindly to Matt. "Look for the baby. She was thrown out, too."

"Hell." Matt rose and hollered for his brother and father.

"No." Susannah clutched weakly at Riley's arm. "The baby's okay. She's with Cora."

Relief took the starch right out of his legs, and he sank back on his heels. "She's okay." He waved off the men starting through the grass around the wagon.

Susannah's eyes closed, her face creasing in pain.

"You're gonna be okay, too." He caressed her cheek, his hand shaking as if he had palsy.

He called out for the other men to help him with Susannah, and bent to her, his voice hoarse. "I'm going to get you to the doctor."

"Where did you come from? Were you chasing those men?"

"Yes, it was the McDougals." He forced away the savage fury that rose inside him at the way they'd endangered her. "Don't think about them right now. Just lay quiet here with me. You're going to be fine."

Davis Lee walked over and knelt beside him. "How is she?"

"Nothing's broken. I'm not sure about her insides." Riley glanced at her, his jaw tightening when he recalled the sight of her flying out of the wagon. "Davis Lee, you can go on. I'll take care of Susannah. Leave one of the Baldwins to help me and go after those McDougal bastards."

His brother shook his head.

"Yes. Don't let them get away with this," Riley insisted.

The other man stared into the distance. "You sure?"

"Yes."

Davis Lee squeezed his shoulder. "I'll be back as soon as I can."

He rose and walked over to confer quietly with the other men. After making sure Susannah was all right, J.T., Russ and Davis Lee mounted their horses and rode off.

Matt walked over. "One of your wagon wheels is busted plumb off."

"How's Pru?" Riley noticed the mare was now standing.

"I checked her. Looks like her right knee might be sprained. I'll take care of her while you get Susannah seen about."

"Thanks."

"You'll have to take her on your horse. This wagon's not any use right now."

Riley laid Susannah gently back in the grass, then got to his feet. He mounted, tensing as Matt lifted her to him.

He tucked her in front of him on the saddle.

"You gonna be able to handle everything?" Matt asked.

"I think so. I'm taking her to Doc Butler at the fort."

"You take care, Miz Susannah." Matt awkwardly patted her foot. "I'll be by to check on you later."

"Thank you, Matthew." Her voice sounded stronger.

Riley prayed there was nothing seriously wrong with her. The black fury inside him wouldn't abate, threatened to swallow him up. Time enough for that once he saw to his wife.

Matt pulled a shirt from his saddlebags and knelt to wrap Pru's knee. Riley headed northeast toward the fort.

Doc Butler said the cut on Susannah's head was minor. The worst of it was that she'd dislocated her shoulder when she hit the ground. Riley had been forced to brace her body with his while the doctor jammed the bone into place. She screamed, then fainted.

Riley would've done the same. He couldn't imagine the pain of such a thing, and hated that she had to endure it. The rage he'd felt upon seeing her helpless in the grass kept nipping at the edges of his control.

Concentrating enough to listen to the doctor's instructions was a struggle, but Riley did it. They rode home slowly, the dun seeming to take extra care crossing the rough grassland. Doc Butler had sent some laudanum with them, as Susannah didn't want to take anything until they got home.

Why had she been out driving? And without Lorelai? Why had she taken the baby to Cora's?

Questions circled viciously in his head, tangling with the fury that snapped at him. He had questions, but now was not the time to ask them. He could wait until she was back on her feet, or at least fully conscious.

He helped her into bed, taking off only her shoes before tucking her under the covers. The doctor had said her head was fine, and he'd ordered rest, warning that her shoulder would hurt like blue blazes for a while.

She slept a couple of hours, and Riley stayed in their room, getting up to pace when the anger rose inside him. He stared out the window, time dragging as day rolled into night. Shadows stretched across the land and the moon floated out from behind a cloud.

"Riley?" she said from the bed.

He went to her, taking her hand. "Doc Butler said you should sleep as much as possible."

"I'm sore, but otherwise fine, I think. I want to know how you are."

"I'm fine, darlin'." He sat on the edge of the bed, his callused fingers smoothing her curls off her face. He wanted this rage inside him to fade, wanted his questions to disappear.

"I missed you." Her fingers moved lightly against his thigh.

He covered her hand with his. The words on the tip of his tongue didn't need to be said right now. It would be best if he didn't talk at all. "Why don't you rest?"

"I want to hear what happened with the McDougals."

The reminder had Riley's emotions boiling over and he felt his common sense ebb away. "Let's not talk about that right now."

"But I want to know."

"They got away," he said in a hard voice, telling himself to calm down.

"Got away? But I thought—"

"Let's talk about something else."

She shifted her head on the pillow, blue eyes clouding. "Are you angry at me?"

He glanced at her shoulder, then away.

"You are. Why?"

He rose from the bed, paced to its foot.

"Riley? Are you going to answer me?"

"I told you not to go anywhere alone, Susannah."

"But your wire said you were coming home. I thought that meant you'd captured them."

"We'd lost them, until this morning. Thank goodness we were hard on their heels when they came across you."

She put a hand to her temple. "Are you angry because you think I got in the way?"

"I'm angry because I told you not to go anywhere alone."

"I took Lorelai to Cora's because I wanted us to have a night together all alone. I thought you'd like that after being gone so long."

"What I'd like is for you to heed instructions once in a while."

"That's unfair." She sat up in bed, wincing. "How was I to know the McDougals hadn't been caught?"

"You weren't. That's why you shouldn't have been out alone until you did know. What if the gang had come upon you with Lorelai in the wagon?"

"They didn't."

"What if they had?" He shoved a hand through his hair. "When I couldn't find her, I thought she'd been thrown from the wagon, too." A numbing blackness had consumed him. "She could've been killed. You have to think about more than yourself now."

"I know that!" She grimaced, obviously in pain. "How dare you imply that I would risk Lorelai's life!"

"Well, you did, didn't you?" He hated himself even as he said the words, but he couldn't stop them, couldn't stem the sensation that life was draining out of him. "It was foolish, especially knowing the McDougals were on the loose."

"I didn't know they were right here," she said hotly.

"You're so damn stubborn."

"It wasn't like that. You said you were coming home. I thought that meant the gang had been caught. I didn't think there was any danger."

"Something like this wouldn't have happened in St. Louis."

"Don't be ridiculous." She slid her legs to the floor. "We have outlaws up there, too. Haven't you heard of the James gang?"

"Don't get out of bed." He wanted to stop her, but hesitated to touch her, afraid he might cause her pain. "In St. Louis, if you'd been out, you wouldn't have been driving alone. You certainly wouldn't have been away from town and people to help you."

Bracing herself with her right hand on the mattress, she stood. "I'm perfectly capable of taking care of myself."

"A matter of opinion. There are too many dangers here, Susannah. You've got to take them into account."

"And you've got to take into account that I'm doing the best I can. Are you telling me you've never made an error in judgment? Or been caught up in events, like I was today?"

"It wouldn't have happened if you'd stayed in like I told you. You don't understand how it is here. You don't understand what this part of the country is like. After what you did today, I have to wonder if you ever will."

Her chin came up. "You still think I don't belong here. That I'll never belong here."

"I'm just trying to protect you and the baby." He picked up his hat and opened the door.

"Where are you going?"

"To get Button. That'll help me clear my head."

She held her injured arm close to her left side, the hurt in her eyes pulling at him. But he couldn't stay. He was suffocating, and he didn't want to say anything else hurtful.

Hearing the thud of his boots down the stairs, Susannah walked to the window. In a few seconds, he stalked off the front porch and stopped, head bowed, shoulders stiff. Moonlight played over his strong neck, washed the blue of his shirt to nearly white.

Grief pulled at her. Riley would never really believe she could meet the challenges here, never believe she belonged. And their daughter would grow up seeing that.

Her daughter, Susannah corrected. Not *theirs*.

She would always love him, but he would never return her feelings. That had been made painfully clear in his hard-edged words, in the disappointment that darkened his eyes today.

She'd been wrong to marry him. She knew what she had to do, and it broke her heart.

Chapter Nineteen

He'd returned with the baby and they'd shared a cold supper. Lorelai had fussed every time he and Susannah were in the same room together—because the baby sensed the tension between the two of them, Susannah decided. She stayed the night in Lorelai's room, still hurting over the realization that his opinion of her wasn't going to change. It was late when she heard him come upstairs, then pause outside the baby's door. After a few seconds, he walked away and their bedroom door closed.

The next morning, he left after breakfast to go to Whirlwind and see if Davis Lee had returned. Despite her injured arm, Susannah had her bags packed within a half hour. It took her longer to write the letter. Miss Wentworth would disapprove of addressing such a problem by letter, but Susannah knew if she told Riley her decision to leave in person, she wouldn't be able to resist him or any arguments he made on behalf of the baby.

As she finished writing, her vision blurred and she looked away before a tear could fall and smear the ink. Nearly numb, she sprinkled sand on the letter and left it to dry on his desk.

The sling Doc Butler had fashioned for her arm had given her the idea to try something similar as a way to hold the baby while she drove the wagon. Since she wouldn't be able to use both hands, she would have to trust the mare to do most of the work.

It took awhile to hitch Pru to the wagon, but Susannah did it by focusing on her actions and trying to block her painful emotions. She led the mare right up to the porch and managed to topple her trunks down the steps into the wagonbed.

The ink on her letter was dry now. She folded it and took it upstairs, leaving it in the middle of their bed. The tears she'd fought all morning flowed down her face. She pulled a knotted length of linen over her head and slid her good arm through, settling the sleeping baby securely against her breast.

Susannah climbed carefully into the wagon and drove away.

Riley took longer in town than he probably should have. Davis Lee and the Baldwins had trailed the McDougal gang north, past Tascosa in the Panhandle. There, they had run into Jericho and another Ranger on the outlaws' trail. Wanting to check on Susannah and get back to keep the citizens of Whirlwind safe, Davis Lee had been happy to turn the chase over to their cousin.

Riley had dallied on purpose, staying to talk to Davis Lee about nothing because he wasn't ready to go home. Seeing Susannah deathly pale in the grass yesterday, with no sign of Button, he'd been scared spitless.

He knew he had come down too hard on Susannah last night and he owed her an apology.

Three hours after he left for town, he walked into the house, peeling off his gloves. An eerie quiet surrounded him. "Susannah?"

The slate floor of the foyer was spotless; his heavy coat

hung where it should on the coat tree behind the door. Nothing seemed out of place in the sitting room or the dining room. He went upstairs, hit with a sense of desolation.

Upon walking into their bedroom, he knew immediately that she was gone. The armoire stood open, emptied of her clothes and shoes. Her brush and mirror were missing from the dresser. No cotton wrapper was draped across the rocking chair he'd moved up here for the baby's midnight feedings.

He saw the letter and grabbed it, walking across the hall. Button's cradle was empty, her blanket and tiny clothes gone.

What the hell was going on? He opened the letter, reading quickly, hardly able to take in the words.

Dear Riley,

I've gone to St. Louis for good. I married you for the wrong reasons. After what happened yesterday, I see now that you'll never believe I belong in Whirlwind. I know you love Lorelai, and you're welcome to see her anytime you wish. I was wrong when I thought all she needed was a mother and father who loved her. What she really needs are two parents who love each other. Pru and your wagon will be at Cora's. I'm so sorry. Thank you for all you've done.

Love, Susannah.

The words merged in a haze of red, pain gouging deep. How could she do this? He hadn't taken their vows so lightly.

Fury and hurt tangled. Well, she'd finally gone back to the city, as he'd urged her to a dozen times. His fist closed over the letter, crumpling it. Why had he ever taught her to drive that damn wagon?

He'd known not to fall in love with another city girl.

St. Louis. That's where she belonged.

His anger carried him through that day and night, but when he woke the next morning, he knew he had to go after her. She belonged here with him.

It wasn't just sleeping alone that made him realize how much he needed her. She meant more to him than he'd allowed himself to think. To feel, even.

He slid out of bed, standing naked in the center of the room as images melted away the last of his anger. He missed watching her brush her thick curls. Missed the sound of her padding softly across the floor to check on Button.

On the trail with Davis Lee, Riley had ached for the feel of her beside him, the gentle scent of her early in the morning, her silky hair tickling his chest when she snuggled into his shoulder. Her smart-aleck remarks when he least expected them. Her laugh. That determined look in her blue eyes.

He'd known his feelings for her were changing, but he had forgotten all that when he'd seen her lying in the grass yesterday. The realization that he could have lost her as easily, as swiftly as he'd lost Maddie had slammed into him. It was pure-dee fear that had spurred him to tell her she was foolish, accuse her of not thinking about the baby's well-being.

He was an idiot. He loved her and he'd driven her away.

When had his admiration, his lust for her changed to something else? He loved Button, but he had never examined what he felt for Susannah. Had refused, in fact.

During his marriage to Maddie, he'd been set upon to prove things. Those were the years he'd worked his fingers to the bone to establish his reputation for prime horseflesh and quality beef. Providing for a wife had been a priority and he'd wondered over the years if he had really been such a good husband. Then there were the times he'd held it against Maddie for being a city girl, for dying and leaving him. He was ashamed.

Something about Susannah forced him to look deep into himself, come to terms with things and put them to rest.

He'd told himself he couldn't get close to another woman,

couldn't risk such a loss again. But he *had* gotten close to her. And now he'd lost her.

Without ever telling her that he loved her.

She thought he didn't want her in Whirlwind, that she didn't belong. That had been true, once. But she'd made a life for herself here, for *them*. How many times had she proved him wrong? Shown him a deep core of strength beneath that soft exterior?

He loved her and he was going after her.

"Please tell me how long she's been gone, Cora," Riley demanded of his friend a few hours later.

"Since yesterday morning. She took the stage and thought she could catch the afternoon train out of Abilene." The woman's lips flattened.

"I'm going after her."

Cora's hazel gaze considered him, then she said grudgingly, "I had a wire from her last evening. She didn't make yesterday's train and plans on leaving this morning. I don't know why I'm telling you anything, you stubborn, mule-headed man. You never shoulda let her leave. I oughta blister your hind end."

"You're right, I shouldn't have let her leave."

"Humph."

"Who drove the stage?"

"She had plenty of volunteers, I can tell ya."

"That figures. Who drove?"

"I think Pete Carter. He and J. T. Baldwin were coming to terms about it last I saw. They've been taking turns driving Ollie's route since he passed on."

"Thanks." Riley pressed a hasty kiss to her cheek and she pushed him away.

She slammed the door behind him and he mounted Whip,

heading for town. If Susannah was half as mad as Cora, he had a lot of begging to do.

Reining up in front of the saloon, he hitched his horse and strode past the swinging doors, heading for the post office. And the telegraph machine.

"Where you going in such a hurry, Holt?" Matt Baldwin stepped out of the saloon.

"You're not chasing Miz Susannah, now, are you?" J.T.'s big voice boomed down the street.

Riley turned, looking at the elder Baldwin. "I guess you didn't drive her to Abilene."

"What did you do to her, Holt?" Russ asked.

"That's between me and—nothing!" He pivoted and stalked into the post office. "Tony, I need to send a telegram to Abilene, ask Susannah not to board that train."

The rotund man lifted one dark eyebrow. "I don't think she wants to hear from you."

His jaw dropped. Was everyone in Whirlwind mad at him? "Just send the damn wire. Here's my money." He slapped a coin down on the counter and leaned over, saying softly, "You best send it."

Tony snatched the coin and pounded out the message, his lips flat and disapproving.

Riley turned, heading out the door. He'd ride like hell to Abilene and see if he could stop her, though he feared it was too late.

"Well, well, did you come to your senses, little brother?"

Who had told Davis Lee? Cora, most likely. Riley walked past his brother, who held Whip's reins, threading them through his fingers.

"I'm going after her."

"It would serve you right if she didn't hear you out."

"Yes, it would." Riley looked at his brother. "I'm surprised you didn't hightail it out to the ranch when you learned she'd left.''

"I thought about coming out there to pound some sense into you, but I reckon y'all need to work this out for yourselves.''

"I love her, Davis Lee. I'm an idiot for taking so long to realize it, but I do. And I don't plan on coming home without her.''

He took the reins from his brother. "There's no telling how long it'll take me to convince her, if I can. You might need to check in with Joe and Cody about the ranch.''

"I will.'' Davis Lee pulled the watch from his vest pocket. "That train's already left Abilene.''

"You think she really boarded?''

"I'm afraid so.''

"Then I'll ride to St. Louis. That way, I won't have to make all the train stops and I might reach St. Louis the same time she does.''

"Good idea.''

Riley swung into the saddle.

Davis Lee stepped into the street and stuck out his hand. "Good luck. You're gonna need it.''

"Thanks.''

Nothing in the room where she'd grown up had changed. The same ice-blue satin covered her walls and her bed. The blue drapes were open to let sunshine stream through the mullioned windows.

When she'd arrived at the train depot in St. Louis, she'd gone straight to Adam, but when her parents had learned of her return, they had come there also. They'd wanted to talk, and though she dreaded another scene like the one they'd had before she left home, it hadn't happened. Hurt still lingered in all of them, she knew, but they had made a start.

There was no disguising Ginny's and Edward's immediate

love for Lorelai. They had actually argued over which of them should hold the baby first. Susannah knew that seeing their granddaughter had gone a long way toward softening the animosity between herself and her parents. They had begged her to reconsider staying at their house and, once Adam promised to rescue her at the first sign the truce might break, she had finally agreed.

Things were a bit awkward among the three of them, with everyone trying to be careful of each other's feelings, but Susannah appreciated the effort put forth by her mother and father.

Even after five days, she still didn't know what she would do about Riley and her marriage. She instinctively knew he wouldn't give her a divorce. Her heart ached. She missed him, and she missed their home. She missed the rugged plains around Whirlwind and the small town she'd come to love. She'd never before noticed how close together the houses were on her parents' street. Never noticed how people seemed to press in on top of her. In Texas, she'd been able to breathe, and now felt constricted.

She tried to stay cheery for Lorelai's sake, but the baby sensed her unhappiness. And probably missed the only man she'd known as a father, Susannah acknowledged. It was five days since Lorelai had heard Riley's voice or felt his touch. Didn't that have to affect her? It certainly affected Susannah.

The baby slept fitfully in a lovely crib next to her bed, but it wasn't the cradle Riley had repaired. She had left that one at his house, having no room for it on the stage or the train.

The sound of voices drifted upstairs to her room. She peered into the mirror, glad her shoulder had healed enough that she could go without the sling for short periods of time. It was still tender, so she smoothed her hair using her right hand, then walked out to greet her brother and sister-in-law for dinner. No amount of pinching put any color into her pale cheeks, and the strain of the last few days drew tight lines around her mouth.

On her first night away from Riley, she'd cried herself to sleep. But she knew he would never love her as she loved him. Somehow she'd gotten through hour after hour, then an entire day. She was grateful for Adam and the efforts he'd made on her behalf with their parents, but she didn't know if she would ever forgive him for pushing her at Riley Holt.

She started down the broad sweeping staircase, freezing halfway down at the sound of a familiar male voice. It didn't belong to Adam or her father.

She saw him then, standing in her parents' foyer. Holding his hat in his hand, dressed in dusty Levi's and boots and a grimy white shirt, he appeared to be arguing with her father. Adam, standing quietly to the side, looked up at her.

She spun.

"Susannah?"

Her hand closed tight on the gleaming wood rail. She closed her eyes at the pain his husky voice brought, a voice she hadn't expected to ever hear again.

"Please hear me out, darlin'."

Darlin'! She looked at him sharply, tears of hurt and anger stinging her eyes. She caught her skirts in both hands and ran up the stairs.

Footsteps pounded behind her.

"Young man!" Edward Phelps bellowed.

"Let him go, Father," Adam said.

Why had Riley come here?

"Susannah, please?" At the top of the stairs, he closed his hand over her arm.

How had he climbed those steps so quickly? She tried to shake him off and he tightened his grip, turning her to face him as he backed her into the wall.

Anger and hurt burned in his eyes. "I know you don't want to see me, but I came here to say my piece. I'm not leaving without saying it."

"Say it to Adam." She opened her bedroom door and marched inside, attempting to slam it shut.

Riley slapped a hand against the wood and pushed his way in.

She gasped. "You are not invited!"

"You're still my wife. I don't have to be."

Staring into the blue eyes she loved so, she nearly broke. He smelled of horses and man. Whiskers shadowed his jaw, giving him a rugged, dangerous look.

Concern darkened his eyes. "Your shoulder isn't bound."

"It's doing better."

"Still sore?"

She didn't want his compassion; it made her want so much more. "Did you come to see the baby?"

"You didn't let me tell her goodbye."

So *that* was why he'd come. Trying to keep her face from showing the stark pain his words inflicted, Susannah studied her fingernails. "I didn't think I'd be able to resist you if I told you in person. Resist your arguments, I mean," she added when she saw a flare of male satisfaction in his eyes. "I'll get Lorelai."

"Not yet. I came here to talk to you. To talk about…us."

Us? She eyed him warily.

"First, I apologize for what I said to you the day of the accident. Seeing you lying on the ground, and no sign of Button, put the fear of God in me, but I had no right to say those things. I know you would never put Button in jeopardy. And I do know that you can take care of yourself."

Her eyes narrowed. "Since when?"

"Since you put me in my place." He gave her a crooked smile.

Not wanting him to see how her nerves jumped at his nearness, she balled her hands into fists. "You didn't have to come all this way to tell me that."

"That isn't all I want to tell you."

She wanted him to hold her once more, and at the same time she wanted to get as far away as she could.

"You signed the letter 'Love, Susannah.'" He fished a crumpled piece of paper from the front pocket of his trousers. "Do you? Love me?"

She turned away.

He moved in front of her, putting a gentle hand on her right arm. "You said you married me knowing that I didn't love you, but hoping I'd come to."

She closed her eyes, trying to regain some sense of balance. "Why couldn't you let me get close? You had no problem doing that with Lorelai. Why?"

"I don't know. All I know is the way I feel about *her* doesn't scare the hell out of me. The way I feel about you does."

"Well, that's promising," she muttered.

His hand slipped to her wrist, his thumb stroking the bare skin below her sleeve. "I just mean—listen, I'm no good at this stuff. I was afraid something would happen and I'd lose you."

"You mean like you lost Maddie?"

"Yes."

"Don't you think something bad could happen to the baby?"

Her question put fear in his eyes and he said tightly, "I never thought of you as cruel, Susannah."

"I'm not being cruel or wishing anything bad to happen. None of us ever knows what might happen, good or bad."

"Woman, you are confoundin'." He released her, bracing his hands on his hips. Frustration stamped his features. "The fact is, if something happened to you, I couldn't survive it."

"I feel that sometimes, too," she said gently, "but I can't accept less than I'm willing to give, Riley. I want all of you, all of your heart. I settled once, and I won't do it again."

"Well, why do you think I rode like hellfire to get up here?" He stepped close, this time catching her hand when she tried to step away. "I want all of you, too."

"What you feel is for the baby—"

"Darlin', let *me* tell you what I'm feelin'." He stroked a knuckle down her cheek. "What I'm trying to say is, I love you. I was just too much of a damn fool to realize it before you left."

"You love me?"

"Yes."

She stared into his eyes, searching hard for doubts.

"Your leaving like to ripped my heart out."

"You miss the baby."

"I miss *you,* Susannah Holt. My wife. I'd marry you all over again, for the right reasons this time. I never thought I'd want to let someone close again, but you plumb stole my heart. I don't think I had a chance."

His words took her breath. "And what about Lorelai?"

"I love her, too, Susannah. You know it, but this is about us. You were right when you said the best thing for her is two parents who love each other. That's what I had with my folks, though I didn't realize it until you put it into words." He took her hands, bringing them to his lips. "Please don't turn me away. Please tell me I'm not too late to change your mind and take you home."

"I want to believe you," she said tremulously. "But it seems too good to be true."

"You know I wouldn't say it if it weren't true."

"It's not that I don't trust you, but—"

"Darlin', do you think I could love Button if I didn't love you so much?"

She stilled. "Yes. She's a child."

"She's *your* child, Susannah. And yes, I want her to be ours. But more than that, I want you to be my wife. Please believe I love you."

Her head and her heart, in perfect accord for once, urged her to believe him.

"Just say yes, Susannah," Adam called from the other side of the door.

She huffed indignantly.

Riley grinned. "I guess we have an audience."

"I guess so."

His hands went to her waist, easing her against his hard length. "I need to kiss you, Mrs. Holt, but I won't until you're sure."

What would her life be without him? She would live it, she knew, but it would be lacking. The love she'd wanted for so long shone fiercely in his eyes, poured down on her. "And we'll go back to Texas? That's where I want to be."

"Absolutely." He lifted her hands and brushed his lips across her knuckles, the stubble of his whiskers tickling her.

"I love you, Riley," she whispered. "Kiss me."

"You're sure?" he teased.

She slid her arms around him. "Never more sure."

"I'd be obliged." He covered her mouth with his, tasting of peppermint and sweet desire.

Maybe her brother's heavy-handed attempt at matchmaking hadn't been such a bad idea.

* * * * *

HISTORICAL

HISTORICAL

BOUGHT FOR THE HAREM
by Anne Herries

After her capture by corsairs, Lady Harriet Sefton-Jones thinks help has arrived in the form of dashing Lord Kasim. But it's out of the frying pan and into the fire... Kasim has a plan of his own: he wants Lady Harriet for himself!

SLAVE PRINCESS
by Juliet Landon

For ex-cavalry officer Quintus Tiberius Martial duty *always* comes first. His task to escort the Roman emperor's latest captive, Princess Brighid, should be easy. But one look at his fiery slave and Quintus wants to put his own desires before everything else...!

THE HORSEMAN'S BRIDE
by Elizabeth Lane

Not even a remote Colorado ranch can shelter Jace Denby while he's on the run, but one danger this fugitive doesn't see coming is impulsive Clara Seavers! Clara doesn't trust this hired horseman, but she can't deny he ignites her spirit. Even though Jace seems intent on fighting their mounting passion...

On sale from 5th August 2011
Don't miss out!

Available at WHSmith, Tesco, ASDA, Eason
and all good bookshops

www.millsandboon.co.uk

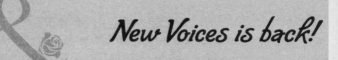

2 FREE BOOKS
AND A SURPRISE GIFT

We would like to take this opportunity to thank you for reading this Mills & Boon® book by offering you the chance to take TWO more specially selected books from the Historical series absolutely FREE! We're also making this offer to introduce you to the benefits of the Mills & Boon® Book Club™—

- **FREE home delivery**
- **FREE gifts and competitions**
- **FREE monthly Newsletter**
- **Exclusive Mills & Boon Book Club offers**
- **Books available before they're in the shops**

Accepting these FREE books and gift places you under no obligation to buy, you may cancel at any time, even after receiving your free books. Simply complete your details below and return the entire page to the address below. You don't even need a stamp!

YES Please send me 2 free Historical books and a surprise gift. I understand that unless you hear from me, I will receive 4 superb new books every month for just £3.99 each, postage and packing free. I am under no obligation to purchase any books and may cancel my subscription at any time. The free books and gift will be mine to keep in any case.

Ms/Mrs/Miss/Mr ——————————— Initials ————————————

————————————————————————————————————

Surname ————————————————————————————

Address ————————————————————————————

————————————————————————————————————

——————————————————— Postcode ——————————

E-mail ————————————————————————————————

Send this whole page to: Mills & Boon Book Club, Free Book Offer, FREEPOST NAT 10298, Richmond, TW9 1BR